'Now, Sophie, I want you to give Julie six hard strokes of the martinet on her backside. And when I say "hard" I mean very hard. Miss Chapel will repeat any strokes that are not up to scratch. And Julie, I want you to count the strokes and thank Sophie after each one,' instructed Miss Walters.

Julie took up her position and sensed with a flush of shame that all attention was on her bottom, fully displayed in the most humiliating position. She felt her stomach clench with fear as she waited, wondering what was to come. Suddenly there was a whirring noise and a loud smack as the leather thongs of the martinet fell. A burning sensation spread rapidly across the whole of Julie's seat. She bit her lip, determined not to cry out. Remembering that she had been instructed to thank Sophie, she cried out, her voice quavering, 'One, thank you, Sophie.'

JULIE AT THE REFORMATORY

Angela Elgar

This book is a work of fiction.
In real life, make sure you practise safe sex.

First published in 1995 by
Nexus
332 Ladbroke Grove
London W10 5AH

Reprinted 1998

Typeset by TW Typesetting, Plymouth, Devon

Printed and bound by
Cox & Wyman Ltd, Reading, Berks

ISBN 0 352 33134 8

Contents

The iron chain and the silken cord are both equally bonds.

SCHILLER

Only one who is in pain really senses nothing but himself; pleasure does not enjoy itself but something beside itself.

HANNAH ARENDT

1

The Party

Julie was watching the news on the crystal display television in the kitchen, while the cook rustled up a prawn salad sandwich in place of dinner.

'I'm going on a diet,' Julie had gaily announced to the cook that morning. 'From now on, I am going to eat nothing but prawn salad sandwiches.' The cook had smiled, indulgently. Julie's fads usually only lasted three or four days.

The main item on the news was the PM's rousing speech at the party conference at the National Reconciliation Centre in Birmingham. After every sentence, the stern-faced ladies in the floral hats would burst into ecstatic applause. The younger generation of activists at the back of the hall, wearing their uniform of crisp white shirts, black ties and cropped hair, chanted inarticulately, as they punched their fists to the sky in their trademark salute.

'We will cut crime at a stroke.'

This was received with a huge cheer.

'No longer will we listen to the half-baked theories of the social workers and woolly-headed liberals.'

– Prolonged cheering and stamping.

'We will fight fire with fire. Criminals will get their just desserts.'

– Sustained clapping.

'From now on, anyone caught breaking the law or taking part in politically inspired mob violence, will face the full rigours of the penal system. And they will not be released until they are completely cured.'

– Hysterical cheering.

'To this end, we are implementing the kind of rigorous regime that was once so effective in the penal systems of bygone ages, when being caught was something to fear. This was when the deterrent of the reformatory or prison kept the crime rate low.'

– Renewed cheering.

'Of course, those were the days before the trendy, pot-smoking academics and unpatriotic pacifists had any influence and Britain was truly a great nation. Well, let me tell you, Britain will regain her national pride. Britain will be great again. And we will be proud to call the land of Britannia Great Britain once again.'

– Overwhelming cheers and chanting.

Everything had seemed so stable, so boringly unchanging – or at least it had, until the change of government. Julie took for granted the large, detached house in the leafy London suburb of Richmond, with her father's Ministry-subsidised Rover parked in the drive and Prissie, the Filipino maid, to take her coat when she came home from lessons. True, the newspapers would report the huge rise in unemployment and increased poverty, but fortunately these unpleasant aspects of society did not impinge on life in the private estate with its uniformed security officers or the country club with its squash courts and jacuzzi. Changing back from metric measurement to imperial, 'in the interests of national pride', during the Back to the Best of British campaign, was the only minor inconvenience that affected Julie. The scenes of the tax riots on the television, the armoured cars and clouds of tear gas, were extremely frightening though, and Julie felt deep pity for all the people who had been attacked by the riot police. Her father had pointed out to her that the march was illegal

2

and that the protesters had no right to be there. It was not as if they had not been warned by the authorities what the consequences would be. Anyway, the new government formed by the National Reconciliation Party would change everything for the better – given time.

It was later that evening, at about ten o'clock, when the immigration police came and took Prissie away. There were four of them: three burly men and a policewoman, almost as large, wielding a leather sjambok. Quite unnecessarily, they also had a snarling Rottweiler dog that barked incessantly throughout the whole brief operation. This scared Tonto, the family cat, so much that it would not emerge from under the satinwood escritoire cabinet for hours afterwards. It was all due to some irregularity with Prissie's work permit, apparently. Her anguished face as the police dragged her out of the front door, and into their van, with her hands cuffed behind her back and wearing only a brief burgundy chemise that rose up to reveal her trim Oriental figure, was a sight Julie would never forget. Julie felt sorry for Prissie, of whom she had grown very fond over the years. She also felt upset and angry at the unnecessary brutality of the immigration police. Her father, pouring himself another whisky, explained that the innocent had nothing to fear from the authorities and that the agency could soon provide a replacement maid. He was rather more concerned that the police in their haste, had caused a certain amount of damage to her bedroom door. Taking another gulp of Scotch, he settled himself in his favourite armchair and prepared to spend the rest of the evening dozing in a semi-drunken state.

It was at precisely that moment that Julie knew her father was wrong, deeply wrong. He was no longer the kindly figure who always had time for her when she was a little girl. She realised that over the last few years he had become corrupted by the system. He was seldom at home now and, when he did come home, he often reeked of whisky and had a strange, hard look. It was as if scales had been lifted from Julie's eyes. Until now, her mind had blanked out the suspicion that her father was part of the increasingly powerful state machine, but now she knew he was not the person she had loved as a young girl. He was almost a stranger. It was the oppressive regime, Julie now realised, that had corrupted him. The long tentacles of state power were reaching into every corner of life and nobody escaped its pervasive influence. Julie's mind raced. Yes, it was true, nobody was immune to the might of the totalitarian state. She delved into her own consciousness and recoiled as she realised that, as much as she blamed the system for corrupting her father, taking Prissie and trampling on the liberties of the whole population, something inside her was drawn to the crisp uniforms, spectacular rallies and confident power of the new political masters. Julie emerged from her reverie, angry and confused. It was not true: she hated the police, the politicians, the youth rallies, the uniforms, the banners. She hated the posters on every wall, the military brass bands on every radio station, the keep-fit classes in every park, the flags on every building.

'I hate you. I hate you. I hate you,' Julie shouted, as she swept the tumbler of whisky off the side-table with one wave of her hand. 'I hate the whole bloody system. Don't you realise what's happening to you? Don't you realise what's happening to everyone? Can't you see what they have done to us? Can't you see anything any more?' Her father opened one bleary eye. Julie ran sobbing from the room, slammed the door behind her and locked herself in her bedroom.

Throwing herself on to her bed, Julie stifled her sobs with the pillow and used the corner of the sheet to wipe away her tears. Why was everything going wrong? Why did she feel this depth of frustration? Everything was so unfair. Reaching under the pillow, she pulled out a crumpled letter that bore all the signs of having been read and reread many times. Unfolding it and smoothing it out with the palm of her hand, she read it yet again:

Dear Julie,
This breaks my heart, but I have to tell you that our relationship must come to an end. I cannot be your lover any longer because I cannot treat you in the way that you want. It's no use, I cannot be cruel to a woman – let alone to the girl I love. You say that you want me to spank you, that you cannot be satisfied sexually unless you are cruelly treated. You plead with me to tie your wrists, rip your blouse, blindfold you and put you over my knee – don't you understand that I am completely dedicated to the political struggle against the domination of the weak? Don't you understand that man's traditional power over women is all part of the very system that I am committed to fighting? Don't you understand that I would be forever branded a hypocrite if anyone ever found out? My whole future political career depends on sticking firmly to my principles. If we don't stick to our principles, how can we blame others for reneging on their promises? I have thought about this problem long and deeply. Don't you see that when you come to me wearing those skin-tight jodhpurs, urging me to treat you like a slave, that you are trying to tempt me into sacrificing everything I believe in? Now that I am at university, I can see things much more clearly, though I have missed you like mad. I must end now – I am late for a lecture. I can't say any more in this letter. I hope you understand and I hope that we can still remain friends.

Love always

Roland

X X X X X

PS Ma and Pa are away next weekend – off to a 'political re-education' course in Blackpool. The house is empty, so we are having a monster bash (must not miss the opportunity). I want you to meet my friend, Jack. So please come along, you'll like him. Please don't take this too badly, it's all for the best, really it is.
PPS Little sis has used her 'creative talent' to design the invitations. No doubt she will be in touch with you this week.

Reading Roland's letter rekindled Julie's passionate longings. As she lay on the bed, her hand crept down to lift the hem of her tartan mini-skirt. Her index finger pressed against her lilac silk panties exactly where her clitoris had begun to tingle. Seconds later, the same finger was sliding smoothly up and down, spreading the wetness of her vagina to lubricate her clitoris which she began to flick rapidly. As her climax began to build, familiar fantasies, which she had honed and polished since puberty, swam into her mind. Now she was the European princess captured by Turkish pirates on the high seas. She was being tied to the main mast for a flogging with the cat o' nine tails, for refusing to sleep with the pirate captain. Seconds later, the scene dissolved into a Victorian workhouse where she was bound to a trestle to receive the birch. Julie's climax came with a deep sigh and a shudder, at the usual point in her fantasy, as she pictured herself as a white slave on a sugar plantation. Her ankles were shackled and she waited in line with the slaves who had not picked their daily quota. The overseer was dismounting from his horse, a long leather paddle in his hand, while his two muscular and half-naked black assistants picked Julie up, ripped off her skirt and stretched her on the ground . . .

The next morning, Fiona called by and passed on the invitation to Roland's party. The two girls had been great friends ever since Julie had joined the pony club.

Fiona had wasted no time in introducing Roland, her handsome elder brother, to Julie, but now that he had started his first term at university, Julie had not seen Fiona for several weeks.

Julie knew there would be lots of older boys from the university at the party. She also knew that it would be huge fun. Almost certainly, her father, who was extremely suspicious of students, would not approve. Her mother believed in taking the line of least resistance and was always careful never to contradict her husband. Julie had never seriously lied to her parents before, but on this occasion she felt that it was justified. After all, she was getting older now.

'Can I sleep over at Janet's place so that we can revise for the exams together all evening?' she simpered in her most innocent voice.

Julie's mother looked up from her romantic novel and replied, 'Now don't work too hard, and give our regards to Janet's parents.'

This was exactly the answer that Julie had hoped for.

In order not to arouse suspicion, Julie did not take her party clothes with her. Fiona was roughly the same size and had a huge wardrobe of expensive clothes. For a whole hour, Julie and Fiona experimented with every combination of diaphanous underwear and party outfit. Posing in front of the cheval mirror, they would dissolve in fits of giggles and have to hold on to each other to avoid falling over. Fiona had a bottle of Serbian Riesling, smuggled up from the wine cellar, and both of them were soon in a very jocular state.

As the guests arrived and the sound of partying grew louder the two girls joined the throng. The wine and the novelty of the situation had made them feel rather daring and they had picked outfits which they judged to be sexy and sophisticated. Fiona was wearing a slinky black dress with a plunging cleavage. A special bra pushed her breasts up in an inviting way and a gold pendant hung tantalisingly between them. Black tights with a silvery sheen, black thong-back silk knickers with a little bow at the front and high heels completed her outfit. Julie finally opted for a sheer white blouse with flared cuffs, which being fairly transparent, showed off her slim waist and her generous bust in a white half cup bra. A tight black mini-skirt, scarlet tanga briefs and red tights showed her shapely legs to perfection. Proud of her pretty, snub-nosed face and lustrous dark hair, cut in a bob, Julie felt confidently attractive.

Downstairs, the party was in full swing. Roland's university friends certainly knew how to let their hair down. Julie and Fiona were both highly flattered to have the attention of some of Roland's male friends who were slightly older and impressively intellectual. Most of them belonged to Fightback, the youth wing of the secret anti-government society, the Provisional People's Army. They were full of jokes and sarcasm about the heavy-handed methods of the state regime. This, in itself, was a novelty to Julie, who had seldom heard a word of criticism about the government except from Roland. However, given her new-found hatred of the state, it was all music to her ears. It seemed tremendously exciting to be mixing with the kind of people the newspapers and television called 'the self-deluding enemies of the people'.

It seemed that whenever Julie had almost finished her glass of wine someone would top it up and chide her for being a slow drinker. It was hard to keep up with the rest, but how could one refuse to knock back every glass without appearing young and unsophisticated? Julie's head soon felt rather strange. Luckily, Roland's friend, Jack, who apparently was a very gifted medical student, gave her some aspirins to swallow which he said would clear her head in no time. Julie felt a strange attraction to Jack, who seemed to embody a charismatic magnetism, and felt greatly flattered when he whispered that he needed to talk to her privately on a matter of the greatest importance. He ushered her into the warm darkness of the deserted conservatory and lowered his voice confidentially.

'Look, Julie, Roland has told me a lot about you and I have been dying to meet you for ages. From what he has told me, you have a rebelliousness that is all too often missing from the pampered classes. I can't imagine that you are taken in by all the garbage that passes for news these days. I admire people who can see beyond their own comfortable circumstances and feel solidarity with those who are oppressed every day of their lives. And I know that you hate the system – you do, don't you?'

'Yes, I want to see it destroyed. I want everything to go back to how it was when I was a little girl, when everything was peaceful. When the police didn't patrol the estate in armoured cars, people cared for each other and propaganda was not poured down everybody's throat all the time. Everything was happy at home and people were allowed to speak their minds at work without being arrested ...' Julie stumbled to a halt, wondering if she had made a fool of herself with this outburst.

Jack cast his eyes suspiciously around the darkened conservatory and lowered his voice even further. 'Fantastic, Julie. You know, when that strength of feeling comes through, you could really inspire others. You have massive potential and I'll be frank with you. I know that I can count on you to keep this absolutely secret. It's really important that you tell nobody, otherwise it's curtains for me. I'm the leader of the London cell of Fightback. The PPA has begun to organise resistance in the prisons and they want Fightback to help them by mobilising our forces in the reformatory system. That way, we can make the enemy fight on two fronts at the same time. We have already recruited many volunteers willing to sacrifice themselves for the greater cause, but we still need more. Roland has said that you would be well suited for this type of mission. We need people tough enough to stand up to the rigours of the reformatory system, discreet enough to keep secrets even under severe provocation and bright enough to help organise the resistance. It won't be easy, being an agent for Fightback. What do you say?'

Julie agreed without a hint of hesitation, her voice tremulous with excitement.

Jack clutched Julie's arm and, looking into her eyes, said, 'We are hoping to get some more people into our ranks tonight. This is mainly why we are having this party. Are you with us or would you like to leave before it's too late? You could think about it for a while, and get back to me. I want you to be absolutely sure of what you are getting yourself into. If you are successfully infiltrated into the reformatory system, life will be very harsh. The information from our agents already in the field is that the regime is sadistically severe. Some of the women who run them are complete bitches. It is testing our most committed volunteers to the absolute limits. Some of them are even pressing Fightback to spring them. However, once you are in, it's virtually impossible to get you out. The reformatories are all in remote places and the security is horrendous.'

'I'm ready now. And willing, if need be, to sacrifice myself for the greater good,' replied Julie. 'I suppose,' she whispered, blushing deeply, 'Roland has spoken to you about my – well, the way I am; my desires.'

Jack squeezed Julie's hand and said, 'Yes, Roland has been most frank about you. He has told me everything that I need to know. I have a complete file on you and it seems that you could be one of our best recruits. We pride ourselves on good information and attention to detail in our cell. That is the best defence against the secret police. It has taken us a long time to get the operation organised because our volunteers are hand-picked for their affinity to a cruel regime. They are all natural masochists or sado-masochists who are willing to put their natural talents to the use of the party. Some of the girls here tonight have similar desires to you. Roland felt that by serving the party in this way you might also satisfy your deepest needs. Everyone has some talent or characteristic that can be used to further the cause. Once you are successfully infiltrated into the reformatory system, and when we can be sure that the enemy have not seen through your cover, someone will make contact with you. This agent will give you further instructions and co-ordinate the actions of all our activists in whichever institution you are sent to. Until then, do not give away your true mission to anyone, not even to those who may be arrested with you. In the absence of any specific orders, gather as much information as you can. Make detailed plans of the buildings and try to establish whether and how the inmates would support a nationwide insurrection.

'We must get back to the party before we are missed, but there is just one more thing.' Without pausing, he stooped his tall frame and kissed Julie full on the lips. As he did so he reached down and squeezed the cheeks of her bottom through her tights with one hand. Then, without further words, he led Julie, her mind reeling, through the tropical plants of the conservatory, back to the party.

When someone proposed a game of 'spin the bottle' it was the funniest suggestion that Julie had ever heard. This was an intellectual version of the game, whereby if the bottle pointed at you, you had to answer a question from the Trivial Pursuit bank of questions. Every question was hilarious and out of the twenty or so people in the circle, Julie and Fiona found that the bottle came to rest pointing at them surprisingly frequently. Being the focus of so much attention made Julie feel wonderful, and the way everyone laughed at her jokes was even better. When someone explained that the second stage of the game was the forfeit stage, in which you had to remove an item of clothing whenever you got an answer wrong it seemed churlish to complain especially as all the others nodded and were behaving as if it was the most natural thing in the world. Obviously, intellectuals would not be hidebound by suburban morality. Anyway, Julie and Fiona had not got a single question wrong yet, and it would be funny to see everyone else have to take things off whilst they kept all their clothes on. Before long many of the others had taken off a sock here or a shoe there. It was hilarious. Julie's whole body tingled with an excitement she had never felt before. She could not remember ever having laughed so much in her life. These new friends were truly the most entertaining people in the world. Her whole being felt imbued with a new sense of purpose as the adrenaline surged through her.

Soon, however, the bottle seemed to be stopping at no one but Fiona or Julie. For some reason, their previous skill at answering the questions deserted them and their answers were invariably wrong even when they felt sure that they knew the answer. Julie felt a bit sheepish when she and Fiona had to start removing items of clothing, especially when they found themselves down to their bras and panties, but it was no good being shown up as a bad loser. Some of the other girls were also now in their underwear and they did not seem to be too bothered. Julie wished that she had chosen a more modest bra instead of the half-cup one, which hardly contained her breasts and did not really cover her nipples properly. However, the flattering comments of Roland and Jack (who had got one answer wrong and had daringly removed his jeans) intoxicated her with the power of her own attractiveness. On the other side of the circle, Julie could see Fiona in her black silk undies, also getting a lot of attention and wiping tears of laughter from her eyes. Uncannily, the very next spin of the bottle stopped when pointing at Fiona. The question was unbelievably difficult, something to do with the translation of a Latin proverb, and predictably Fiona got the answer wrong.

'Off with your bra,' someone shouted. Fiona stood up, swaying slightly, but then shook her head rather coquettishly, wagged her finger and covered her chest with her arms.

'Make it double or quits. Have another question and if you get it right you can put it all back on again. If you get it wrong you take the whole lot off,' suggested a handsome fellow sitting next to Fiona.

There was a sense of inevitability to the next few minutes. Of course, Fiona gave the wrong answer, although to Julie's slightly woozy mind it sounded like the right one. Fiona was suffused in giggles but shouted out that she had kept her fingers crossed and so she did not have to keep her bargain. The others, not to be disappointed, set up a chant of, 'Get 'em off, get 'em off.' Fiona blushed but held her ground. Julie saw two of the girls from the university in a similar state of undress creep up behind Fiona. Quickly, they had her by the arms whilst one of the boys reached up and unhooked the front fastener between the cups of her well-filled bra. The cups flew apart and Fiona's ample breasts swung free, wobbling wildly as she struggled with the girls who had her arms pinioned. A second later, her black silk panties had been tugged down and lay at her feet, exposing her neatly trimmed pubic curls and the outline of her bikini bottom from last summer's holiday in the French Riviera town of Frejus.

'Give her the bumps for trying to double-cross us,' someone shouted. Fiona looked beseechingly to Julie for help. Julie felt on top of the world, and capable of anything. She rushed over to Fiona and attempted to release her from the grip of the girls holding her. Somehow she was not as strong as she felt and all her movements seemed to be in slow motion. Dimly, she became conscious of the fact that someone was tugging at her own panties. In fact, as her eyes focused on them, they slid right down to her ankles, pulled by someone's hand behind her. She bent down to retrieve them, but immediately straightened up when she felt a hand caress her bottom and a finger inserted audaciously between her sex lips. Julie turned to confront the source of this impertinence, which turned out to be Jack. She tried to tell him off in a sarcastic and sophisticated way but found that she could not utter a word, as a fit of the giggles came over her and would not go away. Jack's face seemed to go in and out of focus, but she could see that his eyes were not meeting hers. He seemed instead to be intently studying her chest. With a start, Julie realised that in the struggle someone must have unclipped the fastener at the back of her bra, which had now risen up to expose her breasts completely. As Jack reached out to cup and gently lift the almost perfectly rounded globes, it slowly registered on Julie that she was now entirely naked in a roomful of people, most of whom were also in a state of undress. It also dawned on her that instead of feeling embarrassed, she felt proud of her body and the admiring attention that she was receiving. Roland had often commented that she had the most perfectly voluptuous breasts anyone could hope to set eyes on. Now, looking at the admiring faces around her, she felt instinctively that the comment may have been not far off the mark.

'Give them both the bumps,' a voice shouted.

Jack put his arm around her protectively and retorted, 'No, leave them alone now. This is getting out of hand. There is no need to overplay the role. Everything is running to plan perfectly, already.'

14

Somehow he was pushed aside in a wild *melée* and Julie felt herself grabbed by many hands at her arms and ankles. Rapidly, she was lifted clear of the ground, turned horizontal and launched upwards towards the ceiling, then let down to bump the ground. Up and down, up and down she went as the revellers counted each bump. She then realised that Fiona was getting exactly the same treatment, since she would pass her friend coming down as she was on her way up. Julie realised that this activity was not particularly intellectual and that her veneer of sophistication had worn rather thin, especially as she could see a crowd of faces positioned beyond her ankles gazing down the length of her naked body. When the count reached 35, those jerking her aloft began to slow down, which pleased Julie as her fit of giggles had now subsided and a new feeling of queasiness had replaced it.

A violent crash rent the air as the door was smashed in. Julie felt a jarring impact as she was dropped on the floor. Looking up she saw a circle of unsmiling policemen wearing jackboots, helmets and gun holsters and carrying riot batons. The discordant sounds of fighting, screams and furniture breaking filled the air. Julie was hauled to her feet, her hands pulled behind her back and handcuffed together, a position which had the effect of pushing her bosom proudly forward. One of the policemen, his face leering, ran his hands appreciatively up the inside of Julie's legs, slowly over her pudenda, and upwards to tweak both nipples, while another policeman gripped her tightly from behind. Julie was outraged but bit her lip; she had read in the papers about the 'accidental' injuries that happened to many people when they were arrested. The uproar of the raid had now subsided and Julie could see that all of the party guests were now handcuffed. Some of them had cut lips and nosebleeds, and poor Jack was on the floor with two fat policewomen sitting on his chest. Several of the other girls were also naked and were being subjected to humiliating body searches despite their protestations.

Without warning, a short bespectacled figure carrying a megaphone and wearing an elaborate police uniform, which featured yards of gold braid, strutted into the room and climbed on to a chair. His voice sounded harsh and unnatural through the hisses and clicks of the megaphone.

'You have all been arrested and will be charged with holding an illegal meeting and breaking the morality laws and the alcohol laws. We have enough evidence to have you all put away for a long time.' Holding a transparent plastic bag containing papers in the air he went on, 'You will also be charged with subversive political activities, which is an even more serious offence. We have seized various treasonable pamphlets which are full of outrageous slanders against our much respected political leaders. That alone will send most of you to institutes of correction until you are cured of your delusions. And don't think that you will be able to deny your part in seditious activities because we have an undercover agent who has been here from the start. Take them to the interrogation centre.'

They were then marched, each between two police officers, out to the Black Maria van parked on the big semi-circular gravel drive. The cold air on her bare skin and the sensation of the sharp gravel crunching under her feet began to clear Julie's head rapidly. They were herded, most of them naked or semi-naked, into the van. Julie was frightened, especially as about thirty of them were crammed into the confined space together, in semi-darkness. She found herself pressed tightly, cheek to cheek and breast to breast, against Sophie, one of the other girls from the party who seemed only to be left with the remnants of a sheer, black nylon bodystocking. Large holes had been ripped in it during the raid and

16

now her firm, melon-like breasts were jammed hard against Julie's rather softer orbs.

After a short interval, the van doors slammed shut and the vehicle started up. With a jerk and swerve that pressed everyone even tighter together the van sped off. Every bend and roundabout caused the chaotic bodily friction to get worse, particularly as being handcuffed the occupants of the van could not fend each other off. Within a few minutes, Julie found that she was no longer pressed up against Sophie, who had slipped sideways between two boys. Instead, she was now pressed even more tightly against Jack. His shirt, which was all he now wore, had been torn to shreds during his valiant struggle with the two fat policewomen who had arrested him.

'Don't worry, little Julie,' he said. 'You are so young and innocent and yet you will be able to do great things for the movement.' Julie began to cry with emotion, her head nestled into Jack's neck and her nipples rubbing against the rough hairiness of his chest.

'There, there,' cooed Jack. 'It's worth it all to meet you, and to strike at the heart of this corrupt system.' Julie then realised that she felt an overwhelming desire for this handsome and so gallant young man. The motion of their two bodies rubbing together and Jack's kind words kindled a flame of lust in her. She squeezed her pelvis more tightly against Jack's and gradually added her own movements to those dictated by the rocking of the van. As a virgin, Julie was not over-familiar with the variations and norms of male sexuality, but she had touched Roland's penis on a number of occasions, during petting sessions, and was always amazed at the way it could grow so quickly. This was what seemed to be happening with Jack's penis. Gradually, it rose up until it was pressed vertically, throbbing between their stomachs. It was frustrating not being able to use their hands to caress each other, but they were able to kiss with undiminished passion which inflamed the sensations that Julie felt in her clitoris as it pressed against Jack's balls. The overwhelming, roaring lust that surged through them both obliterated all consciousness of the other occupants of the police van as their movements became increasingly urgent. As the motion of their bodies massaged Jack's penis, Julie felt its hardness pulsing against her soft stomach and heard low animal-like growls emanating from Jack's throat. Suddenly, with a squealing of tyres, the van swung round and entered what must have been a cobbled road or courtyard for a strangely rapid vibration was transmitted through the floor and up through their legs.

'Oh, Julie,' Jack gasped as his body jerked and his legs almost buckled beneath him. Julie felt a tremendous pulse flow through the rigidity of his penis and a hot jet of semen shot up between her breasts and bathed them both in its slippery warmth. Simultaneously, her legs turned to jelly and waves of intense pleasure rippled through her in powerful convulsions. A shrill cry broke from her lips. If it had not been for the tight press of bodies in the van, Julie felt certain that she would have sunk to the floor as her legs gave way. As the waves of her orgasm receded, the van screeched to a halt, the back doors were flung open and powerful lights shone into the interior.

'Right, you lot, the party's over,' a coarse voice shouted. 'Welcome to Feltham interrogation centre. Out you get where we can see you. Don't be shy. We need our luxury coach to give some other lucky folk a trip to our luxury hotel.' This was followed by peals of raucous laughter from the outside which was not echoed by those inside the van. Julie nestled her head against Jack, treasuring every precious moment of contact. She revelled in the love she felt for this handsome young man who was so protective and attracted to her in spite of the circumstances. She could not help wondering if she would ever see him again, and at the back of her mind she wondered whether she would lose her virginity to him. Whatever happened, she knew that she would never let Jack down.

2

The Interrogation Centre

The experience of the interrogation centre was, in fact, perfectly dreadful. The policemen, warders, wardresses and plainclothes detectives who ran it seemed like utter yobs, completely ignoring Julie's demands to be able to telephone her parents. Apparently under the new laws, suspects could be held *incommunicado* for up to five days. Julie did not relish her parents finding out about her deception and her wild behaviour. She knew that both her father and mother would be livid. But she was more frightened of the police and was particularly shocked by the conditions at the centre. Her parents would, of course, try to use their influence with the authorities and take her back to her own cosy bedroom with its pink en suite bathroom. Julie fervently prayed that they would not be successful as this would ruin the whole plan for Jack, Fightback and for herself.

After being released from the crush of the Black Maria, the boys were separated from the girls in the glare of the sodium floodlights of the interrogation centre courtyard. Julie noticed that the courtyard walls were at least twenty feet high and topped with a bulbous anti-grappling hook profile. Above this was an array of razor wire and a laser beam parallel with the wall that glowed red against the night sky. There was obviously no point in trying to escape. The night now seemed very cold, after the sweltering heat of the van interior. Having to line up in two lines, one for the boys and one for the girls, still handcuffed and still half-dressed while the police counted and recounted them, only served to make Julie feel colder and brought her arms and thighs out in goosepimples. They were forbidden to talk to each other and so they just had to stand there while the officers strutted up and down the line, leering at them and making infantile personal comments. Two particularly obnoxious, plainclothes agents in their late twenties, with lank, greasy hair, stood in front of Julie while they smoked their cigarettes, making obscene comments the whole time.

'Hey Frank, take a look at this pair of beauties, they're a pretty good size aren't they? How big are they, love? Does your boyfriend like them? I bet he can't wait to get his mitts on them. Not answering, eh? I bet they're 36 or 38 inches. What would you say, Frank?'

Frank, who was absurdly overweight, had the squashed nose of an ex-boxer and spoke with the gruff tones of a gangland 'heavy', held his thumb up in a mock measuring charade. 'Well you don't get many of those to the pound, they could be 38 inches. But I prefer these ones on this blonde bint over here, they might be smaller but they're kind of pointed and she's got terrific nipples. The cold air is making them stand out like organ stops. I prefer small, pointed tits myself, like big half-lemons, with little pink hard nipples. You can keep your big ones. Do you fancy me, darling? You not speaking either? Another stuck-up bitch, are you? Well you won't be so stuck up where you'll be going, I'll guarantee that. I bet you've got no idea what these new reformatories are like, you stuck up bitches with your la-di-da accents from your private estates. You don't mix with the criminal classes, do you? A pity, 'cos they would have probably warned you what happens to people who don't toe the line these days. It's no more kid glove treatment. It's no more bleeding heart social workers and psychiatric reports and being let off with

21

suspended sentences or community work. You are in for a bloody big shock, I can tell you. They take it out on your backside these days and a good thing, too. That'll teach you. I've heard some stories from people who work at some of them places and what they say would make your toes curl. They really know how to tame rebellious little tarts like you lot, and they don't care if you do come from a fancy background. Everyone's equal now, and from what I've heard they will have you screaming under the birch just the same as slags from the slums. What do you think to that? You don't look so stuck up now, do you? You wait till you're on the flogging bench about to get a good lesson on your backside, then you'll wish that you had never taken liberties with the law and had a bit of respect for the officers of the law. They don't advertise what actually does go on at these reformatories but mark my words I know what I'm talking about. You are going to pay for your mischief girls. You won't want to go back for another taste of it, make no mistake. None of them want to go back, they're as good as gold when they come out. What they do in those reformatories works a treat. They should have brought them in years ago. The same goes for your boyfriends over there. And don't think that you'll be seeing them for a while, because you won't.'

Julie exchanged glances with Sophie who was standing next to her in the line. Whether the leering policeman was just trying to frighten them she did not know. Sophie looked pretty scared and so did the bespectacled skinny girl wearing just a barely-filled, floral-patterned bra standing on her other side. Julie wondered if they were volunteers working for Fightback as well. Julie could not see what had happened to Fiona but thought that she was probably at the other end of the line. She could not see her friend without stepping out of the line which would be likely to land her in more

22

trouble. Julie knew that the new reformatories were supposed to be tough and give a 'short, sharp shock'. The newspapers had run articles on the new regime supposedly based on the old reformatories which practised corporal punishment, but Julie had always found it safer to assume that anything in the newspapers was just propaganda issued by the Ministry of Information.

Presently, another officer with a clipboard came down the line getting names, addresses and ages from everyone. He was accompanied by an attractive young nurse in a crisp starched white uniform who made everyone blow into a breathalyser device and then logged the result. When they were finished, they were all led through a heavy steel door into the centre, marched along miles of corridors and divided up into separate cells. Julie found herself sharing with Sophie and the skinny girl who had been on her other side in the line, whose name turned out to be Andrea. The cell was very basic, merely having three low wooden benches to sit or lie on and a plastic toilet bucket with a lid. The walls, painted a dismal green colour were covered in graffiti, much of it of a rather despairing nature. There was no window and a bright bulb under a wire mesh in the ceiling burned with a harsh light. Their handcuffs were removed as they entered the cell and all three girls were soon rubbing each others' arms and wrists to help restore the circulation. Unfortunately, the generosity of the police did not extend to providing any clothes, so the three were wearing what they had been clad in when they were thrown into the police van. Sophie still wore the remains of the black nylon body stocking, Andrea retained her bra and Julie had not one shred of clothing to keep her warm. Huddle together as they might, they could still not find enough warmth. The benches were hard, the cell was cold, the bare light bulb was bright and what was worse, the cover of the spy hole in the door was constantly being moved aside as lascivious officers took it in turns to look over the charms of the nubile occupants. Whenever Julie heard the spy hole cover move she tried to cover her nudity with her hands, but the attempt was futile, as her breasts were too large and her hands too small. Although it was now the early hours of the morning there seemed little hope of getting any sleep so they swapped life stories and pondered their fate. Sophie turned out to have a wry sense of humour and was normally the life and soul of any party. She knew that she would not get off lightly since the police had found revolutionary leaflets in her handbag, which she said were planted by them. Furthermore, she was not endearing herself to the warders by shouting obscenities at the door whenever the spy hole cover moved aside. Andrea was a complete contrast to both of her cell mates, being studious and inclined to intellectualise about the iniquities of the police state, ballot-rigging, media manipulation and the oppression of the masses. It transpired that she was heavily involved with Fightback and was partly responsible for the political literature found at the party. She was rather shy, not a regular party-goer, and was naturally finding the whole experience traumatic. Not having an ounce of fat on her, her ribs showed clearly and her skinny frame shivered in the cold. Her skimpy floral-patterned bra with lace trimming did little to keep her warm, so Julie and Sophie sandwiched her between them as they cuddled up together to share their body heat. Jack had warned Julie to keep her mission a secret, even from fellow prisoners, since it was not beyond the wit of the police to plant a spy as a fellow prisoner in order to trick someone into speaking frankly. It was also rumoured that every cell was electronically bugged. Julie resolved to be vigilant in order to not give anything away. She felt sure that Sophie was another agent for Fightback but was a little suspicious of Andrea. Julie wondered whether, by criticising the authorities so openly, Andrea was trying to trick the others into speaking indiscreetly and giving their mission away. On the other hand, the girl might be completely genuine. Julie realised that she had now entered a world of trick and counter-trick, where appearances may be deceptive and could never be taken on trust. Indeed, Julie herself was now in the deception game. Her imprisonment was part of a deception, and her secret craving for domination and pain was the most deceptive part of her character.

After what seemed like the longest night of Julie's life, three breakfasts on a tray were brought in by an Amazonian female warder who announced that the three girls would shortly be arraigned in front of the judge for the formality of a trial. The breakfast did little to raise their spirits, since it only consisted of some tepid tea in plastic beakers and six slices of stale brown bread thinly spread with cooking margarine.

It was only a few hours later that Julie found herself back in handcuffs and being marched by two rather masculine wardresses down long corridors towards the courtroom. They informed Julie that clothes would be found for her in the annexe of the court but meanwhile she would have to stay in her present state. They also pointed out that it was not their fault Julie was arrested in a state of undress. 'If you will go taking all your clobber off at a political agitator's Roman orgy then that is your lookout, young lady. You ought to be ashamed of yourself,' one of them had said.

The very worst part was being led down one of the very long men's corridors, called C-Wing, which had about fifty barred, American-style police cells down each side. Each cell appeared to contain about four inmates. Julie felt hundreds of pairs of eyes roaming over her jiggling breasts and the slight wobble of her curvaceous bottom as she walked. She felt her face burning up with embarrassment. To hear the noise of the wolf-whistles and catcalls emanating from those cells, it was as if the inmates had never seen a woman in the nude before.

Julie protested vehemently to the wardresses. In response one of them replied nonchalantly, 'Don't you fret, young lady. They can't get at you. It's not so surprising that the men get a little bit excited. Some of them have been on remand for over a year, and have hardly seen a woman of any description, let alone one in the nude, for that time.'

'Don't walk so fast, we're not getting our money's worth,' Julie heard one of them shout and she wondered if this was a joke or whether the prisoners had bribed the wardresses to force her into this embarrassing display.

Seeing the look of extreme discomfort on Julie's face, one of the wardresses turned to her and whispered, 'I suggest that you plead guilty, supply the names of all your confederates in crime, and generally co-operate as much as possible while you are here, otherwise you'll get the same treatment that a young lady just like you got last month.'

'What treatment was that?' Julie stammered.

'Well,' replied the wardress, 'she was about your age and even looked a bit like you. The silly young thing wouldn't take any advice. She wouldn't co-operate at all, wouldn't name her accomplices, wouldn't even tell us who gave her the pamphlets or why she had been videoed by a surveillance camera at the home of a dealer in stolen goods. What's more she bit one of my colleagues. Silly girl.'

'Yes, but what happened to her?' said Julie, impatiently.

'Well, it seems that some of my colleague's friends who were on duty that night made a bit of a mistake with the locking up arrangements. These mistakes are very easy to make, what with being short-staffed and having more and more inmates to deal with every day. Anyway, what happened was that they forgot to lock the cell doors in A-Wing, which is another men's wing. The doors to the wing itself were locked, of course, otherwise the prisoners would have tried to escape. Guess who was left in the wing wearing only her bra and panties and with her hands cuffed behind her around a pillar? Of course it was our friend – the biter. Naturally, they realised their mistake in the morning and rescued her. It seems that the men on that wing had been keeping her most entertained because she was completely exhausted, and minus her bra and panties. It must have been quite an interesting night. The funny thing was that she was totally co-operative from that time on, she was most insistent to tell us all about her fellow activists and even apologised to the wardress who she had bitten.' The wardress smirked, knowing that Julie would take every word as the gospel truth.

Julie felt nervous but excited at the thought of what might happen to her if she did not co-operate. She knew she had to admit to anything that she was accused of, to prevent herself being found innocent and released. That would spell the end of the whole adventure. After walking down several more long corridors and going up six floors in a crowded lift, in which her bottom was pinched by someone behind her, they arrived at the court area. Julie was supplied with a denim shirt several sizes too big which had no buttons, a tight pink micro-skirt one size too small and a pair of white shoes with impossibly high stiletto heels. Julie could barely walk in the shoes and wobbled and lurched as she tried to keep her balance.

'It's a shame that we couldn't find any better clothes for you, dear,' laughed one of the wardresses. 'You look like a drunken little tart in that outfit. I do hope that the judge doesn't get a bad impression. You really should be wearing a bra, panties and some tights. I always think creating a good first impression is so important, it's a pity that you will look like an incorrigible little minx who needs some firm discipline.' The two wardresses wheezed with laughter at their own leaden wit and frog-marched Julie into the courtroom.

Her parents were both present, their expressions of concern quickly replaced by expressions of outrage when they saw her brazen outfit. Their shock was further deepened when the state prosecutor read the charges of immorality and political agitation. The judge was a thin-faced woman in her early forties with her greying hair tightly drawn in a severe bun and an obvious dislike of the type of skimpily dressed young woman in front of her, who would appear before the bench in an outfit implying that no knickers were worn under the skirt. Some legal argument with the so-called defence counsel then ensued, during which the prosecutor produced the political pamphlets that had been seized at the party. In the end, no amount of argument would have changed anything. The judge saw the case as simply one where, in spite of having a privileged start in life and caring parents, a brazen young hussy had been caught red-handed at a debauched orgy, had associated with political criminals and then had the effrontery to walk into her court improperly dressed. It was well known that the judge, despite diets and workouts at the gymnasium, could not shift the fat and cellulite from her own bottom, and would feel a sense of relish that the bottom so round and firm, so impudently on display under the skin-tight skirt would soon be shuddering under the birch, benefiting from the disciplined regime of the new reformatories that were proving so effective. A governmental crash programme of building and conversions had ensured that dozens of reformatories were now dotted around in remote parts of the country. Old boarding schools, dilapidated stately homes and old derelict hospitals and institutions had all been quickly adapted to cater for the new influx of delinquents. After all, if the Government's promise to eradicate young criminals from the streets was to hold water, it must have the institutions to put them in. After at least two minutes' careful consideration, the judge announced that she had determined what the due punishment would be. Three years was the sentence, with the possibility of only serving two years if the headmistress considered that a particularly quick change of personality had been achieved. For the inmate to qualify for this reduction, the headmistress had to be completely convinced that the old personality had been permanently erased and had been replaced with total humility and unquestioning obedience. In fact, it was rare for the head teachers to report that they felt absolutely convinced there had been an early change in personality because they had a vested interest; more pupils meant more power and more staff, so most pupil inmates served the whole term.

Julie was allowed a few minutes with her parents after the verdict. Naturally they were enormously upset, especially her mother, who cried into her handkerchief whilst repeating, 'What will the neighbours say?' and 'What will they say down at the club?'

Her father could only stare open-mouthed at Julie's outfit and mutter, 'What do you look like? A common streetwalker and strumpet, I should judge. What got into you?'

Only one visit for the whole sentence was allowed at reformatories, and that depended on good behaviour, so Julie made the most of the few moments allowed and tried to reassure them that she would strive to be on her very best behaviour and so get an early release. The wardresses gleefully informed Julie on the way back to her cell that she would be going to Roughton Hall Reformatory on the island of Barrough, which apparently had an excellent reputation for discipline.

'Just what you need, young lady. You won't see any young men for three years and you'll get birched if you so much as breathe out of turn. And a good thing, too, if you ask me,' volunteered one of them.

Julie's heart sank as the cell door slammed behind her. Would it be as bad as everyone was saying?

Julie sat feeling very lonely, trying to make sure that the buttonless shirt kept together at the front because every so often the spy hole opened and an inquisitive eye would look in. The owner or owners of the eyes had an uncanny knack of knowing when she was sitting on the toilet bucket and so Julie was trying to use it as seldom as possible. Some hours later, Julie was pleased to see Sophie, wearing an ill-fitting red micro-dress which barely covered her bottom and matching red high heels, returned to the cell after her court appearance. After a further interval, Andrea, wearing a bedraggled blue blouse and thin skirt, was thrown roughly into the cell. Sophie reported that she had admitted everything in an attempt to get a lighter sentence and had also been sentenced to three years at Roughton Hall, which seemed to have plenty of vacant places for recalcitrant girls. Andrea had pleaded innocent and, somewhat foolishly, had then gone on to accuse the judge of being a fawning agent of the state and the warders of being jackbooted, fascist thugs. She was worried that the wardresses would seek some revenge on her but Sophie and Julie tried to allay her fears. However, they were realised when, late in the evening, four wardresses and two warders burst into the cell. The leading wardress leapt at Andrea and pinned her to the wall.

'Don't struggle you little bitch. We thought that the male inmates on B-Wing could benefit from your political analysis of society, so we are going to introduce you to them and let you get to know each other really well. You could, of course, tell us the names of your co-

conspirators and we might change our minds and let you stay here instead.'

'Get lost, you fascists,' shouted Andrea. 'You can't break my will. One day this corrupt regime will be swept away and you will have to answer to the people.'

'Enough! Help me hold her down,' screamed the first wardress and slapped Andrea hard across the cheek. The delicately-built girl could not resist the burly wardresses, who quickly restrained her and then proceeded to strip her and cuff her hands behind her back. When Andrea was completely naked, Julie watched with horror as one of the warders produced a black felt tip marker pen and wrote in large capitals on Andrea's tiny, pert breasts, COME AND GET ME, BOYS. She was then turned over and GIVE IT TO ME GOOD FROM BEHIND was daubed down her back, complete with an arrow pointing down towards her slim buttocks. Julie rose to protest but was sent flying backwards with a blow to the stomach which made her fight to catch her breath. Seconds later, Andrea was bundled out of the cell, screaming, and followed by the rest of the warders and wardresses.

Julie and Sophie clung together and wept, wondering what was happening to Andrea. It seemed as if there was no point in trying to resist the demands of the system. The system was an implacable and emotionless master. The freedom of the past, together with its attendant crime and strife, were gone and had been replaced with a relentless totalitarian state. Julie felt a sudden wave of pessimism. Her mission to gather information was already bearing fruit but organising resistance in the reformatory seemed like a hopeless task. It was only an hour later that Andrea, bruised and weeping, was unexpectedly thrown back into the cell.

'I've told them everything, it was horrible. Those men are wild animals. I've betrayed everybody. I can't live with myself any more. I'm a traitor to the resistance movement, but I couldn't help it. It was too awful. They put me in a tall cage about the size of a public call box. The men's hands were coming through the bars, groping me all over. I couldn't stop them, I was still handcuffed. There was a timer on the lock of the cage door set for thirty minutes. When it unlocked, I screamed for the wardresses to rescue me and promised to tell them everything. But the bitches took their time coming, just to show me. It must have been a minute or so before they came to me, and it felt like ten times as long. Those men are disgusting brutes. It would have been easier to have told them everything in the first place. The fascist bastards.' Andrea collapsed weeping into Sophie's arms as both she and Julie tried to soothe her, telling her that she had bravely done her best to resist and really could not be blamed for giving in, considering the circumstances. Meanwhile, Julie felt an elemental thrill as she imagined herself in Andrea's place, bound and helpless to resist the advances of the sex-starved inmates.

The next morning, Andrea was sentenced to three and a half years with a judge's recommendation for no remission and extra hard labour at a different reformatory, called St Theresa's Institute for the Correction of Young Ladies, situated on Dartmoor. When the tea tray came round Julie asked the wardress what had happened to Fiona and, even more crucially, Jack, the new love of her life, but was promptly told to shut up and mind her own business. The girls said a tearful goodbye to Andrea later that day. Julie felt at a low ebb but was soon cheered up when Sophie put her arm around her, and pulling her close whispered, 'Well, it looks like it's just the two of us left for the time being. Roughton Hall, here we come.'

3

The Journey

Two days later Julie and Sophie found themselves on a
train bound for the north of Scotland in order to be
shipped to the Isle of Barrough. The girls and their
escorts were delivered direct to the platform of King's
Cross station by one of the prison-service vans. Julie
noticed with some fascination that the train was pulled
by a steam engine, as were now commonly used on lines
frequented by tourists. Julie had previously only seen
them in black and white films and was entranced by the
spectacle of the billowing clouds of steam and the acrid
smell of the coal smoke. Julie and Sophie were attached
to each other with one pair of handcuffs and Julie's
other wrist was similarly attached to one of the two
wardresses who were accompanying them. During their
short stay at the interrogation centre they had realised
that most of the wardresses were lesbians, and mainly of
the butch, crop-haired variety. It transpired that these
two on the train, Officer Potter and Officer Muir were
two uncompromising lesbians who wasted no opportunity to molest their two nubile young charges. They both
wore the dark blue uniform, black seamed stockings and
brogue shoes of the prison service and each carried a
vicious-looking baton. The two young prisoners had not
escaped the attention of a crowd of football fans on the
same train, especially as they were still wearing the
revealing outfits that had been provided at the interrogation centre. The two massive, uniformed wardresses

were not entirely inconspicuous either. Since Julie's hands were constrained it was not easy to maintain her modesty when the front of her buttonless shirt drifted apart to reveal spectacular views of her naked breasts bouncing with the motion of the train. The two girls writhed with embarrassment and entreated the fans to leave them alone, but to no avail. The threats of the wardresses, who were enjoying the spectacle themselves, and therefore had ignored Julie's pleas to cover her up, had little effect on the exuberant fans, who persisted in calling out their appreciation and chanting, 'Get your tits out for the lads'.

Eventually, the wardresses arranged with the train guard to move to an empty first-class compartment which was a great relief to Julie and Sophie, but profoundly disappointing for the football fans.

The journey continued interminably. At lunch time Officer Muir went off to the buffet car and returned with some cans of diet cola and a pack of chicken and salad sandwiches each. This feast they duly ate, although not without difficulty due to the handcuffs, which the wardresses refused to unlock. The train passed through the industrial regions of the north of England, through the moorlands and up into the mountainous regions of Scotland. The scenery was breathtakingly beautiful as they passed beside lochs and forests. Inverness, where travellers previously had to change trains to continue north, the Moray Firth, Cromarty, the Cromarty Firth and the Dornoch Firth all passed by in their bleak grandeur. Gradually, the landscape became more and more rugged and craggy peaks towered over the single-track railway line. Most of the passengers, including the football fans, had already left the train at the stations serving the more populous areas and only those wanting the most remote stations or the ferry remained. Around tea-time Officer Muir paid another visit to the buffet car, this time returning with toasted tea cakes, strong tea in polystyrene cups for Sophie and Julie and a clutch of scotch whisky miniatures for themselves. The air became noticeably colder as they continued north and the cloud became thicker and lower. Soon it became so dark that the carriage lights came on. Minutes later, peals of thunder shook the air and torrential rain lashed the carriage windows. The wardresses, who had knocked back at least four of the whisky miniatures each, had long since run out of conversation.

Suddenly, Officer Potter shivered and remarked with a thin laugh that it was a pity that the girls had not wrapped up warmly. Looking out of the window at the rocky, uninhabited expanse of rain lashed mountainside, she added, 'Take a look at that, you two baggages. If you ever think of trying to escape just remember what this looks like. You couldn't get off the island anyway, but if you did escape, what chance would you have of getting back to England before the helicopters and dogs caught up with you? All you would achieve would be to almost die of starvation, exposure and blistered feet. And, what's more, you would get your just desserts when they took you back, a double dose of the birch at next morning's assembly at least and probably another year added on to your sentence.'

'We've passed Dunbeath so we'll be at the harbour station before long,' said Officer Muir winking at her colleague. 'It's time for the bonus we get for having to come out of our way when we could be taking it easy back at the centre.' So saying, she pulled down the carriage blinds, produced a key and unlocked both sets of handcuffs.

'Thank you,' sighed the two prisoners, rubbing their wrists.

'Not so fast, you cheeky pair. You can save your breath,' barked Officer Potter and immediately hauled Julie up by the hair. 'Stand on the seat and raise your arms.'

Julie obeyed and watched with horror as Officer Potter handcuffed one wrist, passed the links over the luggage rack rail and snapped the other cuff on to the other wrist. Officer Potter then quickly tugged Julie's skirt off and tied the denim shirt behind her. Julie shuddered at her helplessness and ridiculous posture, standing virtually naked, bouncing slightly on a train seat, her breasts shaking as the train clattered and swayed. Within seconds, the two wardresses had secured Sophie, naked in a similar way, on the opposite seat. Julie exchanged glances with Sophie, who had a look of apprehension on her face and looked faintly ridiculous as her body bowed slightly forwards so that her breasts hung down, swinging from side-to-side. She seemed to be shaking like a jelly with the motion of the train on the uneven mountain railway track.

'Better secure the door, Rose,' giggled Officer Potter, and proceeded to tie the handle with her belt. Having done that, the two wardresses turned towards each other and immediately clasped in a passionate embrace, showering kisses all over each other's face and gasping with pleasure. Growing increasingly frenzied, the kisses became longer and deeper, their heads seemingly locked together, occasional moans escaping and their hands excitedly pawing each other's head and back. The next minute their heads had parted and they fumbled madly with the buttons and belts of their partner's uniform. Within seconds the uniforms lay in a tangled heap, kicked into the corner of the compartment. Julie noticed with some surprise that the two wardresses wore matching underwear – no-nonsense white underwired bras designed for a large bosom, white navel-high waisted knickers cut high on the leg, white silk suspender belts and black seamed stockings. They hugged each other in a passionate squeeze, whilst each reached behind and unclipped the triple-row hooks and eyes of her partner's bra. The tightly stretched straps of the bras twanged apart, and as they were discarded their heavy breasts swung free, swaying and rippling with the vibration of the train. Again the lovers embraced squeezing their massive breasts together so that they bulged in great mounds out to each side. It was not long before the two pairs of knickers were edged down and kicked aside to reveal the big, rounded buttocks of the wardresses. Miss Potter had by far the largest breasts, at least 44DD thought Julie, and the biggest, roundest bottom of the two, whilst Miss Muir's whole back and chest were covered in little freckles. Although Miss Muir's breasts were slightly smaller, they hung down more pendulously, like two sacks of flour, and had a faint lattice work of blue veins running across them. Julie and Sophie looked on with increasing fascination as the lesbian lovers, while smothering each other with kisses, reached down and began to caress the other's pubis. Slowly they increased the pressure over the moist clitoris and inserted fingers deep within the slippery entrance of the vagina. Gradually the movements became frantic and the panting and cries more intense. As their orgasms seemed to be imminent, Miss Muir, who was directly in front of Julie, turned around, her face flushed with passion, and embraced Julie in a tight hug, her fingers slowly sliding down to cup the girl's firm bottom. She began to suck frenziedly on one of Julie's nipples which quickly responded by growing stiff and throbbing. As she did so, she inserted one finger deeply into Julie's bottom and two fingers of the other hand into her vagina, the thumb pressing and stroking her clitoris. Miss Potter moved round to kneel behind Miss Muir, and began to perform an impassioned act of cunnilingus, her hands gripping the backs of Miss Muir's thighs and her head buried deeply between the cheeks of her bottom. Julie was disgusted by the gross lesbianism of the wardresses, but with her hands shackled was in no position to do anything about it. Gradually, however, the skills and experience of the older woman overcame Julie's initial resistance. She felt herself lubricating between the legs, her nipples were aching more and more and her breath was coming in short gasps and pants. Looking across to where Sophie was swaying she saw the look of disbelief on her face as both she and Miss Muir erupted in a simultaneous howl of orgasmic release. Her body writhed and her legs turned to jelly as the waves of erotic sensation flooded through her. Seconds later, she hung limply from the luggage rack as Miss Muir staggered back to lean against a shocked Sophie. Miss Potter, meanwhile, rose from her kneeling position and embraced her lover.

For a while the two wardresses just clung together, supporting themselves with one arm each around Sophie. However, as Miss Muir recovered her breath, they both began to caress Sophie's wobbling breasts, paying particular attention to her large, dark nipples which were rapidly becoming engorged. This, in turn, caused the surrounding areolae, which were also a dark, almost chocolatey brown, to wrinkle. Sophie, meanwhile, studiously avoided meeting their eyes as a mark of defiance. After some minutes of this dual attention, in which the two older women became increasingly excited, Miss Potter grasped Sophie tightly and sank her head between her breasts while Miss Muir moved behind her colleague and inserted her hand between her legs, stroking the wet pouting labia and jutting clitoris from behind. The movements of Miss Muir's fingers grew increasingly rapid and muffled moans escaped from Miss Potter, her head still buried between Sophie's breasts, which were glistening and dripping with saliva. The moans soon became a series of squeals and drawn-out whimpers as Miss Potter's limbs began to jerk uncontrollably. She sank to her knees with the force of her climax, her head resting on Sophie's feet, which were perched on the edge of the seat. It took Miss Potter some minutes to recover, but when she did she crisply announced that it was time to get dressed and give the prisoners a farewell memento and mark of appreciation. They carefully put on their suspender belts, bras and stockings and as they donned their skirts they unthreaded the wide leather belts from their retaining loops.

Miss Muir, taking both, joined them and folded them double and said menacingly, 'The next two minutes will be your memento, since you will not easily forget them or the people who made them unforgettable, namely myself and Miss Potter. They will also provide a degree of appreciation since the mark – or marks, should I say – will probably last three or four days if my right arm is in good fettle. The mistresses at the reformatory could do with a little reminder that they are not the only ones who can wield a bit of discipline. Set your watch please, Katherine, time me for two minutes exactly, and let me know when the first minute is up.'

Miss Potter, leering at Julie and Sophie, took her watch in her hand, studied the dial for a few seconds and then announced, 'Ready, three, two, one – give it to them.'

Miss Muir swept her arm forward and, with a whirr and a crack, slashed the two belts across Julie's buttocks, drawing a shrill yelp from her. Without a pause she applied a second stroke across the front of Sophie's thighs which resulted in an even shriller yelp from the girl. By the time Miss Potter had shouted that one minute was up, Miss Muir had managed to deliver ten full-blooded strokes to each girl and the yelps had turned to howls and cries for mercy. As the full minute was announced, Miss Muir wiped the beads of perspiration from her forehead and stepped to the other side of the carriage. Now she was delivering strokes to Sophie's bottom and Julie's thighs and both the backs and fronts of each girl's legs were turning a deep shade of burning red with livid blotches standing out. By the time that the second minute was up, both girls were sobbing noisily and writhing, their faces contorted.

'You may as well get used to it, there will be plenty more of that where you are going,' crowed Miss Muir as she buckled her belt back on. 'Your pretty little rumps will be used to the taste of a good leathering by the time you get off the island.'

When the wardresses had finished dressing themselves they detached Sophie and Julie from the luggage rail and told them to get back into their clothes. Soon they were all sitting demurely as if nothing untoward had happened. Only the most astute observer would have noticed that the two younger members of the party were having a lot of difficulty sitting still and tended to squirm about as if they were sitting on something extremely uncomfortable, as indeed they were.

Before long, the train pulled into Thurso station, where almost all of the remaining passengers alighted. The few that were left were all travelling the last ten miles to Scrabster, the station for the Thurso Bay ferries to Torshavn or Stromness. Julie and Sophie gazed at the wonderful view from the right-hand window and took deep breaths of the fresh sea air occasionally tainted by smoke from the engine as the train skirted the rugged coastline. Eventually, with a metallic squeal of brakes and a sharp hiss of steam the train stopped at Scrabster, the small harbour station. The single platform station was within yards of the harbour wall and Julie could see the fishing boats and a couple of ferries moored a short walking distance from the train itself.

'Here's your reception committee, coming on to the platform now. They're usually so punctual it's just as well that the train has arrived late,' said Miss Potter, opening the carriage door. 'Out you get, this is where we have to leave you.'

'It's been nice knowing you, I expect you will miss us,' said Miss Muir with a laugh. 'At least, you will miss us when you realise that you have had it soft up to now.'

The 'reception committee' consisted of three women in their late twenties or early thirties. Julie and Sophie immediately noticed how tall and unusually athletic they looked. They were all wearing extremely tight navy blue shorts which showed off their long, tanned legs and slim buttocks. Tight black leather belts emphasised their narrow waists and their large jutting, firmly-brassièred busts strained at their white ribbed jumpers. They all had impeccably neat hairstyles and a curt military bearing. The railway staff were used to seeing the comings and goings of the inmates of the reformatory and so did not pay much attention except to look them up and down with a trace of a leer as the two prisoners were handed over to the three women from the reformatory. Various papers were signed, Miss Muir removed the handcuffs and, after a few whispered pieces of gossip between Miss Potter and one of the reformatory staff, the two wardresses climbed back on to the train for the long journey back to the south. Julie shivered, there was a stiff sea breeze blowing and a hint of rain in the air. There was much activity around the steam locomotive as it took on more coal and water with frequent hissing and the letting-off of steam. A replacement driver and foot-plateman in their blue jackets and caps stood waiting, their food for the journey in tin boxes under their arms. Julie looked out to sea beyond the harbour wall and observed a thick sea mist rolling in towards the shore. Seagulls, uttering their piercing cries, were swooping near the boats eager for bits of fish offal and a lighthouse ship that was just visible in the distance sounded its hooter. The noise echoed eerily against the bleak cliffs.

How different this is from Richmond, thought Julie. I wish I was back there now. At least I would be a bit warmer.

One of the women was holding two thick leather belts. Stepping forward, she ordered the two frightened girls to turn around to present their backs to her. She then buckled the belts around their waists with the buckle at the back. At each side of the belt was a leather band with a buckle, into which the girls were told to put their wrists. When these buckles were drawn tight the girls found that their hands were firmly attached to their sides as if they were standing to attention.

One of the women introduced herself as Miss Chapel and then barked the order, 'Quick march.'

With some alacrity, since the expression on Miss Chapel's face showed that she would tolerate no resistance, the two girls marched in the direction indicated, along the harbour perimeter towards the moored boats. Miss Chapel strode in front and the two other women followed behind. The few fishermen and harbour workers in the vicinity followed the progress of the party with ill-concealed interest. As they paused in their work to stare, Julie did not know whether they were mainly interested in the statuesque examples of feminine athleticism represented by the three mistresses from Roughton Hall or the dejected prisoners in their skimpy clothes and with their wrists tightly attached to their sides.

Occasionally the stentorian voice of one of the mistresses behind would shout, 'Keep your heads up, you sluts, don't look at your feet. Heads up and look straight ahead. Keep those backs straight, too, slouching is not allowed at Roughton Hall. You may as well learn that now.' This shouting only served to increase the interest of the harbour workers and ensured that everyone, unless they were deaf, would be aware of the approach of the group. Julie felt that the mistresses basked in the admiring glances of the men and surmised, correctly as she was soon to find out, that there were no males present at Roughton Hall.

They passed a small huddle of young construction workers repairing the slipway beside the diesel storage tanks. Some of the younger ones were quite attractive, thought Julie, but her face soon burned with embarrassment as a bellow of, 'Eyes to the front, Semple, I told you before. That disobedience will cost you three strokes of the cane across your bottom, on the bare,' echoed across the harbour.

Julie heard a snigger from the group of young men, followed by a wolf whistle and a muttered comment, 'Nice arse.'

Finally they stopped at a large cabin cruiser which bore the legend *THE CHRISTIAN MAID* – ROUGHTON HALL STATE REFORMATORY FOR GIRLS on a plaque at the stern. It looked to be an expensive vessel with a radar dome mounted high on a mast. It also had a small launch with a black outboard motor marked with the name *Mercury* hanging from davits over the stern.

'Right, you two. You can run on the spot until I tell you to stop, while we get the engine going and the cabin sorted out. Start now!' barked Miss Chapel. Julie and Sophie started to run on the spot on the quayside while the three mistresses busied themselves preparing the boat.

'Don't face this way,' shouted Miss Chapel. 'Face the diesel tanks. We don't want to have you staring at us with your ugly faces. And put more effort into it or else you will feel my strap across your backsides before you get on this boat.' Julie and Sophie turned in the direction of the tanks and were acutely aware of the group of young men in the middle distance enjoying the spectacle of the two girls bouncing up and down with their hands pinioned to their sides. The men had now stopped working completely and were sitting on oil drums, rolling cigarettes and pouring tea from their flasks as if they had seats at a cricket match or race meeting.

43

'What's your name?' one shouted with a broad grin as he nudged his mate in the ribs, but Julie and Sophie were not foolish enough to shout back and wished fervently that they could be swallowed up into a hole in the ground where no one could see them. Running on the spot was rather uncomfortable as having large breasts, no bra and her hands pinned to her sides made Julie's whole chest and back ache. In addition, both girls were getting very out of breath.

'When will those bitches let us pack this in?' whispered Sophie. 'I'm feeling wretched and I'm brassed-off with those jerks staring at us. Look at that one on the left, the one putting his cigarette out. He's got a massive hard-on like he's got a cucumber in his trousers, and he's not making much effort to hide it.'

A sudden flash of lightning followed by a clap of thunder drowned out Julie's whispered reply and a deluge of icy rain started pouring from the sky. A voice from the boat shouted, 'Don't even think of stopping, you two trollops. Keep those knees up. A bit of rain won't hurt you, but my strap will if you slow up just one iota.'

Within a few seconds the scant clothing of the two hapless girls was saturated and clinging tightly to every contour of their lithe bodies like a second skin. Every moment increased the discomfort as they squelched and shivered. Julie could see that both her own nipples, and Sophie's, were clearly visible through their wet clothes, especially as they were fiercely erect with the freezing wet material rubbing on them. Rainwater was pouring down Julie's neck and trickling down her back, and her hair was sticking to her face. The cotton skirt was clinging to her thighs and buttocks. Every step was accompanied with loud squelches and she could not remember when she had ever felt so miserable or so uncomfortable. The rain had not deterred the onlookers who, now sheltering under some old tarpaulin, were even more engrossed with observing the plight of the prisoners whose every bodily detail was shown off to glistening perfection by the thin, wet material.

Julie was just feeling that she could not run for a second more when the cabin door was thrown open and a voice bellowed out, 'Get in here, you two, double quick. Stop displaying yourselves to those vulgar workmen, you dirty sluts. You won't be seeing any more men for a good long time now, so I would try to remember what they look like in case you forget. And if you like being fucked by a man you can forget that, too. You two won't get any fucks, not from a man at least, for a very long time. You'd better get used to the idea, because there are no men on the island. There's plenty of female company, though, so you won't be too lonely.'

As soon as the girls stumbled into the cabin the ropes were cast off, the engine was opened up with a roar and the craft lurched forward towards the harbour entrance. As they passed the harbour wall the waves became higher and the boat was tossed and buffetted by the pounding of the waves.

'With this sea and headwind it will take about two hours to get there,' shouted Miss Chapel who was seated at the wheel. 'We will get thrown about quite a bit so you had better go below and lie on the bunks. Miss Sullivan will come with you and tie you. It's a rule of the reformatory that you must be restrained on the boat. Perhaps some girls tried to overpower the crew once upon a time, I don't know, but don't worry, you will be quite safe. We go out in much rougher weather than this without any difficulty. This boat can easily handle these waves so you won't go down with the ship.'

Miss Sullivan, who appeared to be in her late twenties, made her way gingerly across the deck clutching on to the chromium rails. She had shoulder-length, dark brown hair and a pretty face with high cheekbones.

Julie could not help noticing as Miss Sullivan passed by that she had the most beautiful deep blue eyes which seemed to twinkle as she spoke.

'Follow me,' she shouted above the roar of the engine and waves. Leading the way into the cabin, she closed the door behind them muting the roar and shutting out the cold wind. The interior was warm and the noise of the engine was now a comforting low throbbing. Mahogany panelling and polished brass fittings gave the cabin an air of opulence. A thick pile rug adorned the centre of the floor and some chesterfield-style seating with deeply buttoned and padded cushioning followed the perimeter of the cabin. A gentle vibration quivered through the polished wood floor.

Miss Sullivan turned to the shivering prisoners and said with a trace of a kindly tone, 'You are new girls, unused to the ways of Roughton Hall as yet. I don't want you to do wrong through ignorance and inexperience forcing me to have to punish you, so listen carefully to my instructions. You must obey them in their entirety without hesitation – that is the way of the reformatory. Failure to do so will have serious consequences. In the past, some new girls have tried to test the resolution of the reformatory mistresses with small acts of defiance without realising that they were earning a severe birching. I am sure they felt that they had been unfairly treated. So that is why I am warning you. And, incidentally, it is another rule that you always answer the staff by name, so for instance you call me Miss Sullivan. Do you understand?'

'Yes, Miss Sullivan,' chorused the two girls.

'Sophie, I am now going to undo your restraint belt, so hold still.' Miss Sullivan quickly undid each buckle in turn and as the belt swung free she said softly, 'Your clothes are dripping wet. It would probably give you a bad cold or flu if you kept them on, besides making the whole cabin wet. I am going to count to ten. Strip naked

46

and stand to attention before the count is up if you want to avoid punishment. One, two, three, four, five ...' Sophie struggled in a frenzy to beat the count and just made it, standing up straight by the count of eight.

Miss Sullivan turned to Julie and, after unbuckling her belt said, 'Now it's your turn, Julie. One, two, three ...' Julie seemed to be all thumbs but, perhaps due to not having many clothes on to start with, managed to reach the required state of undress and posture by the count of seven.

'Good, you seem to be getting the idea already. That will make life easier for you. It's the ones who fight the system who learn the hard way. They are the really silly ones. It's much better to just accept that you are going to be reformed whether you like it or not,' lectured the mistress. 'Stand next to each other. That's better. I see that you are both in reasonable shape; not too fat. You could lose a little bit of weight, both of you, but the reformatory will soon take care of that. Probably with a bread, water and lettuce diet for a couple of weeks, coupled with our usual physical exercise regime. You would be surprised how overweight some of the girls who get sent here are, and even more surprised to see how soon they lose it. A ten-mile run, naked except for a thirty-pound backpack with twenty press-ups every fifteen minutes on a diet of bread, lettuce and water plus a half-hour aerobics session at two in the morning every day for two weeks is all it takes. You do look shocked! Don't worry: neither of you would fall into that category.'

Miss Sullivan moved nearer, exuding a faint scent of sandalwood perfume and cupped one of Sophie's breasts in one hand and one of Julie's in the other.

'In fact, you two are in rather nice physical shape. Sophie's breasts are extremely firm. No sag at all, which is unusual considering their size, and a nice big, dark areola. I like them very much. Julie, yours are a bit softer, but still pretty firm for their size and what a perfect shape. I'll probably send for the two of you one evening, to attend me in my study. Turn around, both of you. Ah, marks of a recent strapping! How nice the red stripes look against the lily-white skin of those pert little bottoms. Now, stay still while I put these belts back on you.'

She then buckled and locked with a small padlock one of the leather belts around each girl. Next, she moved the wrist bands to the back of each belt and, ordering the girls to stand closely face to face, she then attached Julie's wrists to the back of Sophie's belt and Sophie's wrists to the back of Julie's belt so that the two prisoners appeared to be embracing each other. Julie found the position somewhat uncomfortable with their faces touching and her breasts squashed hard against Sophie's, making them bulge out at the sides. Miss Sullivan steered them with some difficulty across to the couch and helped them to lie on their sides. She then draped a thick eiderdown over them and tucked the edges in tightly.

'There you are,' she said. 'As snug as bugs in a rug. You both look so pretty in that position and you are keeping each other warm as well. You can kiss each other when I leave you if you like. I do think that the ability of girls to comfort each other is so important, especially at Roughton Hall. There are no men there, after all, and when a girl gets a whipping – and no one escapes it, of course – she naturally wants some comforting. Who needs men anyway? They are such vulgar brutes, and can never satisfy a woman as well as another woman can. They are too rough and ugly. Disgusting, bony creatures if you ask me. I find that many a girl, after a whipping, especially if I have had to administer it myself, is most grateful for the comfort and solace that I give her. Of course, that is assuming that I find her pretty and to have an agreeable little personality.

Some of the girls are just hardened little sluts who can neither give any kindness nor deserve to receive any. But you two look to be rather innocent and naive. You will get the same severity of treatment as anyone else of course, but I may on some occasions be able to give you some treats and comfort in my study if you show the right inclinations and willingness to learn. After all, there is a lot that an experienced, older woman can teach a couple of pretty young things. Sapphic delights are, naturally, an infringement of the rules at Roughton Hall but there is an element of flexibility as well, depending on the ruling of the headmistress, Miss Spenser. For example, she believes in some cases that the close attention of a particular mistress to a particular girl can help the process of reformation and submission. Any unauthorised relationships are, of course, dealt with severely for all concerned.' Miss Sullivan broke off in mid-flow as an impatient call from the deck could be heard faintly through the door. She immediately turned and was gone.

'All the women who get these reformatory and prison jobs seem to be raving lesbians,' whispered Sophie. 'Either that or they soon turn into one, it would seem.'

'Perhaps it's because there are no men there,' whispered Julie. 'At least Miss Sullivan seems a bit nicer than the other two; they seem very strict.'

'It feels funny being pressed together like this, doesn't it? When we move, our tits bulge funny ways like four balloons being pushed together. Do you think Miss Sullivan is trying to turn us into lesbians, Julie?'

'I don't know. I suppose it does feel nice in a way. After all the mean treatment we have had to endure together, it is sort of comforting to feel you warm against me, and when you move I can feel your mound rubbing against mine and it gives me a kind of warm feeling inside. But I don't think that I could turn into a lesbian, I like boys too much,' murmured Julie dreamily.

'I wonder what it will be like at the reformatory. I bet it will be really horrible with really strict teachers and rotten food,' Sophie continued. 'It's making me feel nervous, the nearer we get. Why do the wardresses and these mistresses and all the others keep going on about punishments and straps and whips and so on? Do you think that they really use them all that much? Perhaps they don't use that sort of punishment except as a last resort, such as when someone tries to escape. I hope that it is something like that. My bum and thighs still hurt from that strapping that those old cows gave us in the train. I would rather do anything than have a worse whipping than that.'

Julie gave Sophie a squeeze and said, 'I suppose there is no point in worrying until we know what is going to happen to us, but I can't help feeling nervous, too. It would be nice to think that all this talk about punishment with whips and things is a lot of hot air but I doubt if it is. Those Roughton Hall mistresses look as if they mean business, and I doubt if it is just escapers who get the birch because I don't think anyone would try to escape. It would be totally futile from an island miles out in the North Sea. Besides, do you remember what Andrea was saying back in the cell about the way the government had got all these ideas from that nineteenth century convent which ran those reformatories where they thought that a good whipping brought you nearer to God and their motto was "spare the rod and spoil the child"? The Convent of the Righteous Sisters, I think she called it. The sisters were all cruel and mean religious fanatics, so a spell in one of their reformatories was not something that anyone would wish to repeat. No wonder they were considered an effective answer to juvenile crime. Anybody who had been in one of those reformatories never committed any more crimes because they were too scared of being sent back. So they were all "reformed", well and truly.'

'Perhaps it's not so surprising that the new government has picked up the idea,' whispered Sophie. 'With the crime and urban terrorism rate being so high, people will go along with anything to bring back law and order, however extreme.'

'Yes, and it's also a reaction to all those ideas of the last government, who said that all young criminals were victims of capitalism and needed some understanding and a holiday in the countryside to help them lose their anger against society,' replied Julie.

'I think we are going to be "reformed" whether we need it or not,' Sophie concluded with a deep sigh and gave Julie a tight squeeze.

4

The Isle of Barrough

Julie must have fallen asleep, because the next thing that she was aware of was being shaken by the shoulder and Miss Chapel's face looming over her.

'Your clothes have been hung over the engine cover since we left harbour and are now dry. You can put them back on now, because we are nearly there.' Miss Chapel threw the clothes mixed together in a pile on the cabin floor, unlocked the two waist-belts and tersely ordered, 'Clothes on and standing to attention by the count of ten, one, two, three . . .'

Julie and Sophie scrambled to obey within the time allowed and by the count of ten were standing to attention, facing Miss Chapel.

'Look straight ahead. It is not allowed to look the staff of Roughton Hall directly in the eye except in specific circumstances,' instructed Miss Chapel. She walked around the girls inspecting them in minute detail and lifting Julie's skirt commented, 'No knickers. How suitable since knickers are not allowed for new girls at Roughton Hall. It's just as well you are already getting used to it.' Walking behind Sophie, she lifted her red dress and frowned.

'Oh dear, this just will not do. Your knickers are back to front. In your haste, you have obviously omitted to take care. Sloppiness is not tolerated at Roughton Hall in any circumstances. Careless actions are a sign of a careless mind, and a careless mind is an intolerable characteristic in a girl. I will therefore punish you to teach you a lesson. Now remove those knickers and give them to me.'

Sophie hastily removed the offending article of underwear with trembling fingers, almost falling over as one of her high heels caught on the elastic. She handed them to Miss Chapel, who strode over to the cabin window, slid it open, letting in a gale of cold sea air, and hurled the knickers out.

'You won't need those again,' she said. 'Now assume position one.'

A look of confusion overcame Sophie and with eyes cast down and blushing she squeaked, 'I'm sorry Miss Chapel, but I don't know what position one means. No one has told me.'

An expression of impatience passed over Miss Chapel's face and she said with a sigh, 'I thought Miss Sullivan had been giving you some lessons in the ways of Roughton Hall, she was down here long enough. Well, you will get your proper induction tomorrow morning when you will be told all of the rules and ways of the reformatory. However, for the moment let me give you some preliminary instruction. The various positions a girl must adopt when ordered to do so are numbered to save time and to ensure that there is no deviation from the positions as laid down by the founders of the Ancient Order when they set up the original reformatories. Position number one is the quickest and most basic position for a peremptory, routine and mild application of the instrument of correction to the buttocks. Follow my instructions. Turn to face away from me and stand with your feet twelve inches apart. Now, bend at the waist and hold on to your ankles.'

Sophie slowly bent forward at the waist; as she did so, her red mini-skirt rode up completely exposing the twin globes of her buttocks. Her legs trembled slightly as she strained down to clasp her ankles without bending her legs.

'Lastly, raise your head so that it is looking at the wall and not at the ground,' continued Miss Chapel. 'It is forbidden to move or change position in any way until you are given permission. When I do give you permission to rise after I have punished you, you will thank me by name. Oh, and you can count each stroke as well. It's not usually necessary with so few strokes but you may as well get the hang of it. You will say, "One, Miss Chapel, two, Miss Chapel," and so on. Failure to observe these rules, however slight the infringement, means a doubling of the punishment at the very minimum. Do you understand, girl?'

Sophie had followed the instructions to the letter and, with her head straining up to look at the wall, croaked, 'Yes, Miss Chapel.'

'Good, I'm glad you are a quick learner. That may save you some painful episodes in future. You have got the position very well – nice straight legs and head well up, that's good for a new girl. I'm going to give you three strokes on the bare with the cane, a junior one. I'm being very lenient. Remember what I said about keeping your position and the necessity of thanking me. You may scream or cry out if you wish, I don't object to that. In fact, I quite like to hear it because I know that the cane is doing its work effectively when I hear a girl cry out. I especially like it when a proud young hussy has been gritting her teeth, desperately attempting to deny me the satisfaction of hearing her cry, and finally she gives way with a hoarse scream or a plaintive sob. And you, Julie, I want you to kneel down in front of Sophie, arms by your side, looking into Sophie's eyes. I want you to see the expression of a girl being whipped. It will be most instructive and serve as a lesson to you. You can also tell me if Sophie's eyes deviate from looking straight ahead as position one requires. Now move!'

Julie scrambled over to kneel facing Sophie. Sophie's face was flushed with the exertion of bending down for so long, keeping her balance as the boat rolled and the strain of forcing her head up to look straight ahead. Her lips trembled with fear and a tear rolled down one cheek. I wish I could say something soothing or give poor Sophie a hug, thought Julie, but I can't, otherwise I would get the cane myself.

Miss Chapel strode across the cabin, her long, tanned legs covering the distance in a few strides and reached into a brass-bound sea chest. She rummaged around for a few seconds and Julie stole a glance at the sight of Miss Chapel's slim bottom straining the tight cotton of her shorts as she bent over. Straightening up, she held a pale yellow, bamboo school cane about 24 inches long, with a crook handle, in her hands. Julie quickly returned her gaze to meet Sophie's frightened eyes.

Striding back, Miss Chapel remarked casually, 'A nice, rounded bottom, just made for a pliable junior cane to wrap around. The junior cane is the shortest and most lenient in use at Roughton Hall, and I am only going to give you three strokes, but you will find that it will nevertheless still sting like a hundred bees. I've got the right arm of a seasoned squash player. You are about to get a taste of some real punishment, not the half-hearted slaps on the backside that you may have received up to now. This will be a good introduction to the Hall's rigorous methods and convince you that the mistresses of the reformatory are not to be trifled with. If I say get dressed I don't mean get dressed with knickers on back to front. In future you will instantly obey any order correct to the absolute finest detail. Do you understand me, girl?'

'Yes, Miss Chapel,' came the croaked reply.

'Louder, girl. I can hardly hear you,' bellowed Miss Chapel, flexing the cane in her hands so that it formed a big letter 'C'.

'Yes, Miss Chapel,' repeated Sophie a little more loudly, her voice quavering.

'Good, and God help you if you get up before I say you can. Now begins the process of turning you from a useless slut into an upstanding and penitent, fully reformed member of society.' Miss Chapel adjusted her stance and measured the cane against Sophie's bottom, gently touching the centre with the tip of the cane. Slowly, she brought her arm back behind her shoulder and then, rising on to the tips of her toes, she slashed the cane with a whistle through the air to curl evenly around Sophie's buttocks with a sharp crack. Sophie was nearly lifted off her feet and she staggered to maintain her position without falling over. A choked scream split the air, followed by a loud intake of breath. Looking directly into Sophie's eyes, Julie saw a pained expression pass over her features and her face turned an even deeper shade of crimson. Julie feared that her friend would forget Miss Chapel's instructions and incur a worse punishment but then Sophie, through gritted teeth, gasped, 'One, Miss Chapel.'

The mistress again flexed the cane and ran it through her hands evidently relishing the springy power that could be unleashed with it when handled by an enthusiast. Again she measured the cane across Sophie's twin globes and quickly cracked it across them. Again Sophie rocked forward emitting a loud scream which ended with a strangled cry of, 'No, no, please ... I'm sorry ... Two, Miss Chapel.'

Miss Chapel edged forward and with an expression of pure sensuality slowly ran her hands over Sophie's burning buttocks for half a minute while the girl uttered a few gasps and tried to bite her lip.

'A couple of rather delicious stripes. Pretty good for a junior cane even if I do say it myself. And we are not finished yet,' announced Miss Chapel with a smug expression. Julie wished that she could turn her eyes away from the look of fear and misery on her friend's face as she struggled to maintain her posture. She also wished that Miss Chapel would hurry up and get it over with, instead of making it stretch out. Her prayers were answered when the mistress resumed her stance. Raising the cane high and swivelling her shoulders, she brought it down again with all of her strength. The bamboo landed with another loud crack on its trembling target. Sophie shot up on her toes, her hands almost unclasped from her ankles. A howl broke from her lips and a dribble of saliva hung down and finally dropped from her mouth.

'Three, Miss Chapel,' she managed to force out through a choking sob, her whole body shaking.

'Very well, you may straighten up, young lady, and turn to face me,' said Miss Chapel calmly. Sophie turned to face the mistress her face crimson and eyes puffed up with tears.

'Th- th- thank you Miss Chapel,' she just about managed to blurt out, her chest heaving with stifled sobs.

'You are welcome, Sophie, it was a pleasure. I make no secret of the fact that I thoroughly enjoy caning sluts. I feel sure that I have already started the process of turning you into a good little girl again, a process which I find most satisfying and which is also for the greater good of society. We are almost at our mooring point at Barrough, so I am now going to handcuff you and take you up on deck. Turn around and place your hands behind your back.'

Having turned around, Julie felt the cold metal of the cuffs as they clicked on each wrist. Following Sophie and Miss Chapel up the steps to the deck was especially difficult in high heels and with no hands to steady herself, but finally Julie found herself standing next to Sophie on the rear deck. They watched the seagulls circling around them noisily as the boat edged alongside a wooden landing stage, on which a drab green Land Rover with ROUGHTON HALL REFORMATORY FOR GIRLS painted in maroon on the side, was parked. A trailer with a tarpaulin cover was hitched to the rear of the vehicle. There was only one building on the quay; a low breeze block shed with a diesel tank and pump alongside it. Barbed wire hung in great loops over the side of the shed's roof and a huge padlock fastened the door. Directly outside the building was a large lorry painted in a similar colour scheme; and several high stacks of wooden pallets were lined up as if waiting to be returned to the mainland. A number of large notices announced, PRIVATE PROPERTY. TRESPASSERS WILL BE PROSECUTED. BY ORDER OF THE HOME OFFICE. From what Julie could see through the mist and the rapidly failing light, the island had a coastline of craggy cliffs, dense undergrowth and no obvious signs of general habitation. All in all, it was a scene that would evoke despair in even the most optimistic of characters.

As the boat was tied up to concrete bollards fore and aft, Miss Chapel ordered the two girls to step ashore and walk over to the Land Rover. On reaching the vehicle, Miss Chapel assisted Julie and Sophie into the back of it, where they sat on the vinyl-covered benches on each side. Julie noticed that Sophie sat down very gingerly and winced as her bare skin touched the vinyl. Miss Chapel strode back to the boat to help the other two load the trailer with several large sacks and carrier bags; obviously the result of a shopping trip to the mainland supermarket. Having done that she climbed into the Land Rover.

'Hold your heads still, I am now going to hood you both. It's a simple precaution and probably unnecessary. It's so that in the event of an escape you would not know the way from the reformatory to the landing stage,' Miss Chapel explained. Julie watched as she reached under the dashboard and produced the hoods. Reaching over to Sophie, Miss Chapel first put a soft, elasticated cotton band over her head and pulled it over her eyes.

'Can you see anything through that?'

'No, nothing, Miss Chapel,' came the reply.

'Good. And now to make doubly sure, here comes the hood,' continued the mistress. She then, carefully, fitted a brown leather hood with a large mesh for breathing over Sophie's head. Miss Chapel next turned her attention to Julie, firstly slipping the elastic headband over her eyes, plunging her world into total blackness, and then fitting the leather hood over her head. Julie felt trapped in a world of darkness, all she was conscious of was what she could hear. For a long time she could hear only the gulls wheeling around the bay and the crashing of the waves. Finally, however, the other two mistresses climbed into the front of the Land Rover, the engine was started and Julie felt a lurch as it began the final leg of the journey to Roughton Hall. For what seemed like half an hour, the vehicle lurched and bumped over what were obviously rather poorly maintained roads. At times, Julie almost fell off the slippery vinyl seat especially when the vehicle raced around a bend, of which because of the blindfold, she had no warning. The three mistresses were talking in low voices together. Julie strained her ears to catch what they were saying but she could only make out the odd phrase here and there as the noise of the engine and the rattles of the bodywork were very loud. Some of the talk seemed to be about what they had seen or bought in the shops that day. Other snatches of conversation seemed to be gossip about fellow members of the Roughton Hall staff and various pupils.

Finally the Land Rover came to a halt. Julie heard a window being wound down and some muffled conversation with someone outside the car. After that came the creaking of a gate or perhaps a barrier and then they continued, this time over gravel. Julie assumed that they would soon come to a halt, but they motored on for about another ten minutes, eventually halting with a skidding noise on the loose stones. The engine was cut, doors opened and slammed and Julie felt herself being assisted out of the back of the vehicle.

'Welcome to Roughton Hall,' Julie heard someone say as she felt the hood being removed. Suddenly, she could see again as the elasticated band was pulled off. Blinking in the murky twilight, Julie gasped with surprise as she found herself looking at an enormous stone mansion the size of a stately home with tall leaded windows, stone lions, ivy-clad walls, battlements and turrets.

5

The Arrival

Roughton Hall had a grand stone frontage some twenty steps high, guarded by two stone griffins and rising up to a massive oak-panelled double door.

'On your knees, both of you,' commanded Miss Chapel, as she removed the handcuffs. The two girls duly sank to the ground, wincing as the sharp gravel chips pressed into their knees and palms. Sophie rubbed her wrists where the steel of the cuffs had been tight and looked sulkily at the ground. The bumpy ride on the hard vinyl seat had not soothed her bottom at all – rather the reverse.

'The tradition at Roughton Hall, and remember, this place is based strictly on tradition, is that new girls crawl into the reformatory when they first arrive so that they know their place. We could have stopped the car further down the drive like we did when we brought those two girls who mugged the old lady. It took them an hour to get to the door. However, we have decided to be lenient with you and have parked within ten yards of the steps. So you can thank me and get crawling immediately,' said Miss Chapel.

Julie and Sophie feeling totally overawed by the scale of the building and their own helplessness both quavered, 'Thank you, Miss Chapel,' and started crawling on all fours towards the flight of steps. Progress was painful both to the knees and hands and Julie soon fell behind Sophie who was crawling a lot faster. Julie could see Sophie's naked bottom, with the marks of the caning glowing against the whiter skin, swaying from side to side as she crawled in front. Suddenly, she heard the gravel crunch behind her and immediately felt a searing pain across her buttocks. Julie yelped and quickly accelerated her crawling, almost catching up with Sophie.

'That will teach you to hang back, you lazy baggage,' shouted Miss Chapel as she walked past Julie swinging a leather strap. They reached the steps neck and neck and raced on all fours, their palms and knees stinging, up the grand stairway. Finally, they reached the top side by side, whereupon they both collapsed, panting, in front of the main entrance.

Abruptly, Julie became aware that the enormous door was slowly opening. An imposing figure stood silhouetted against the light of the lobby. It was a tall, stern-faced woman of about 40. As Julie's eyes adjusted to the light of the interior she saw from her position on the floor that the woman was wearing black shoes with a very high heel, a tight black sheath skirt and a white starched blouse, with a buttoned collar and cuffs, against which her large bust strained. An academic gown was draped over her shoulders and she carried a pair of black leather gloves in her hand. The three mistresses each performed a deep curtsey and stood respectfully erect.

'The two new pupils, Julie Semple and Sophie Adams, Headmistress,' announced Miss Sullivan.

The Headmistress cast her eye critically over the whole party for what seemed like an age before saying in a dignified voice, 'So, Miss Sullivan, Miss Chapel and Miss Walters, back at last. And what, may I ask, has caused you to be one hour late? No, don't bother explaining now; I will see you all tomorrow morning at seven o'clock sharp in my office. Now take these two specimens to holding-cell number four. It's too late to get through any induction now, I will arrange it for the morning.' Without pausing, she quickly turned on her heel and walked away, clicking down the stone-flagged corridor, her gown billowing out behind her.

'On your feet and follow me,' ordered Miss Chapel. Julie and Sophie began following the mistress down a corridor that ran off to the right of the entrance door. Miss Sullivan and Miss Walters followed on closely behind. Between them a loud cacophony of clicks echoed off the stone walls as their heels clattered on the hard floor. At intervals on the left of the corridor large oil paintings of saints and eminent clerics hung, while on the right stained glass windows depicting religious scenes from the Old Testament were set into the stonework. At the end of the corridor they descended a long flight of steps, which brought the party into another corridor illuminated by wrought iron lanterns hanging from the whitewashed walls. The walls were occasionally enlivened by paintings and needleworked proverbs although the subject matter was not designed to raise the spirits. The paintings all depicted various scenes of torment of religious martyrs and the proverbs consisted of sentiments such as 'Spare the Rod and Spoil the Child', 'Ye Shall Suffer for Your Sins', 'The Day of Judgement is at Hand' and 'Blessed are the Meek'. Julie felt her heart sinking with the oppressiveness of the atmosphere and the knowledge that there was no way of escape back to the mainland.

What a dismal place, like a cross between a medieval monastery and a stately home, Julie mused. What on earth have I let myself in for? She glanced at Sophie and could see that she was probably thinking the very same thoughts.

The corridor turned a corner and stretched off into the distance. They continued their way clattering along at great speed. This place is vast, much bigger than I would ever have imagined, thought Julie. I do hope that they are not too strict, in spite of the ghastly appearances. This hope was somewhat dashed as they turned another corner and approached a strange scene.

In the middle of the corridor were two inmates, naked and on all fours, facing away so that their two very feminine, paper-white bottoms were displayed to the approaching party. The display was even more brazen as both girls were wearing strange attachments to their legs. These consisted of two leather bands which buckled above each knee, joined by a metal bar about twelve inches long. A similar bar joined each ankle. The effect of these so-called 'legspreaders' was to hold the legs apart so that the crease of the bottom and anal dimple was on full show. One of the girls had a further device attached, which was a leather belt with a strap which passed up tightly between the legs attached to the front and rear of the belt.

'This item of restraint is called a saddle,' Miss Chapel explained. 'It comes in various forms. Some are relatively lenient, such as the plain leather strap, and others are more uncomfortable, such as the rope or chain saddles. Woe betide you if you are sentenced to wear one for longer than a day. Everyone can always tell if you are wearing one under your skirt by the way you walk, and they will see your discomfort if you have to bend over.'

As the group slowed to pass the obstacle, Julie obtained a closer view of the whole spectacle. The saddle was, in fact, one which had a thick, penis-shaped butt plug attached. It was held in place almost fully inserted into the bottom and greatly distended the anal ring. Julie noticed that the bulbous, veined rubber penis had an enormous pair of black rubber testicles hanging down at its base which bounced against the girl's smoothly depilated sex with every movement. At first, Julie could not make out what the girl was doing, her head was almost touching the ground and was making vigorous side to side movements. Getting closer, however, Julie saw that the girl was holding a toothbrush

64

clenched between her teeth and was scrubbing the stone floor with it. A bowl of soapy water lay beside her and at intervals she dipped the brush into the water to renew the lather. The other girl was obviously receiving a less severe punishment since she did not have a saddle or a butt plug fitted. She also had a toothbrush and was working alongside the first girl, sharing the same bowl of soapy water. However, whilst the first girl was relatively flat-chested, the second girl had a magnificent bust which hung down so that her nipples were rubbing against the rough floor as her head moved. The constant friction had clearly made them very tender and they stood erect and crimson. By their expressions both girls seemed to be in considerable discomfort but did not dare stop as they were watched over by a prefect holding a leather tawse. Each prisoner had a small notice on a chain hanging around her neck. The slimmer girl with the saddle retaining the dildo had a notice that said, I AM LAZY AND DISRESPECTFUL and the bigger girl had a notice that said, I AM VERY LAZY. I wonder if they have to clean the entire corridor, Julie thought. If so they will be working all night, since it is at least thirty yards long. Their whole bodies must be aching already. Poor girls, I do feel sorry for them.

As the new arrivals passed this sorry group the prefect jumped to attention and looking straight ahead said, 'Good evening Miss Chapel, Miss Sullivan and Miss Walters.'

'Good evening Abigail,' replied Miss Walters. 'And what have we got here?'

'Amy Durrant and Jennifer Haley, Miss. They are on report for slacking in Miss Jackson's lesson. When they have finished scrubbing the corridor, they are to be escorted to Miss Jackson's study for a beating. I am under instructions to make sure that every inch of the corridor has been thoroughly scrubbed and to use the tawse on their backsides if they slack.'

'Very good, Abigail, carry on. I hope for your sake that they can finish the corridor before midnight. Be a bit more generous with the tawse, I suggest, otherwise you will be standing here all night,' replied Miss Walters with a smile as the party edged by. The group moved on down the corridor. The prefect Abigail must have taken Miss Walter's advice to heart because within a few seconds Julie heard the unmistakable sound of leather applied to bare skin and anguished shrieks echoing up the corridor.

Finally, the little group halted at a small wooden door set into a pointed arch, such as one might have found in a monastery or convent. Miss Chapel fumbled in her pocket and brought forth an antique key. Unlocking the door revealed an austere cell with a vaulted ceiling and whitewashed walls containing only four bentwood chairs set back to back in two pairs. The chairs were ordinary bentwoods similar to those used in cafés, except for the fact that each back leg had a short strap with a buckle at its base. A similar pair of straps adorned the base of the backrest where the wooden struts joined the seat. There was one other addition which made Julie's heart miss a beat and caused Sophie to gasp and mumble, 'Oh, no,' under her breath.

Set upright in the seat of each chair, nearer to the back than to the front, was a polished, penis-like erection several inches long and roughly as thick as a cucumber.

'Go to a pair of chairs – that's right, so that you're back to back – and then straddle them,' ordered Miss Chapel. Julie and Sophie obeyed mechanically, each standing astride a chair.

'Lift your skirts waist high.' Standing as instructed, Julie and Sophie waited as the mistress surveyed them in a leisurely manner with a trace of a sneer.

Meanwhile Miss Sullivan edged close to Julie, and,

66

stroking Julie's pubic hair said, 'You can say goodbye to this little bush tomorrow. It will make you feel more naked when it's gone. I am sure that you have a beautiful little twat underneath, crying out for some attention.' She then produced a bottle of baby oil and proceeded to pour some over each of the phalluses until it ran down over the seat of the chair, collecting in a puddle at the base of the wooden erection. 'Some lubrication,' explained Miss Sullivan. 'I believe in showing some kindness on your first night at Roughton Hall – after all, you might be a couple of little virgins. You have both been very well behaved so you can sit your little honey pots on the dildoes and feel it filling you up all night. Just like a particularly well-endowed lover. New arrivals usually have to sit their tight little bums on the prong until it slips slowly in at first and then suddenly they sink right down, well and truly impaled for the night. Very uncomfortable. That soon puts the girls from the estates in their place. You should see their faces in the morning.'

She poured some more oil over her fingers, then put each hand between Julie's and Sophie's legs and slowly drew them up between their bottom cheeks. Julie felt the globes, slippery against each other.

Miss Chapel then stepped forward and laid a hand on Julie and Sophie's shoulders. 'You know what's coming next, so do it now or you will feel my cane across your breasts and have another dozen on your hindquarters tomorrow.' Sophie whimpered but did not dare to speak, she could feel the massive dildo prodding at her sex lips. 'Do it,' thundered Miss Chapel, applying some pressure to each shoulder. Gradually, the girls sank down, slowly impaling themselves on the phalluses until their buttock cheeks rested on the hard wooden seats. Julie heard Sophie whimper again but Miss Chapel strode forward and slapped her across the face.

'Stop your blathering, girl. Thousands of others have

sat on these chairs before you. Almost all new girls spend the first night in here and have it tight up their dainty bums, so you can stop that snivelling immediately. The erections are getting quite worn away, even though they are made of ebony. I am sure that they were longer and thicker when I started here, so you should be grateful.'

Julie made an effort to restrain any cry for fear of getting slapped as well, but the discomfort of being so deeply impaled by such a thick and unyielding priapus, combined with the sensation of slipperiness on the hard seat, was intense. By bracing her feet against the floor, Julie was able to relieve some of the penetration of the phallus. However, Julie and Sophie soon found that the reformatory had thought of that method of relief, when the three mistresses busied themselves at the base of the chairs. Julie and Sophie found that their ankles were being pulled back, to be attached by the leather straps to the back legs of the chairs so that their entire weight rested on their oiled bottoms and the phalluses achieved maximum penetration. Their wrists were then attached in a similar way to the cuffs at the back of the chairs. Finally their jaws were prised open to their fullest extent and ball gags were strapped around their heads. The feeling of helplessness was overwhelming. Julie could barely move a muscle, could not speak and, worst of all, there was that terrible feeling of being slowly split and engorged inside. The discomfort was beginning to make her perspire copiously and Julie could feel the sweat combining with the oil to make the whole of her lower body feel slippery against the chair.

The three mistresses stood aside and surveyed their handiwork. Miss Chapel, who seemed to be the most unpleasant of the three, had a particularly self-satisfied look on her face and taunted, 'There you are, nice and cosy for the night. You may not get much sleep, but that is all the better for being able to reflect on your sins at leisure. Perhaps you will think twice before breaking the law again. You certainly will after your sentence is up, even if you don't yet. This is just the start. Try to get some rest if you can, because lack of attention or drowsiness tomorrow will not be tolerated and will be punished with our usual rigour. You haven't seen anything yet, so be warned.'

All Julie could do was to stare back, her jaws racked wide open with the ball in her mouth. Miss Walters turned out the light, the mistresses strolled out of the cell and the door was slammed shut with an almighty crash. The cell was now in absolute darkness except for a minute speck of light in a strip at the bottom of the door. Julie looked down but could not see anything, not even her legs. Silence and darkness was all there would be all night.

I wish that Sophie and I could at least speak to each other and share our misery and fears but even that is not possible, thought Julie. If only I could get some sleep, so that I could put an end to the torment until the morning. This bunged-up feeling is worse than the gag and that on its own is pretty awful.

Julie must have dropped off to sleep with sheer exhaustion because she woke with a start as the cell door swung open and crashed against the wall. In a trice, her situation flooded back with shocking clarity. Here she was buckled to a hard, oily chair with a thick prong inside her and a rubber ball in her mouth, quite unable to move. Miss Chapel stood in the doorway, her legs apart. One hand was on one hip and in the other she held a flexible riding crop with a plaited leather tip. Her hair this morning was tied back in a pony tail. She wore a Victorian-looking white blouse with a high neck, a black mid-calf length skirt, seamed black stockings and black leather, stiletto-heeled shoes.

Tapping the crop against her thigh she enquired

rhetorically, 'Did you have a comfortable night? Have you thought about the errors of your ways? Are you beginning to realise that you are nothing until you are released from the reformatory? You are the lowest of the low here, and if you don't obey in every way with complete submission, your release date will be later rather than sooner. Good, I can see from the look in your eyes that you are starting to see things our way. You are going to be taken for your induction training, during which you will be informed of the rules of the reformatory. You will also be told something of the proud history of the Ancient Order whose wise principles and rigid morality are the basis for the pioneering work of the new reformatory movement so effectively encouraged by the Home Office. When the present government said that they were going to tackle crime, who would have thought that they actually meant it? Now people realise that the Party of National Reconciliation, of which I am proud to say that I am a member, is not like the half-hearted political parties of the past. Oh no, it is a party that stands by its word. It doesn't promise what it is unwilling to deliver. When Harold Fletcher gives his word, that word is his bond. He is a man of unbending principle and morality such as this country has never seen before. People should be proud to say that he is their leader, their guidance and inspiration. I know that I am. Every night I pray to the Almighty to lend strength to our great leader, our rock, our cornerstone, our shepherd.'

Julie took a quick glance at Miss Chapel and saw the look of religious fervour in her eyes, she seemed to be looking up at the ceiling as if her leader was watching from above. She is really obsessed, thought Julie. She has the look of a fanatical Nazi stormtrooper, and we are at her mercy.

Seconds later, the other two mistresses from the previous day, Miss Sullivan and Miss Walters, appeared behind her. They seemed to be decidedly less fanatical and more concerned with practicalities. Miss Sullivan had an upset expression on her face and she began to whisper earnestly to Miss Chapel. Julie, straining her ears could just make out the gist of the conversation. Miss Sullivan was saying, 'You don't have to be a party member to be a good reformatory mistress thank goodness. I still believe that the punishments have the most beneficial moral effect when coupled with some kindness and tender care. Now, let's get these two upstairs to the Headmistress' Study before we all get in her bad books again. We have already been punished once today and that is easily enough for me. She is not in the best of moods, I can tell you. You know it was all your fault that we got back late. We covered up for you but that meant we all got the same punishment. A whole week of twice-nightly cold swims is a lot to endure when the offence was not really mine or Annie's fault.'

Julie saw Miss Chapel's face darken and heard her hiss a reply in Miss Sullivan's ear, 'I hope that does not imply a criticism of the party. Don't forget that I have some influence with the district commissioner on the mainland. I sometimes feel that you would try to undermine the precisely laid down regime that has been approved by the party and which has been shown to be so effective over two centuries of unbroken reformatory practice. I also suspect that at times you allow your own preferences and, shall we say, "little affections" to influence your strict application of the regime as set down so clearly in the handbook. If you are not careful you might find yourself in the prison for female political offenders. It would probably do you good – you would come out as committed to the party as I am. Their methods may be harsh but it's the result that counts. You probably wouldn't believe it, but even I once had my doubts about the motives of the party. And now I am glad that I was reformed. The experience was

71

unpleasant, I wouldn't deny it, but now I can see things so much more clearly. I am a happier person for it and, incidentally, much fitter too.'

Miss Sullivan's face blanched and she retorted, 'I don't doubt that you do have some influence with the party. Isn't that why we always waste so much time on the mainland whenever you are on the boat detail? Why you go off for so long while Annie and I have to do most of the shopping and why, when you come back you have such a smirk on your face?'

Miss Chapel rounded on her colleague in such a fury that she could barely keep her voice down, 'What I do is my own affair, it is no business of yours. You are just jealous that the party sees a lot of potential in me. They can see that I follow the dictates of the Home Office reformatory committee efficiently and without deviation. They know that I believe in the principles of the government implicitly and that my loyalty would never be in question. That is why I will be promoted to senior mistress as soon as a position is available, while you will always be just a mistress. And when I am a senior mistress I will make sure that when you displease the headmistress you pay dearly for it. And if you have to be punished by me it will not be just cold swims, bread and water, and a dozen over your little silky panties. Oh, no, it will be a lot more besides. I will also see to it that you get all the worst duties and that your little friendships with some of the sluts are the subject of a severe reprimand. "Kindness and tender care" as you put it, are certainly not beneficial to moral reform. On the contrary, cruelty, severe punishments, total despair and rigid discipline are the key to the reform of delinquent girls.'

Julie could see that Miss Sullivan was close to tears and unable to bring herself to pursue the argument any further.

Miss Walters put a soothing hand on Miss Sullivan's

shoulder and said in an artificially jolly voice, 'Let's not fall out any more. We must get these girls up to the Head's office double quick or we will be in even more trouble and none of us will ever be senior mistresses.'

The three mistresses set about unbuckling the leg and wrist cuffs and then with a hand under each arm slowly hauled Julie up. She could feel the slippery phallus withdrawing and the relief as, with a barely audible pop, she was lifted clear of it. Next the ball gag was removed and Julie felt the sensation return to her numbed mouth. She then watched as Sophie was also released, noticing her friend's look of exquisite relief as she was lifted off the black prong and was able to smooth down her dress to cover her modesty.

Miss Walters cleared her throat and speaking earnestly as if addressing a group of schoolchildren leaving for a day trip at the zoo, said, 'Right, you two, we are taking you to the headmistress' study. We will go via the kitchens so that you can have a sandwich and some fruit juice to help stave off the hunger until your eating regime has been established. Of course, it goes without saying that you must be on your very best behaviour when you meet the headmistress or the consequences will be very painful. Remember to only speak when you are required to and to keep your eyes respectfully cast down except if you are told to look up. The headmistress should be addressed simply as "Headmistress" and you should curtsey as you enter and when you leave. Anything the headmistress tells you to do must be done without hesitation. Anything she asks you must be answered without hesitation and in a clearly audible voice. Unless you are told otherwise you should stand with your legs together, your hands straight down by your sides and your head slightly down. I am telling you this for your own good. The headmistress does not tolerate anything other than perfect behaviour, therefore it is not easy to stay in her good books. If she takes a dislike to you at this early stage it is bad news and you might have to work extra hard for the whole of the next year just to redeem yourself. So be warned.'

Julie gulped. Her tender regions were still hurting from the ingeniously sadistic overnight seat and her jaws still ached from the ball gag. She also fancied that she could still feel the bruises from the strapping in the train and the extra stroke received whilst crawling from the Land Rover. And now an audience with a dictator of a headmistress. Where would it all end? This domination was a nightmare, but she had to admit it was also her dream come true.

After a long march through immaculately clean corridors, through the extensive kitchens with first-year girls on washing-up duty, through ivy-draped cloisters and up a marbled staircase, they finally halted in front of an oak door bearing a brass plate simply inscribed HEADMISTRESS. There were not many pupils about and Julie assumed that most of them were in class or assembly. Immediately in front of the door was a lobby area with a row of seven school chairs against each wall. It was there that a strange sight met Julie and Sophie's eyes. On one side were two girls sitting, fidgeting with their trembling fingers and looking distinctly nervous. Every few seconds they would glance at the door and then over to the chairs on the opposite side of the lobby, where on each of four chairs stood a girl facing the wall and with her hands placed on her head. Each of the four wore just a white blouse, white knee-length socks and black shoes with an ankle strap and were thus stark naked from their waists to their knees. At the base of each chair lay folded a navy-blue pleated gymslip. Every so often one of them would emit a great sob and fight to catch her breath. The reason was staring Julie in the face, for each of the four had six livid red welts across her bare buttocks that would surely glow in the dark if it were possible. At intervals, groups of pupils passed by the lobby and Julie heard the occasional snigger and a whispered name or names. The three mistresses sat in silence beside the two nervous girls, which seemed to increase their agitation and hand wringing. Miss Chapel signalled for Julie and Sophie to stand at the end of the row with their hands clasped demurely in front of them, facing the row of punished bottoms.

After waiting for some five minutes Julie heard very faintly through the thick door a swish followed by a sharp crack and a shriek. This was repeated five times over the space of some two minutes. A few minutes later, the door opened and a red-faced and tearful girl clutching a folded gymslip stepped out. The girl seated nearest the door gulped and turned a shade paler as her fellow pupil bent to place her gymslip at the base of the next vacant chair and, in doing so, displayed a thoroughly punished bottom. Biting her lip and choking back the tears, she stepped up on to the chair, placed her hands on her head and, facing the wall like the others, displayed her striped bottom to whoever passed. A minute later a buzzer sounded and a panel that had previously displayed a red light above the door turned green. The girl seated nearest the door, her face a picture of apprehension, got up, turned the handle, pushed open the door and slipped in. About ten minutes later Julie again heard the unmistakable sounds of corporal punishment and soon after, the girl emerged in a similar condition to the others. As she stepped on to the sixth chair wincing and blubbing the buzzer sounded again and the last of the seven pupils rose up, emitting a little whimper and exhibiting a greenish pallor.

As the girl entered the room Miss Chapel leant conspiratorially over to Miss Walters and whispered, 'The last is the worst position to be in, I always think. Waiting, listening to your companions being punished, seeing the results and knowing that your turn is getting ever nearer all adds to the punishment. What do you think, Ann?'

Miss Walters considered and then whispered back, 'Yes, at least it's all over with sooner if you go first, but some reckon that the first one gets it laid on harder because the mistress' arm is not so tired. Anyway, I hope that caning these seven has put Miss Spenser in a better mood than she was first thing this morning. I hate the cold swims.'

'I don't think the headmistress is susceptible to moods,' said Miss Chapel suspecting that Miss Walters may have said something detrimental to the system. 'Those swims will tone us up, making us mentally and physically leaner and tougher. Remember it was our fault – well my fault mainly I suppose – that we wasted time. Without a doubt Miss Spenser is one of the fairest headmistresses in any of the reformatories. I admire her tremendously.'

Ten minutes later the last girl emerged, clutching her gymslip, with her bottom striped and her eyes puffy. Behind her towered the woman who Julie recognised as the headmistress. Julie could see her more clearly now and could not help but admire the statuesque figure she saw before her. Miss Spenser must have been at least six feet tall, with a proud, upright posture which emphasised her imposing bust. The right sleeve of her white blouse was rolled up and she carried a long cane in her right hand. A tight, black, knee-length skirt with a slit on one side showed that, despite her age, her thighs and behind were as firm and toned as a 25-year-old athlete's. High cheek bones, dark hair and dark eyes contrasted with her mouth, which was lined with dark red lipstick. Miss Spenser was the sort of figure who would attract attention in any situation. Addressing the line of burning posteriors she said in a calm and gentle voice, 'I hope that will be a lesson to you. Don't you dare whisper in assembly again, whoever it was. It is a pity that the culprits didn't own up. If they had, I would not have been forced to cane the whole row. Now, put your gymslips back on and run along to Matron. Ask her to rub some cold cream on those bottoms and then get back to class as quickly as possible.' So saying, the headmistress turned on her heel and strode back into her study without a glance at the three mistresses and their nervous charges.

6

The Headmistress

Julie, Sophie and the three mistresses sat silently waiting for the signal to enter. It had begun to seem an eternal wait when the buzzer sounded and the red indicator turned to green.

'Now, remember what we told you,' whispered Miss Walters as Miss Chapel gave a polite knock on the door and entered the room. Miss Sullivan and Miss Walters anxiously ushered the two girls in front of them and closed the door behind. Julie and Sophie found themselves standing in a row facing the Head's desk.

'Curtsey!' hissed Miss Sullivan under her breath, and at once all five performed a neat curtsey.

Julie kept her eyes cast demurely down, but at the same time she was impatient to survey the room without making it too obvious. Her initial impression was that the room was enormous and furnished with antique oak furniture. Miss Spenser's vast desk was especially ornate, being carved with lion heads and shields. Magnificent gilt-framed paintings hung on the walls and several glass-fronted bookcases containing heavy volumes stood at the far end of the room. A number of elaborate brass standard lamps stood in the corners and a large mirror was situated above a roaring log fire where several timbers the size of tree trunks were blazing. More ominously, a rack containing a variety of school canes in various lengths and several leather tawses hung on hooks stood beside the desk. However, the most threatening piece of furniture resembled a leather padded vaulting horse and was placed in the middle of a Turkish rug in front of the fire.

'Yes, you may well observe the flogging horse,' said Miss Spenser, catching Julie by surprise. 'There's no need to lower your heads and squint, you have my permission to look up and to look all around you. I hope you approve of the furnishing – who knows, you may have to visit this room quite often. It would be better if you felt at home –' Her voice sounded quite friendly; not at all as frightening as Julie had expected. But then, in a split second the voice turned harsh, and she continued, '– especially if you are having the evil beaten out of you, beaten out of your lazy insolent bottoms until you beg for mercy. But I digress. I was pointing out the practicality of my flogging horse. Notice that it is much like a vaulting horse except that it is not as long. Notice also that one end, where a girl's head goes, is lower than the other so that her backside is well presented. Notice also the padded step where the knees go, and the straps for each knee – the wider strap to go over the waist and the two leather wrist cuffs low down near the base of the lower end. Yes, it is beautifully made and designed. Goodness knows how many girls have benefited from suffering on that horse, it must be thousands. Look how the leather is polished and worn with so many years of service, so many sweating bellies pressed wriggling and sticking to the leather surface. You see, it is one of the originals, one of the original pieces of reformatory equipment from the Ancient Order of the Righteous Sisters. We are really most fortunate to have it here at Roughton Hall. If I flog you on it, you can consider it a great privilege.'

Julie felt sure that she would not feel that way at all, but since the headmistress seemed to be as fanatical as Miss Chapel she thought it wise not to appear to disagree. Miss Spenser continued, 'Historical roots and tradition are so important. That is why we think that it is so important that every new girl to Roughton Hall is made fully aware of the great historical basis for everything that happens to her at the reformatory. There is a reason for everything. We are not cruel for its own sake. We do not punish because we happen to enjoy it. When we punish and how we punish is determined by the two hundred years of experience bequeathed to us by the Sisters of the Ancient Order. It is a system; not a personal or temporary fashion. And it is a system that the Sisters honed and developed to perfection. There is no doubt that it succeeds in reforming virtually one hundred per cent of the girls who come here. So far, no girl from Roughton Hall has re-offended after release. That compares very well with the previous borstals, approved schools, young offenders institutes and prisons where about one third of ex-inmates offended within two years of release.'

Normally it would be nice to see someone so in love with their job, but not this time, thought Julie. She is obviously a rigid disciplinarian and completely obsessed with the work of the reformatory.

The headmistress was now touching on the history of the Righteous Sisters that Julie had heard so much about, 'They were a religious order of nuns that existed from the eighteenth century to the first decade of the twentieth century. They believed that the way to Godliness was through the persecution of the flesh. They took their creed from the flagellants of the medieval monastic communities which existed from the thirteenth to the fifteenth century and were at their peak at the time of the Black Death. Similar movements were also found in Roman times. Consequently, they would whip each other and undergo other privations such as fasting, taking cold showers, eating plain food and wearing sackcloth and ashes. By conquering the flesh as a penance, they believed that they raised their spiritual awareness and that they were proving their devotion to God. Their harsh lifestyle and the remote locations of their various convents meant that they soon developed a reputation for being able to handle difficult or recalcitrant young ladies in the convent boarding schools attached to them. The upper and professional classes could afford to send a wayward daughter or one who continued to refuse an eligible suitor to one of the convents run by the Ancient Order, where she soon learned to respect her family's wishes. Many a headstrong and spoilt young minx would finally provoke her father too far and be taken struggling and swearing in her finery, fancy bonnets and lace handkerchiefs to such a convent for a year or two, in order to learn obedience. On her return, she would be a picture of demure submissiveness, wearing plain sensible clothes and ready to submit to the will of the head of the family.

'During the nineteenth century some local parishes sent female juvenile delinquents to the convent schools of the Ancient Order rather than send them to a women's prison or Bridewell where they would be mixing with lunatics and dangerously violent older prisoners. Sometimes there was no space at the regular prison and a judge might order the parish to pay the convent's fees out of their education budget, especially if he believed that the offender needed a combination of a sound education and regular doses of corporal punishment. It was also often said that the judges who were most in favour of corporal punishment believed that the young offenders sent to the convents would get more regular thrashings than those sent to the prisons, where, due to the bureaucracy of the system, an offender sentenced to imprisonment with hard labour and two dozen strokes of the birch would get exactly that and no more. It was also suspected, although never proven, that some judges, by contributing to the convent's "charitable funds", could have frequent opportunities to observe the chastisement of the young ladies from peepholes set in the walls of certain rooms.

'Over the years, the Sisters perfected their methods and eventually wrote the sum of their knowledge in a beautifully illuminated manuscript. The manuscript was copied and became the handbook on which the regime in all of the Ancient Order's convent schools was based. All procedures and types of offences and the type of punishment that each one merited were detailed in the book, which became a bible to those committed to the reform of young women. The original manuscript was acquired by the British Museum where it was ignored until the Party of National Reconciliation came to power. The new government, formed at a time when society seemed to be tearing itself apart with rampant lawlessness as the economy declined, was desperately searching for a policy to appease the so-called "hangers and floggers". They were the rich bedrock supporters of the party. The party could see that a draconian penal code would also help to stop political opposition, because political enemies could be swept up and imprisoned along with the great mass of ordinary offenders, especially when anti-government activity was criminalised under the law of sedition. The adoption of the principles of the Ancient Order, which were also used in the reformatories for males, enabled the government to give the new reformatories legitimacy and the stamp of historical precedent.'

The headmistress paused and fixing Julie with a piercing eye said, 'Now you have some idea of the background to this institution. I hope I have made myself clear. Well, have I, girl ?' she barked.

'Y – y – yes,' stuttered Julie.

'And what about you?' turning to Sophie.

'Yes, thank you,' she quavered.

'That's good,' replied Miss Spenser. 'Now I will outline some of the basic rules here. It is important that you commit them to memory because transgressions, whatever the excuse are not tolerated. Firstly, all instructions whatever they are, must be obeyed without hesitation whether they are given by me, a senior mistress, a mistress, senior prefect or prefect. You must address all mistresses by their surname prefixed by "Miss". You must cast your eyes modestly downwards when facing a member of staff unless given permission to do otherwise. When entering or leaving a room in which there are staff members you must curtsey. You must ask permission to speak to a mistress, unless you are in class, in which case you must raise your hand. If the mistress grants you permission to speak and she then considers that the request was frivolous when she hears what you have to say you will be punished – so think carefully before asking permission. When you face a mistress standing up you must keep your hands at your sides and eyes lowered. If asked a question by a mistress you must answer immediately and truthfully. When you are being beaten, if you are not restrained, you must not move out of position. Failure to observe this rule will incur the penalty of extra strokes or an extra punishment session. After any punishment you must thank the person who punished you. You will not talk to your friends in class, in assembly or at meal times. You will not masturbate or indulge in lesbian activities with other girls. When in bed you must keep your hands above the blanket. You will keep the whole area between your legs completely hairless and smooth and the same goes for under your arms. Any hint of a hair or stubble at inspection will mean punishment. You must not deviate from the uniform laid down for your year. As you have been entered at the third-form level, based on your age and length of sentence, the uniform is as follows. At night, you will wear a short transparent nylon night-dress. In the day, you will wear a thin white blouse, dark blue mini-skirt, black suspenders and stockings and black court shoes with a two-inch heel. The first and second years are not allowed to wear underwear but as a third-former you will be allowed to wear a white non-underwired bra and white thong knickers so that the condition of your buttocks can easily be inspected after or before a caning. However, it is a rule that as part of the Welcome process which I will explain later, all new girls are forbidden to wear underwear for the first ten weeks. You will have to let your breasts swing for that time, which I imagine will be quite uncomfortable for you two. When ordered to strip, you will immediately remove all clothing including shoes and put them in a neat pile.

'You must also understand the numbered positions. Position one is bending over with your legs straight, feet apart, holding your ankles and with your head up. Position two is standing with legs wide apart and hands clasped behind your head. Position three is lying prostrate on your front with your mouth to the floor and hands straight by your side. Position four is lying on your back, hands on the floor with your legs in the air and spread wide. Position five is similar but with your legs drawn back by your hands behind each knee and with your feet hanging down. The last two positions are excellent for checking that your vaginal and anal areas are completely hair-free. Position six is kneeling on the floor with hands behind your head. Seven is the same except with your hands at your side. Eight is standing with your hands out to the front, palms upwards, which would normally be used if you were to be caned or tawsed on the hands. Position nine is kneeling on all fours with your back arched downwards so that your buttocks are presented nicely pushed out, an excellent position for a quick six with the cane. You can appeal against any ruling or punishment; I will judge the merit of your appeal. If your appeal is refused you will be punished for abusing the system. Do you understand what I have told you?'

'Yes, Headmistress,' chorused the terrified girls.

'That is good, I would hate you to have any misunderstandings. Now let us put some of this into practice. Let's see if you really understand. Miss Chapel, Miss Walters and Miss Sullivan can help me judge whether you are obeying correctly, and if you are not they can assist in strapping you on to the flogging horse for a swishing. I prefer to have an excuse to demonstrate it. Let's try some commands to see if you remember the instructions. You can do everything together. Perhaps it could be a little competition: the one who performs the best can punish the one who performs the worst. Yes, that is a sterling idea. When a girl has to punish her friend it adds a certain piquancy to the scene and teaches us that one's loyalty is to the reformatory, not to one's friends. Now strip!'

There was no question of disobeying; besides, Julie did not want to be the one demonstrating the efficacy of the flogging horse, however great the 'honour'. Both girls raced to be the first to strip, which did not take long as they were not encumbered with much clothing. Both remembered to place the clothes neatly folded on the floor and to immediately stand upright, hands by the sides and looking demurely downwards. Sophie was marginally quicker but it was very close.

'Position one!' barked Miss Spenser. This one was easy to remember, especially for Sophie who had experienced it on the boat. Quickly both girls were bent over, holding their ankles and looking directly forward. It hurt Julie's neck and she wondered how Sophie had managed to keep the position for so long in the boat.

Without a pause Miss Spenser shouted, 'Position three!' For a split second, Julie could not recollect what the required position was, but then saw Sophie beginning to lie face down on the floor and quickly copied. It was an uncomfortable position with her weight resting on her breasts and her mouth tasting the dust of the carpet.

There was a silence for half a minute. Julie wondered what the others were thinking and felt a rising tide of humiliation. Finally, Miss Spenser said, 'A fine pair of meaty bottoms, made for the whip; not too delicate, you could really lay it on. You have already laid a cane across this one, I believe, Miss Chapel. From the lines I would say that this young lady got off quite lightly. Still, the marks are nicely spaced. Good work Miss Chapel. Let's have a good look at those buttocks. Assume position nine!'

Julie and Sophie looked at each other for a moment. Neither could remember which position number nine was, and neither girl wanted to be the first to get it wrong. Miss Spenser drummed her fingers on the desk. The suspense was nerve-racking. Abruptly Julie remembered and quickly turned over, raised her legs and held on to her knees. Sophie hovered with indecision for a second, then turned round on all fours and arched her back proffering her backside for the delectation of Miss Spenser.

'Very good, Sophie, you learn quickly. Julie! You have got it wrong. Don't worry we can inspect your hindquarters when you are on the flogging horse, as you surely will be in a minute.'

Julie's heart sank and she felt herself blushing.

'Now, both of you assume position six.' Again it was Sophie who had remembered most accurately. Julie lagged behind in order to copy her kneeling on the floor with her hands clasped behind her head and eyes cast down.

'Slow again, Julie,' breathed Miss Spenser menacingly. 'What an excellent position for the display of breasts. Elbows back! That's better. Both pairs are very firm, especially Sophie's. That's good. I hate to see slack, saggy breasts; it indicates that a girl has spent too much time slumped in front of the television eating chocolate and crisps, instead of taking part in healthy activities such as netball and hiking. The morning dip in the pool will tone you both up. It works absolute wonders. The pupils all hate it, but they will thank me when they are middle-aged and possess the firm, taut body of a teenager. I take a cold shower myself every day and that is why my breasts are still in prime shape, just like they were when I was a teenager. Now, Julie, there's not much doubt that you have lost out to Sophie in the obedience test and therefore deserve to sample the delights of your friend's attention to your bottom while arranged on my favourite piece of furniture. What do you say to that, my girl?'

Miss Sullivan nudged Julie and whispered, 'Say "thank you Miss Spenser".'

So, from her knees, Julie heard herself, trying to hide the reluctance in her voice and repeating, 'Thank you Miss Spenser.'

'Sophie, stand up and come over here next to my desk. Select from this rack a suitable instrument to enable your friend to try to remember the position numbers in future. That way, Julie will know that whatever pain she feels it is completely your choice and your doing. Here we have two junior canes, three intermediate canes, a couple of senior canes; light, medium and heavy two-tailed tawses; a long three-tailed tawse, an American rubber spanking paddle and a wooden spanking paddle, a short and a long riding crop; a birch – not fresh, so it is rather brittle, I'm afraid – and a French martinet. I wouldn't recommend the birch as there is rather a knack to it.'

Sophie dithered for a few seconds, terrified of the proximity of the headmistress who was standing right next to her. Mechanically, she put out a trembling hand and grasped the nearest thing: the handle of the martinet. As she pulled it out of the rack, Julie saw that it consisted of a dozen thin strands of leather about a millimetre thick and about eighteen inches long, attached to a wooden handle about twelve inches long.

'An excellent choice, girl. The martinet is the terror of the French youngster, used daily at school and in the home. You have to swing it very hard and follow through, otherwise the little lashes merely caress instead of biting. Go over to the horse and watch as Miss Walters and Miss Chapel strap your pal nice and tight into position over it.'

Julie looked up at Sophie; their eyes met, but Sophie blushed and quickly looked away. Julie knew that Sophie was probably feeling as bad as, or even worse than she was. She wanted to tell Sophie not to feel bad about it. She knew that her friend had been forced into doing this, and that if it was the other way around she herself would not have had the courage to refuse. The girls knew that refusal would only lead to them both getting punished even more severely. In addition, Julie had her own reasons for being there. Sophie avoided meeting Julie's eye but Julie felt that Sophie was aware of her unspoken message.

Miss Chapel grasped Julie by the hair, hauled her to her feet and marched her over to stand in front of the flogging horse. Miss Walters moved to the other side of the horse and enquired, 'Excuse me Headmistress, do you require Julie to say the Righteous Sisters' punishment prayer?'

'Yes, that would be most appropriate, especially for a new girl.'

'Repeat after me,' instructed Miss Walters, 'Please Almighty, make me truly grateful for the punishment that I am about to receive. And please bless those who punish me. And please may it drive the evil from my soul.' When the girl had done as she was ordered, Miss Walters said, 'Good, now kneel up on this padded step and lie over the top of the stool. Let your arms hang right down whilst I strap them to the rings at the base.

Keep your legs still, so that Miss Chapel can do up the buckles on the knee straps.'

The smooth leather was cold to the skin, especially on her belly, but warmed rapidly. Julie was aware of the strong smell of old leather, just like the smell in her father's sports car. Julie felt Miss Walters tugging at her wrists and the tight grip of the leather cuffs binding her wrists to the base of each front leg. Simultaneously, she could feel Miss Chapel tightly buckling her legs just above each knee to the front of the kneeling step. Since the knee straps were a good six inches apart Julie was aware that her bottom cheeks were parted in a way that prominently exposed her sex. Seconds later, Miss Chapel was pulling the broad waist strap so that her lower belly was firmly squashed to the highest part of the horse, which was cleverly constructed in order to throw her buttocks out at the ideal angle for a caning. Julie tried an experimental wiggle but found that it was very difficult to move any more than a couple of millimetres in any direction. Only her feet and head had any freedom of movement.

'Now, Sophie, I want you to give your friend and partner in crime, Julie, six hard strokes of the martinet on her backside. And when I say "hard" I mean very hard. Miss Chapel will repeat any strokes that are not up to scratch, so you will be doing Julie no favours by being feeble – quite the opposite. And Julie, I want you to count the strokes and say, "Thank you, Sophie," after each one. Go ahead, and remember weak strokes get repeated.'

Julie heard the soft fall of Sophie's bare feet on the carpet as she took up her position and sensed with a flush of shame that all attention was on her bottom, fully displayed in the most humiliating position. She felt the depths of her bowels clench with fear as she waited, wondering what was to come. Suddenly there was a whirring noise and a loud smack as the leather thongs of the martinet fell. A burning sensation spread rapidly across the whole of Julie's seat. She bit her lip, determined not to cry out. Remembering that she had been instructed to thank Sophie, she cried out, her voice quavering, 'One, thank you, Sophie.'

'That was far too feeble,' Julie heard the headmistress shout. 'You have got to swing it like a hard volley in tennis. One extra stroke penalty awarded, to be added at the end, Miss Chapel.' Seconds later the second stroke fell. This time the blow was a lot harder and Julie felt a searing pain like a hundred individual stings as the many strands of the martinet flicked sharply around her buttocks.

'Mnnh. Two, thank you, Sophie.' A pause followed and then the third stroke fell. This time the strands seemed to whip in exactly at the cleft of Julie's bottom.

'Oh, no, three, thank you, Sophie.' Julie had now given up all attempts to maintain a stoical silence and as the last three strokes fell her cries became more and more desperate and soprano. As the sixth fell, Julie uttered a final mewl and only just managed to splutter the obligatory, 'Six, thank you, Sophie.'

'Good work Sophie,' congratulated Miss Spenser. 'You seem to be a natural for applying the martinet. See how it produces all those fine striations and little red pimples all over, especially on the right side. Who knows, perhaps you will eventually make it to prefect status and then you will be able to make use of your talents. I expect you are pretty glad you managed to remember the positions better than poor old Julie here. It is undoubtedly better to give than to receive. Now, we must not forget the extra stroke that Miss Chapel will provide on account of your not putting enough effort into the first stroke. What a pity that was, because Miss Chapel will lay it on much, much harder than any of your six strokes. So, you see, you have not done your little friend much of a favour. Miss Chapel, I wonder if you would be so good as to do the honours?'

'A pleasure, Headmistress.'

Julie was trying hard to control her sobs and ignore the throbbing, burning sensation spreading across her now striped globes when there was another loud whirr and an almighty crack. The blow made her squash into the soft leather of the horse, she felt the fat of her bottom shudder like a jelly and thousand stings erupted at once.

'Ow! Seven, thank you, Miss Chapel,' whimpered Julie. If only Sophie had not held back on that first stroke, thought Julie, her mind in a frenzy, Miss Chapel's stroke was worse than three of Sophie's put together.

Julie was immediately released from the bonds of the flogging horse and instructed to resume her position facing Miss Spenser's desk. Her first reaction was to clasp her burning cheeks and dance up and down but Miss Chapel shouted, 'Hands by your sides at once, trollop, and get back in position.'

Miss Spenser frowned as Julie grimaced and said, 'Really dear, that was a mere tickle. You will have to toughen up if you are going to get along at Roughton Hall. At least you both now know that we insist on complete discipline here. You will be reformed, just as all the others have been reformed. Turn around so that I can have a good look to see if the martinet has done its work. Yes, I see it has; your buttocks are scarlet and white like a raspberry ripple. Well done Sophie. Sitting down will be rather uncomfortable for a while. You can turn back now. Now, did you feel that punishment working on your moral character?'

Miss Walters nudged Julie.

'Y – yes, thank you, Headmistress.'

'Good,' replied Miss Spenser. 'The Righteous Sisters were great admirers of the Spartans of Roman times. Although, obviously the Spartans were heathens, but that was through no fault of their own. The Spartans were a great warrior people who existed long before Christ. They tolerated no weaklings, and idolised physical health, toughness, austerity and discipline. Boys as young as seven years old were taken from the homes of the upper classes and trained exclusively in discipline, warfare and austerity. Of course, that was how they were able to win most of their battles and achieve their great place in history. The Sisters would often quote in their writings the fabled story of the Spartan boy who stole a fox. When he and his friends were questioned about it they lied and said that they had not seen it. However, the fox was hidden under the boy's shirt and it bit him. The boy cried out with the pain and the fox was discovered. The boy was then given a whipping, not because he stole the fox, nor because he lied, but because he cried out when he was bitten. There is a great moral in that fable, and the staff here at Roughton Hall are dedicated to inculcating just the sort of grit and moral fibre that will eventually turn the slatterns, good-for-nothings, social parasites, vandals, strikers and loafing socialists into upstanding members of society.

'Well, you have heard the history and philosophy of Roughton Hall and been informed of some of the reformatory rules. This is my welcome to you for what I hope will be a constructive and self-improving period of time here. However, my welcome is not the same as the Welcome, it is only part of it. The Welcome is a tradition which, I believe, the Ancient Order of Righteous Sisters emulated from the eighteenth-century houses of correction in Germany. It is the initiation process during which the old "self" is expunged so that the new, reformed self can be built up on a clean sheet. The process involves a radical change in self-image – a change in clothing, appearance, behaviour, diet, daily routine, friendship group and standard of comfort. Part of the tradition was that every new inmate received a flogging, usually with the bull's pizzle – a type of whip

92

made out of a bull's penis stretched and cured. Otherwise, a rattan cane would be used to "welcome" them to the house of correction. This created an *esprit de corps*, a solidarity amongst the inmates, who knew that every single one of them had endured a similar experience and had had to shed all pride by being flogged on the bare bottom in front of the others. It also signals to the law-abiding citizen that any ex-reformatory woman they meet has had to pay the price for her criminality. However rich and respectable she may have become, everyone knows that at some point she was stretched naked over the horse or birching block crying for mercy. No one, however well behaved and however repentant, leaves a reformatory without a thorough taste of the birch or rod. You will get that part of your Welcome in a couple of weeks' time, when you have settled in a bit and know the ropes. It will be something to look forward to. You must get along to Matron now for the next stage of your induction, which is to get you looking like reformatory girls and not like street tarts. Miss Walters and Miss Chapel, you can get back to your duties now. Miss Sullivan, you can escort the new girls to Matron's preparation room as soon as they have put their clothes back on.'

After a nudge to Julie's elbow and a whispered, 'Curtsey,' from Miss Walters, all five performed a deep curtsey together, turned and left the room.

7

The Transformation

Julie and Sophie were both relieved to be dismissed from Miss Spenser's study. They were then led by Miss Sullivan the considerable distance to Matron's quarters, which apparently consisted of a whole suite of rooms and not just one, as Julie had at first supposed. As they walked Julie was aware that they were the subject of considerable curiosity from the other pupils who passed them in the corridors and stairways.

'Don't worry if the girls stare at you,' said Miss Sullivan reassuringly. 'You will do the same when you have been here for a while. You see, being enclosed as we all are at Roughton Hall, you don't get to see anyone apart from the other girls and mistresses. Every new face is a curiosity when you are cooped up with the same people all the time. It is also a kind of tenuous link with the outside world. There are no televisions or newspapers for the girls here, so the pupils are hungry for glimpses and gossip about the outside world, especially if they have been here many years. The very fact that you are not wearing a Roughton Hall uniform and do not have a reformatory haircut is a potent source of fascination for most of the girls who see you. However, that deficiency is going to be rectified in the next hour or so. You will have to grit your teeth a bit at times – Matron is very thorough. But don't worry, it will all help you to fit in with the other girls.'

Eventually, they reached a wing of the building which

was proclaimed by a brass plate to be Matron's quarters. A whole series of doors with their own brass plates announced the purpose of various rooms. Miss Sullivan ignored these rooms and strode on to the end of the corridor, where a door with PREPARATION ROOM embossed in brass stood a little apart from the rest. A tap on the door from Miss Sullivan elicited a call to enter.

Matron, it turned out, was a tall, rather overweight woman of about 35 years old. She was dressed in a white starched nurse's uniform complete with seamed black tights. The room itself was reminiscent of a clinic or doctor's surgery, having an examination table, weighing and measuring devices, cabinets full of medical equipment and other strange items which Julie could not identify. Matron possessed a brisk personality and would clearly brook no argument.

'Good, I was expecting you to be here somewhat earlier, but no matter. If Headmistress wants to detain new girls longer than usual, that is a matter for her. Now, I don't intend to waste time so you –' she said, pointing to Sophie '– strip and put your clothes in this cardboard box. You will get them back when you leave the reformatory. And you –' she said, pointing to Julie '– can stand in the corner and watch.' Julie moved to the corner whilst Sophie put her clothes in the box and stood facing Matron.

'Stand straighter! I can't abide bad posture,' she bellowed. Sophie who was already standing stiffly to attention struggled to pull her shoulders back a bit more.

'That's better, girl. Now step on to these scales.' Sophie stood on the hospital scales while Miss Sullivan read the dial and Matron recorded the reading on a clipboard. Then Sophie was measured for height against a scale set against the wall with a wooden beam that was brought down to touch the top of her head. Again, Matron recorded the result on the clipboard. Miss

Sullivan then brought out a tape measure from the cupboard and measured every dimension of Sophie's body, and calling the results out to Matron who responded with frequent comments.

'A rather long inside leg measurement, it will have to be the long stockings if I have any left. Medium would be too short. Bust 36 inches with a C cup, I guessed it would be. I'll put a 36 C to one side ready for when the ten weeks is up. I've only got half a dozen left in stock. Size six shoes, that's no problem. Hips thirty-seven; that's the medium, thong-style panties. Again, that's a ten week wait. Now, let's check your ideal weight compared to your actual weight.' Matron consulted a book containing tables and charts and then moved around Sophie, pinching her flesh between finger and thumb, paying special attention to the girl's thighs, midriff and buttocks.

'Yes, I thought so. About four pounds overweight by Roughton Hall standards. We prefer the girls to be slightly lean for their height. Could you enter in the log, Miss Sullivan, that Sophie is to be put on a bread, lettuce and water diet until she reaches the target weight of nine stone, twelve pounds. That shouldn't take long, not with the healthy exercise regime here. About a week, probably. Lack of exercise and too much junk food, that's the trouble with the youth of today. They all need some toning up when they arrive here. Now bend over, I need to give you a rectal examination. That's right, touch your toes and keep still.'

Matron produced a shiny, stainless steel instrument and applied it to Sophie's bottom whilst looking through it. Apparently satisfied, she made a tick in her notes and then said, 'Now, get up on the examination table and put your feet in the stirrups.'

The stirrups were on chromium poles two feet above the table, as found in maternity theatres. Matron donned a pair of rubber surgical gloves and after some exploration, commented, 'Mmmm, a virgin, if I'm not mistaken! Not many of those anymore – at least not many who get sent here.'

Sophie stared at the wall impassively trying to ignore the whole humiliating process. After ticking more parts of her clipboard report, Matron turned to Miss Sullivan and said, 'Is the wax ready yet?' Miss Sullivan passed a bowl to Matron and then busied herself at Sophie's feet. For the first time, Julie noticed that the stirrups had loops of leather attached with buckle fastenings. In a flash, Miss Sullivan had Sophie's feet firmly tied to the stirrups. She then moved to the other end of the table and, drawing Sophie's arms back behind her head fastened her wrists to the underside of the table. Lastly, she drew a broad belt across Sophie's stomach and buckled it down firmly. An expression of acute fear crossed Sophie's face and she let out a whimper. Clearly something unpleasant was about to happen and it soon became apparent what it was. Matron, standing between Sophie's widely parted legs, started to apply a hot glue-like substance with a spatula to the girl's dark brown pubic hair, working her way methodically right down to the crevice between her cheeks. Meanwhile, Miss Sullivan attached a ball gag, inserting it as Sophie moved her head feebly from side to side emitting a muted whimper. The necessity for the ball gag and the tight restraints soon became obvious as Matron began to energetically pull off the solidified wax, together with the pubic hair, in short, sharp ripping motions, dropping it into a kidney bowl. Sophie shook her head wildly and a muffled wailing came from behind the gag. Within a minute Sophie's pubis was as smooth and white as a burnished billiard ball.

'That does the trick beautifully,' announced Matron. 'You can't beat waxing. It takes the follicle out so that the regrowth is much slower and softer. It may be more painful than shaving or depilatory cream but the end

97

result is what counts. Shaving gives such awful stubble after a few days, whereas this will last for a long time and make subsequent treatments, whether by wax or cream, much easier and more effective. I'll just rub some soothing talcum powder into the area to relieve the sting. Oh, yes, now that is silky smooth. You will have to keep it like that for the duration of your sentence. If I, or any of the mistresses, see a single, tiny hair on that lily-white mound, or further back between your cheeks, you will be punished. Typically, for that offence you would get half a dozen of the birch, bread and water for a week and a two o'clock and five o'clock swim every night for a week, so be warned. The headmistress cannot abide hairy girls. She allows it for senior prefects and mistresses if they so desire it, but not anyone else. In fact, all of the senior prefects, to my knowledge, keep their pudenda smooth in deference to Miss Spenser's preferences. The girls all help each other to keep smooth, which makes it easier. You will be able to use the dormitory tweezers and depilatory cream. I see that you are reasonably hair-free under your arms already so I won't bother with that.

'And now for your haircut. I do advise you to keep still while I do it, otherwise the effect is more radical than intended. It is this initial haircut that will make you stand out most obviously as a new girl. After this cut, we allow the girls to cut each others' hair as long as it is kept short in the lower forms. This cut, however, is called a workhouse cut and it is specifically recommended in the Ancient Sisters' handbook for curbing pride, vanity and reducing the lusts of the flesh in those who look upon you. It was the normal procedure in workhouses because those coming in from the streets often had head lice. Cutting the hair very short was a way of detecting the lice and stopping them from infecting the other inmates. When you see yourself in the mirror later, you will see why the Sisters of the Ancient Order recommended it for curbing vanity and lust in others. Essentially, you will look extremely unattractive. Although it will look strange at first, it will gradually grow out over the course of a couple of months. Scissors, please, Miss Sullivan.'

Miss Sullivan took from one of the cabinets that lined the room what looked like a pair of garden shears and handed them to Matron. She then moved to the top of the table and grasped Sophie's head in a firm grip. Without a moment's hesitation, as if she was shearing a garden hedge, Matron proceeded to remove most of Sophie's hair, cutting close to the scalp to leave some bald patches and some short tufts here and there. Sophie's protests were completely muffled behind the ball gag and Miss Sullivan's manipulation of the girl's head ensured that Matron reached all areas, even the back.

When Matron was finished, Sophie's head was almost bald, with bristles and tufts dotted about at random. It looked most bizarre. Julie was horrified at this, even more than she was at the removal of Sophie's pubic hair. She felt butterflies in her stomach as she realised that it would soon be her turn.

Having completed the haircut, Matron brought out from a cabinet a long rubber tube and an object which resembled a hot water bottle. 'Is the enema mixture hot enough, Miss Sullivan?' she asked.

Miss Sullivan nodded and brought from the sink area a large jug with some steam rising lazily from it. Matron, stooping down, parted Sophie's bottom cheeks and slowly inserted the rubber tube some inches up into her rectum. Hanging the rubber bottle on a stand at head height, she then poured the hot soapy liquid into the top from the jug.

'The whole two pints will just about go, I would estimate,' said Matron, almost to herself, as she gently squeezed the bottle. Gradually, the bottle emptied and

Sophie was soon squirming as much as was possible whilst so firmly tied to the table.

'I want you to keep it in for a little longer, Sophie, so that your insides are properly cleaned out. A useful side-effect of this treatment is that anyone who tries to smuggle drugs into the reformatory by hiding them internally is soon flushed out, if you will excuse the pun.' Matron smiled at her own feeble humour and gently withdrew the tube from Sophie. By now Sophie's slight movements were becoming increasingly frantic and droplets of perspiration were running down her brow.

'The chamber pot, please, Miss Sullivan,' called out Matron as she undid Sophie's bonds one by one. Miss Sullivan placed an enamelled metal pot, such as one might see in a nursery, in the middle of the floor.

'You can perform now,' said Matron as she undid the gag and the last of the buckles. Sophie scrambled off the table in a desperate bid to reach the pot in time, sank herself on it with her knees around her chin and filled the pot in one great explosion of soapy liquid as a look of intense relief passed across her features.

'A good clear-out there, I think. Most satisfactory,' said Matron. 'Now for your shower. Get up and climb into this shower cubicle.'

Sophie staggered to her feet, seemingly in a daze, and was propelled by Miss Sullivan into a tiled shower cubicle with a clear glass door at the far end of the room. Unusually, it had several spray heads: one in the centre of the floor, one in the ceiling and one on each wall. The controls were situated on the wall outside and the door had strong bolts at the top and bottom. Miss Sullivan clanged the door shut and slid both of the bolts whilst Matron turned the controls. Immediately, fierce jets of hot water shot out from every angle and clouds of steam emanated from vents at the top of the door.

'Please turn it down, it's too powerful,' screeched Sophie above the din of the water. 'It's like a million pinpricks.' The girl could just be seen through the steam and water jets, vainly trying to protect herself with her hands, moving them from her face to her breasts to her newly depilated vulva and obviously wishing that she had more hands with which to cover her body.

'Have you seen this new power shower, Miss Sullivan? Nothing cleans a new girl like it; we have had it imported from Germany especially. It is really intended for an industrial process in the engineering industry. Of course we had to order its modification in various ways – the cubicle design and so on. Its water pressure is reinforced by electric pumps and the shower-head venturi jets are especially small so that the pressure per square inch on the skin is immense. It's like being sandblasted, it takes off the thin layer of grease and dead skin and leaves the new pink skin underneath glowing. I've tried it myself on quarter power. It certainly takes your breath away and leaves you tingling for hours afterwards. Sophie is right when she says it is like being bombarded with millions of tiny pins, but the end-result is skin like a baby's bot. This is the best bit; the *coup de grâce*. I am now going to turn the temperature down to the "very cold" setting which brings into play the tank of refrigerated water. The effect is almost instantaneous and usually brings forth quite a reaction. It must be extremely stimulating, probably somewhat like jumping into deep snow from a sauna cabin, although I have not felt brave enough to try it myself. Here goes!' Matron rotated a dial and almost instantly there was deafening shriek from the cubicle. The steam cleared and goose pimples suddenly erupted all over Sophie. Her nipples visibly arose and strained outwards, making the areolae crinkle.

Sophie pressed her face against the glass, shrieking, as though she were demented, 'Let me out, please let me out. It's freezing cold. I can't stand it. I'll get frost-bite if I stay in here any longer.'

Julie noticed that Sophie's now unnaturally protuberant nipples were pressed against the cubicle door and
were making circular designs in the frosting up on the
glass as the girl desperately squirmed.

'Another two minutes, Miss Sullivan, and she can
come out,' announced Matron.

'I'm not sure that she can take another two minutes,'
said Miss Sullivan, sounding concerned.

'Nonsense, Miss Sullivan. Please allow me to be the
judge of these matters. Miss Spenser ordered two of the
little sluts to be bound together and put in for five
minutes after a birching, the other day. You should
have seen them struggling – like two rats with their tails
tied together in a sack. Most amusing. And all because
they had forgotten to curtsey. I must say, I never
credited the headmistress with much of a sense of
humour but she laughed out loud on this occasion.'

By now Sophie was frantically hammering on the
glass door and imploring Matron to let her out. When
the time was finally up, Matron shut off the water and
opened the door. Sophie fell out into Miss Sullivan's
arms and was soon covered with a large white towel, her
teeth chattering like castanets, her nipples standing out
dark, hard and rubbery, and her skin pink and glowing.

Miss Sullivan dried Sophie, who seemed almost in-
capable of any movement and just had a numbed
expression on her face. Meanwhile, Matron brought
over a pile of clothes and with Miss Sullivan's help
proceeded to dress the girl. Firstly, the black suspender
belt and black stockings, hitched up high, were put on,
Miss Sullivan taking special care to run her hands up
Sophie's legs to ensure that the stockings fitted smoothly. Then the white blouse, through which Sophie's
unfettered bosom was all too obvious, especially with
her nipples threatening to burst through the thin material, was put on her. Next, the dark blue mini-skirt,
which only just covered the darker band at the top of

the stockings, was fitted, followed by the black court shoes with the modest two-inch heel. Sophie still seemed dazed but this was soon dispelled when Matron guided her to stand in front of a mirror. Sophie clutched her head, let out a loud shriek and burst into floods of tears, hardly believing the sight that stared back at her.

'Don't blubber, girl,' ordered Matron in a no-non-sense voice. 'All the girls here have had the same treatment. You are no different. So let's have less of your stuck-up ways. You have been sent here for punishment to break your rebellious spirit and that is just what you are getting. The reformatory uniform for each particular year is especially chosen to chasten the spirit and to show an inmate's low status. It is worse for the first and second years who are never allowed to wear underwear. The first-year girls are only allowed to wear two items of clothing, namely a shapeless grey sack-cloth smock with no sleeves and extra large armholes so that their breasts are often visible from the side, and a pair of sandals. They are forbidden to wear socks and their hair must be kept especially short. They really do look like waifs from the workhouse. Some of the flat-chested ones could even be taken for boys. The second-year girls wear a short, navy blue pleated gymslip and white knee socks with conventional-heeled school shoes with ankle strap. They are not allowed to wear any underwear, either.

'The perpetual exposure of the body and the denial of modesty as dictated by the demeaning uniforms and the daily regime is all part of the process of breaking the pride and rebellion of the delinquent girl. Given the usual female interest in clothes and fashion, the strict uniform requirements and boyish, cropped haircuts are an effective means to signal that a girl who breaks the law forfeits her pride and self-respect. So, all things considered, you are more fortunate than many of the girls here, as far as the uniform goes. Now that you look like a proper reformatory girl and not like a common tart, you are well on the way to being reformed. Just accept what happens to you and don't try to fight the system. That is really the best way. Other girls, much tougher than you two, have tried to rebel and ended up just as obedient and submissive as the most sheltered and delicate pupils.

'Now stand where Julie is standing and watch while Julie is transformed into the perfect reformatory girl – depilated, purged, measured, barbered, washed and dressed. All the sin is now starting to be washed out and the personality recreated sparkling clean, chastened and cleansed of vanity. Right, Julie, now it is your turn. Strip, put your clothes in the box and step on to these scales.'

The remainder of the session in Matron's room was just a blur. The next thing that Julie remembered was standing next to Sophie in her new uniform, her skin tingling as if every square millimetre had been sandpapered. There was also the unusual feeling of the air and her skirt brushing against the bare cheeks of her bottom. Her head also felt strange; unusually cold and without the strands of hair which normally touched her face. The suspender belt was not part of Julie's normal underwear and the straps felt odd against her buttocks and legs. It was also slightly uncomfortable not to be wearing a bra. In particular, the sensation of her tingling nipples rubbing against her blouse as she moved was most disconcerting. This, together with the unaccustomed sensitivity of her silky smooth pudenda, as if every movement of her skirt produced a field of static electricity, gave Julie an almost unbearable sense of sexual arousal.

'Good, a pair of well-scrubbed and presentable reformatory girls, looking suitably humble and God-fearing. You enter as scrubbers and leave thoroughly scrubbed,' chuckled Matron as she circled around checking the fit of the blouses and the height of the skirts. 'You get a change of clothes every week and heaven help you if you get your uniform dirty before the week is up. As you are aware, you will get your bras and panties when you no longer have new girl status, which is after ten weeks. Until then, the workhouse haircut and the absence of underwear will mark you clearly as being new girls. Being new girls will mean more lenient treatment from some mistresses or prefects but harsher treatment from others. It may mean that some of the pupils will go out of their way to help you but others may take advantage and bully you. Either way, the welcoming period will be a traumatic erasing of your old self, and of your old habits and comforts. We have to be cruel to be kind. The quicker you forget your old life, the quicker you will be cured and reformed from your old, misguided self. You are now dismissed.'

8

The Refectory

Julie and Sophie were led away in a dazed state from
Matron's quarters by Miss Sullivan and taken to join
their third-form year group, who had just entered the
refectory for their lunch. The refectory was on an upper
floor and had leaded windows looking out to the playing fields and a high, vaulted ceiling with darkly stained
wooden beams. The walls were panelled with carved
oak, enlivened occasionally with framed portraits of
severe-looking clerics. A dozen or so long refectory
tables with matching long wooden benches were arranged in lines on the oak parquet flooring. Sitting at
the tables, eating their lunch in silence, were about one
hundred and fifty girls. An unnatural silence reigned,
broken only by the click of cutlery or the exaggerated
echo of the footsteps on the hard floor as the duty
prefects patrolled to ensure that the rule of silence was
not broken. At the end of the room was a raised stage
upon which another long table was set with vases of
flowers, candelabra, bowls of fruit and silver tableware.
This was the table at which the mistresses dined. On
their knees, at each corner of the table, were first-year
girls in their sack-like, grey woven smocks, waiting
patiently for orders to pass the salt or pour more wine
for the mistresses, who were dining on far more extrava-
gant fare than the pupils.

Miss Sullivan directed Julie and Sophie to the serving
counter where girls on refectory duty dished out each

meal on a metal tray. Julie immediately realised that even the food was part of the punishment, as it consisted of a small bowl of tepid stew and a plastic beaker of water. Miss Sullivan reminded Sophie that she was to ask for the bread, water and lettuce diet until she was told otherwise. Accordingly, Sophie's tray held no more than three lettuce leaves, a thick, stale-looking crust of brown bread and a beaker of water.

Julie went to pick up a spoon but Miss Sullivan waved her away and said quietly, 'New girls are not allowed to use cutlery at lunch time. You will have to lap it up like a dog. When your ten weeks are up you can use cutlery. Until then, you will have to get used to eating without it, it's not too difficult. You are allowed to use a spoon for your daily porridge at breakfast time, though. The other girls have all been through the same process. Just don't get too much of your lunch over your pretty little face.' Miss Sullivan smiled indulgently and Julie felt a little wave of warmth flowing from the mistress which momentarily lifted her spirits.

Miss Sullivan led Julie and Sophie to a table at the far side where about thirty girls wearing the same outfit as the newcomers were seated. They had apparently all finished their meagre bowl of stew. No dessert was in evidence and so they were all sitting demurely silent, their hands clasped in their laps. They looked up as Miss Sullivan approached and Julie could see that she and Sophie were being closely scrutinised by their fellow third-formers. Miss Sullivan cast her eyes over the girls at the table and said, 'This is Julie Semple and Sophie Adams, girls. Show these new girls the ropes and help them settle in.'

'Yes, Miss Sullivan,' chorused the girls.

'Remember how you felt when you were new girls and try to be helpful,' added Miss Sullivan as she turned and walked off to the top table. Julie and Sophie sat down with their trays in front of them. Julie tried to whisper a 'hello' to her neighbour but the girl, an attractively slim Asian, rapidly gestured for her to remain silent and looked away flustered. Within seconds, a duty prefect appeared as if from nowhere carrying a short junior cane which she used to incline Julie's head towards her by putting the tip under her chin.

'Look at me, new girl,' she said in a low menacing voice. Julie reddened with embarrassment, feeling that the whole refectory was looking at her. 'Did I see you attempt to speak?'

'N-no,' replied Julie, trembling and stuttering with self-consciousness.

'Don't you mean, "No, duty prefect", new girl?'

'Yes, I'm sorry. I meant no, duty prefect.'

'You're lying, new girl, I distinctly saw you speak. What is your name?'

'Julie Semple, duty prefect.'

'Well, Julie Semple, you can stand over here away from the table and bend over.' Julie stepped over the bench, moved to the space between the tables and slowly bent over, feeling the short skirt rise up over her naked buttocks. Her face went crimson with embarrassment as she felt the eyes of the whole refectory focus on her bottom.

'Ah, I see that you have recently had the attention of the birch or the martinet, or so I would guess from the thinness of the stripes on your backside. Well in that case I shall teach you a lesson somewhere else. As you are a new girl I won't cane over your previous marks. Hold your right hand out. That's right, palm upwards.'

Julie held her hand out and closed her eyes. She knew what was coming and bit her lip, feeling that the whole refectory would be expecting her to be brave. The cane whistled down across Julie's palm; she could not stop a cry escaping her lips and instinctively thrust her hand into her other armpit.

'Now hold your left hand out and keep still.' Again

the cane whistled down and Julie doubled up in pain, both hands now under her arms. 'You can sit down now and be thankful that I only gave you two strokes on account of your being so new. Now, clasp your hands behind your back and get your head into that bowl.' Julie sank her mouth into the now almost cold stew and began to slurp it up, feeling a wave of shame as the others watched her. As she drank the silence was again broken by the menacing tones of the duty prefect.

'Jaleel Halwachi, step over here.' The Asian girl stood up resignedly and stood facing the duty prefect. 'You know that is an offence not only to speak in the refectory but also to be spoken to. Have you anything to say?' Evidently she had not, because the next thing that Julie heard was the command, 'Hold your right hand out,' followed by a whistle, a crack and an intake of breath. This was followed soon after by the sounds of the same treatment being applied to the other hand. 'You can resume your seat now, Jaleel. Remember in future that if anyone speaks to you, the correct thing to do is to raise your hand and report the offence to the duty prefect nearest to you. That way you do not implicate yourself in the crime and thus you escape punishment.' Jaleel returned stiffly to her seat, blowing on her hands and casting a reproachful glare at Julie.

The silence was now truly palpable as everyone had finished eating some time ago, even Julie and Sophie, who had started late. Everyone was sitting up straight, hands folded in laps while the duty prefects prowled around. The top table was now deserted, the mistresses having left, leaving the first-year table monitors to clear the plates. Abruptly, the silence was shattered by a shrill bell. The girls rose up en masse and began to file out of the refectory. Julie and Sophie followed the rest of the girls on their table out of the door, down a flight of steps, along a corridor and into a classroom.

* * *

The classroom was very old-fashioned, containing wooden forms with lift-up desk lids and hinged benches attached in pairs. Maps of the world and Home Office posters extolling THE WORK OF THE POLICE and A DAY IN THE LIFE OF A DAIRY FARMER, amongst others, decorated the walls. Julie and Sophie sat side by side near the front. A moment later, a tall, slim, blonde woman with a strikingly beautiful face walked in. The girls rose up and with one voice chanted, 'Good afternoon, Miss Davies.'

'Sit,' commanded Miss Davies in a haughty and educated but still rather beautiful voice. She cast her eyes around the room with an imperious stare as if searching for a miscreant.

'Ah, I see we have a couple of new girls. Yes, I remember the head did mention it this morning. Julie and Sophie, isn't it? Good, well let me make it clear in case you are under any illusions, I run a very tight ship in this lesson. Anything short of best behaviour and total concentration is not tolerated, as the other girls will tell you. I pride myself on being able to reduce the toughest girl to abject tears in minutes so make sure that you work hard in my lessons and do nothing to displease me, for I can assure you that you will regret it. Geography is a very important subject and demands a lot of intellectual effort, therefore time-wasting and daydreaming are inexcusable. I set a test every Friday, normally consisting of thirty questions, and anyone who scores less than twenty-five is caned depending on the number of wrong answers. I can tolerate up to five errors but any more earns one stroke on one hand and one on the bare buttocks for each wrong answer. So you can appreciate that the aim is to get no more than five mistakes, since only those with six or over get punished. Some weeks are very good and nobody is punished, other weeks are bad and almost the whole class is punished. As should be obvious, my methods are most

110

effective and I can justifiably say that my geography pupils learn more assiduously than they do in most other subjects. They certainly work more keenly than they would in any ordinary school or college.

'The next test is on Hastings, which, as it happens, is my home town. Therefore you can expect the test to be particularly tough. There's not much I don't know about Hastings, so you had all better get revising in earnest. Memorise all the details in the textbooks and study the maps in the library. I will be expecting you to have a full grasp of all the pertinent details – population, industry, housing, transport, average rainfall and so on – just like all the previous tests.' Miss Davies paused for breath and glared around the room, studying each face as if she could divine what a girl was thinking. Every face looked determinedly sober and respectful, each individual terrified that the wrong expression would bring down the wrath of the august Miss Davies. The silence was unbearable and the tension in the room could be felt. No one stirred a muscle and not a cough or squeak of a chair impinged on the spell the teacher held over the class. Without warning she yelled commandingly, 'Lisa Butcher, come to the front of the class.'

The girl that Miss Davies was glaring at, a slim, pallid creature with childlike features, gulped and turned a sickly shade.

'Yes, Miss Davies.' The girl rose up, trembling, and walked to the front, evidently wondering what expression or unknown sin had caused her to be singled out. A certain feeling of relief spread through the rest of the class.

'Face the blackboard and lift your skirt up high,' Miss Davies ordered. A look of undiluted terror passed over Lisa's face. Turning round so that her back was to the class, she hoisted up her skirt. It was no surprise to the rest of the class, but Julie and Sophie were shocked

111

to see that Lisa, too, was wearing no knickers. They were further shocked to see the condition of Lisa's bottom, which was swathed in purple and yellow stripes. Miss Davies looked on with an expression of pride.

'This little exhibition is for the benefit of our two new additions to the class, Julie and Sophie. You others witnessed the creation of this pot-pourri of colour. Don't worry, Lisa, I am not going to beat you, I just want to show Julie and Sophie that I do not treat new girls with special leniency; everyone gets the same treatment as everyone else. As you can see Lisa still has new girl status, she has only been with us four weeks and therefore has no underwear. Just under a week ago she did badly in the test on glacial valleys and you can still see the result. Since then, Lisa has scored almost full marks in all tests, so you can see the effectiveness of my methods. Don't learn the hard way like Lisa has done.

'Very well, Lisa, you can lower your skirt and take yourself back to your desk. I hope you can acquit yourself well in the Hastings test, it would be such a pity to have to renew the marks on your rump just as the old ones are fading.'

The remainder of the lesson passed without incident and was in fact quite interesting. Although Miss Davies struck terror into the whole class, she was also a very witty and erudite speaker who could turn any subject into a stimulating topic. Julie and Sophie, like the others, maintained expressions of rapt attention, most of which was genuine and some of which was necessary to avoid the wrath of Miss Davies. It was a double period and the lesson lasted two hours during which no one moved a muscle out of place except to write the various items of dictated notes or to raise a hand to answer a question.

When the bell to mark the end of the second period sounded, Miss Davies gathered up her books and swept out of the room saying as she went, 'And don't forget, girls, revise hard for the test on Friday.'

A feeling of relief suffused the classroom. The short intervals between lessons appeared to be a rare chance to relax and whisper to friends in the daytime without fear of punishment. Julie and Sophie turned and chatted briefly to the girls behind, who were eager to know the circumstances of their arrest and news of the outside world. The newcomers, on the other hand were desperate to learn more about the reformatory. They had not managed to elicit much information apart from the fact that the next double period was the last lesson of the day and was with Miss Hedges before one of the girls, who was positioned at the doorway, gave a short cough and darted back to her seat. Immediately the class fell silent and every pupil assumed a position of rigid deportment with eyes focused on the blackboard, models of exemplary behaviour. Seconds later, Miss Hedges appeared.

Miss Hedges was not as tall or as beautiful as Miss Davies. She was a plump woman with an attractive round face and a massive bust contained within a functional white corset, the outline of which was clearly visible against her cream-coloured blouse. Her black skirt was just above knee length and seamed black tights or stockings descended into black patent leather shoes with a low heel. Clutched under her arm was an edition of *The Complete Works of William Shakespeare*. Under her other arm she carried a set of exercise books and in her hand she held a thin plaited riding crop which was about two feet long.

The class stood up and chanted, 'Good afternoon, Miss Hedges.'

Miss Hedges indicated that they should sit down with a peremptory wave of her hand. Putting the books on the teachers' desk she turned to face the class with a scowl.

'It's a good afternoon as far as I am concerned, but

113

not quite as good an afternoon for you. I have just finished marking the essays which you wrote last week in class titled, "Is there Morality on a Desert Island: are ethics merely a subjective construct?". I was disappointed to find that not one of you has tackled this argument with the clarity of language and logic of argument that I demand from my pupils. You were given two hours to construct a well-structured debate in good English based on the material from the preceding lesson. I gave you plenty of examples of the questions raised by the issue and rehearsed most of the well-known points raised by various moral philosophers, and what do I find in these essays?' At this point Miss Hedges picked up a handful of exercise books and waved them dismissively in the air. 'Let me tell you what I find. I find elementary spelling errors, grammatical errors, illogical arguments, irrelevant examples, woolly-headed notions, errors of fact, discussions that run out of steam within a paragraph, punctuation that shows a lack of appreciation of the use of semi-colons and commas, mistakes of capitalisation and overwhelming superficiality in the treatment of philosophical concepts. Need I go on?'

Miss Hedges paused and cast her eyes around the room with eyes like laser beams. Everyone stiffened and assumed an expression of appropriate shame. Julie noticed that the girl in front of her in the adjacent column of desks had clenched her hands so that the knuckles were white and a bead of perspiration ran down the side of her forehead. Miss Hedges certainly knew how to inspire terror in her pupils. The pause continued as she folded her arms and started to tap her foot lightly on the floor. The class, hardly breathing, felt paralysed like young rabbits caught in the mesmerising stare of a ferret. Miss Hedges put her riding crop through her belt and walked to the other side of the teacher's desk where a number of school canes were hanging over two large

114

cup hooks screwed into the side of the desk. Selecting one of the longer canes, she flexed it in her hands and swished it through the air. Leisurely she returned to stand directly in front of the first row of desks and flexed the cane so that the two ends met, all the time surveying the class with her steely-eyed stare. The tension was overwhelming. Suddenly there was the unmistakable sound of water dripping on to the floor. A girl in the second row turned a deep shade of red.

'Karen Philips, stand up!' bellowed Miss Hedges. A short bespectacled girl stood up nervously, the back of her skirt dripping wet. 'Am I to understand that you have temporarily lost control of your bladder?'

'Yes, Miss Hedges. I'm so sorry, I couldn't help it,' she spluttered.

'And pray tell me what has caused you to disgrace yourself in this way?'

'I don't know, Miss Hedges,' replied the girl still scarlet with embarrassment.

'That will not do, Karen. I expect everyone in an English lesson to make an effort to express themselves clearly in English, the language of Shakespeare. Do you think that he would say, "I don't know" when called upon to explain his actions? No, of course he wouldn't. So let's make an effort this time. Why have you wet yourself in this disgraceful manner? Give me a sensible answer if you know what is good for you.'

Karen cleared her throat and made an effort to control the tremulous wavering in her voice, 'I'm sorry Miss Hedges, it was when you bent the cane. I was so nervous already and when I saw the cane – I can't help it. Last time it stung so much. It always hurts more than I expect – every time I think of it my legs go wobbly and I have to try hard not to wet myself. I'm really sorry, I couldn't stop myself.' Karen's voice finally cracked and she snivelled quietly.

'That's better. At least you have now managed to

115

explain yourself and we all know what a feeble, cowardly creature you are. You obviously need to toughen up and get some moral fibre and backbone in you. Take your clothes off and use them to mop up that disgusting pool under your seat, and when you have finished you will step up here to be caned.

Karen did as she was bidden, crouching, snivelling on the floor, mopping up until her clothes were a soaking wet pile on the desk.

'Now put your uniform back on and step up here,' ordered Miss Hedges, her face stern. Karen struggled to put the dripping clothes back on in evident discomfort. The blouse clung tightly to her back and her breasts, transparently outlining every contour and the darkness and mottling around her nipples. The skirt stuck to her thighs and squelched as she moved to face Miss Hedges at the front of the class.

'What a filthy, woebegone creature you look. Still it's no good snivelling, let's get on with it. Assume position eight.' Karen stood up straight with her hands outstretched palm upwards. Miss Hedges, in a business-like manner raised the cane high and brought it down hard on Karen's left palm before repeating the action on the other palm. Each stroke brought forth a sharp gasp from Karen and caused her to blow on her hands and rub them on her thighs.

'And again,' ordered Miss Hedges, who administered a second cut to each hand, this time causing Karen to whimper and writhe with her hands clasped between her thighs. 'Now assume position nine.' Karen quickly knelt on the floor with her head down and slim, white bottom pushed up. Miss Hedges adjusted the sodden skirt so that it did not obscure any part of Karen's derrière. 'Count the strokes if you would be so kind, Karen,' she ordered.

Julie felt her tongue stick to her dry mouth and a tingle of excitement spreading out from her clitoris as the teacher took up her position and swished the cane though the air experimentally. Karen was shivering, expecting the stroke to sting her quivering globes. Six strokes were then very slowly dealt out, each one making Karen's buttocks shudder and transforming her white bottom into a maze of intersecting scarlet weals. Each stroke elicited an anguished yelp and a squeak resembling the numbers one to six.

'You may return to your desk now, but don't think that you are getting out of the class punishment that I have planned for the end of the lesson. Oh, no, each member of this miserable class with the exception of the two new girls, of course, will pay with her backside for handing in such abysmal essay work,' bellowed Miss Hedges in her most threatening manner.

Karen winced and bit her lip as she gingerly sat back down at her desk, her clothes still tightly clinging to her and her face streaked with tears. Miss Hedges replaced the cane and opened her copy of Shakespeare.

'Now let us get back to intellectual matters. We have wasted enough time dealing with that worthless little imbecile. The class punishment will be at the end of the period since you cannot appreciate the Bard with freshly flagellated buttocks. Open your copies of *Julius Caesar* at the beginning of Act One, Scene Two. Note in particular the dialogue between Brutus and Cassius, especially the words of Brutus around line 84 and line 162. Note the way in which Brutus evinces elements of an embryonic Hamlet in so far as Shakespeare explores the dichotomy between what a man is and what a man does. Both characters are intellectuals ascribing to the intellectual dogmas and fashions of their times, namely classical republicanism in the case of Brutus and liberal humanism in Hamlet's case. And yet both men are more hampered in the world of real politic by their intellectualism than helped by it. However, these passages also show that Brutus is a bad judge of character, something which cannot be said of Hamlet. Cassius, the man who "loves no music" shows elements of the Elizabethan concept of Machiavelli, the figure of political disorder and ruthlessness rather than the high moral standard of republicanism. Yet Brutus does not recognise this flaw in Cassius' character . . .'

The lesson seemed to go on for ever. Miss Hedges appeared to be able to talk on the subject of Shakespeare and Elizabethan drama interminably. Occasionally she would ask a question whilst fixing her eye on some unfortunate, quaking girl who would do her best to stutter an acceptable answer. Julie and Sophie felt relieved that they were excused from the pressure since they had not been class members when the play was studied, and, more importantly, they had not been there when the essay work was done which absolved them from the class punishment. No doubt the other girls felt that time was passing too quickly, Julie pondered, since the end of the lesson would signify the time for an ignominious and painful caning.

Finally Miss Hedges laid the heavy tome of collected works aside and announced, 'Well, a most stimulating session. However, there is a mere twenty minutes to go before the final bell. I will have to cane you all without delay. The two new girls can be of assistance in this matter. Julie and Sophie, I want you to drag that desk, the one with the attached bench, right out to the front.' Julie and Sophie did as they were bidden and stood beside the heavy desk awaiting further orders. 'You two can help by holding your classmates still while I apply the cane. Julie, you hold their arms and Sophie can hold on to their ankles. They are inclined to squirm and wriggle about, I'm afraid.

'Right, girls, you may remember the class caning that I had to give you last term for the bad results in the spelling tests. I see by your faces that you do remember, good. Well, I intend to adopt the same procedure for this one. As you no doubt recall, I do not like skirts, knickers, blouses and so on to get in the way. So all of you stand up and remove everything except your bras, fold your clothes neatly and put them on your desk top and be quick about it. When you have done that, form an orderly line two deep across the back of the class. The last girl in place gets two extra strokes.'

For the next two minutes the only sound to be heard was the rustle of clothes as suspenders were unhooked and knickers removed. This was followed by the sound of bare feet as girls rushed to the back of the class, their cleavages wobbling, eager to avoid the extra two strokes penalty. A mere three minutes later, the whole class, with the exception of Julie and Sophie, were standing to attention, eyes cast down, in two rows at the rear of the classroom.

'Olu Ajadi, you were the last to get in position. Moreover your clothes are not folded neatly enough. It's two extra for you and you can go last,' said Miss Hedges with a sickly smile.

A thick-set black girl with a well-filled bra and a large protuberant bottom curtseyed and croaked, 'Yes Miss Hedges.'

Miss Hedges picked up the cane and placed a spare one by the side of the desk. Addressing the woeful assembly at the back of the class, she flexed the cane and said in a businesslike way, 'Right, girls, you will recall the drill. When I have finished caning the previous girl and she has got up, I want the next girl to walk to the front and lie across the desk. After your caning, you will join the line by the door. The front row can be first, starting with you at the end, Suzy Lodge. You are getting six each, except for Olu who is getting eight strokes. Let's make a start, it will take long enough as it is, and I do not want to be late for tea. Suzy, come to the front.'

119

Suzy, a redhead with a prettily freckled chest and back, self-consciously walked to the front, her buttocks quivering slightly. As she laid herself gingerly across the desk, ankles tucked under the backrest of the bench and hands grasping the front legs of the desk, Julie and Sophie grasped her forearms and ankles firmly. Julie noticed that Suzy kept her eyes tight shut and her hands clenched so that her knuckles appeared white. Miss Hedges wasted no time and, after positioning herself to the left of the desk, delivered six ferocious stingers, evenly spaced across the quivering buttocks, with no more than ten seconds delay as she carefully took aim between each stroke. Suzy struggled in vain as Julie and Sophie held on doggedly to the squirming victim, who yelled loudly to accompany the swish and pistol shot crack of each stroke.

Miss Hedges wiped her brow and said coldly, 'Get up and stand by the door. Don't dawdle.'

Suzy arose from the desk trembling and tearful and, with a curtsey to the teacher and a mumbled, 'Thank you, Miss Hedges,' walked to the appointed place by the door.

The next girl, obviously of Chinese or Japanese extraction, was already walking, eyes downcast, to the front of the classroom. Her jet-black hair, boyish bottom and barely formed breasts were keenly studied by Miss Hedges as she watched the girl position herself on the desk. Julie wondered whether the relative lack of fat on the girl's buttocks increased the intensity of the punishment, since she set up a caterwaul of continuous wailing immediately after the first stroke. This did not seem to deter Miss Hedges, though, who laid on the strokes tirelessly with all her strength. Julie suddenly realised that the girl must be Lin Tsang, whom she had overheard being mentioned in one of the hurried conversations that had taken place between the lessons. The girl had, apparently, fallen foul of the law when working in her parent's restaurant. She had attacked a protection racketeer from a Triad gang with a pan of scalding oil. The judge at the trial had sentenced Lin Tsang harshly for, 'taking the law into her own hands', but had released the racketeer when the police could offer no evidence against him.

For the next twenty minutes Miss Hedges worked efficiently and indefatigably through the whole class like a factory assembly line to the accompaniment of every variety of shriek and wail from contralto through mezzo-soprano to soprano. As each girl arose from the desk the next victim was striding towards it ready to lay across its now sweaty and slippery surface. The only slight delay occurred when it was the turn of Karen Philips, who started crying after the first stroke, and began struggling and protesting that it was not fair to be caned over her recent marks. Miss Hedges, incandescent with rage, added another four strokes to the six she was getting for her impertinence. She also promised her an evening of corridor scrubbing duty, to be followed by attendance at Miss Hedges' study which could mean anything from a motherly cuddle to another dozen of the best.

When finally the whole process was over and each girl had been equally soundly caned, Miss Hedges wiped her perspiring brow and rolled her blouse sleeve back down. After a few seconds to regain her breath she addressed the forlorn line of whimpering pupils.

'Get those shoulders back. I want to see you standing perfectly straight, not slouching. And spread out a bit, you are too bunched together. Sandra Berry! Did I see you rub your bottom? I hope not or it will be another dose for you. You know I don't allow it. Now, I want you all to turn around to face the wall.' The girls turned and presented a row of crimsoned and ridged bottoms. Miss Hedges strolled down the line, inspecting her handiwork with a look of immense satisfaction on her face and occasionally pausing to run a finger over a particularly tender mark or thickly raised stripe.

'Good, everyone seems to have got her just desserts. Nobody has escaped lightly and everyone has got them evenly spaced and well laid on. I am sure that everyone will put in the appropriate degree of effort in future when it comes to English essay work. Now, just to show the rest of the girls in the other years that they had better not produce sub-standard work in my classes you can go into the refectory for your tea, just wearing what you are wearing now. When you have finished, you can collect your clothes from your desks. Now, off you go; you are already late for tea. You new girls, Julie and Sophie, you can follow on behind. Your assistance was most useful. Perhaps it was lucky for you that you were not here when the essay work was done.' Miss Hedges watched as the almost naked line of girls plus Lisa Butcher who, as a new girl, was totally naked, filed out of the classroom and down the corridor en route to the refectory with Julie and Sophie following on behind.

The entrance of the third formers to the refectory elicited some suppressed mirth from the other girls, who were already finishing their tea, especially when they tried to sit down on the hard wooden benches without wincing. A stifled giggle would escape from time to time from somewhere in the hall, which made Miss Hedges' victims feel even more sorry for themselves. Although Julie was grateful that she had not had to endure the pain of a caning or the indignity of sitting almost nude in the refectory, she did feel somewhat guilty that she and Sophie were not sharing in the trials and tribulations of their new-found colleagues. Sophie was again given lettuce, water and dry bread which also made Julie feel bad as she received some bread and margarine, a smear of jam, and an apple, albeit a very small and sour one. After a mercifully short time the bell went and they all hurried back to the classroom to put their uniforms back on.

On the way to the dormitory, Julie and Sophie walked with a pretty blonde girl called Anita Boole, who seemed remarkably jolly considering the events of the afternoon. Whispering confidentially as they walked up the back stairs to the dormitory she said, 'I know it probably seems really awful to you, and you are probably really frightened, but it is not usually quite as bad as this afternoon was. Miss Hedges doesn't usually cane anyone in her lesson at all. She is too bound up in literature to break off from her train of thought. Up until today she hadn't caned any of us in the lesson for at least a month. She's quite sweet, really. Miss Sharp is the English teacher who we all dread. We had her for English language last year. Bloody hell, was she a stickler for punctuation! One comma out of place and you were really for it. Still, we learned a lot from her – we didn't have much choice. There are a lot of teachers worse than Miss Hedges. Some of them are real bitches – Miss Chapel, for example. You have probably already met her. Most days no one gets it, but you must remember to be on your best behaviour at all times. Don't relax in the presence of prefects or mistresses or you could find that you are punished frequently until obedience becomes second nature. Some girls rebel when they first come here and they don't half pay for it. Afterwards, they are as meek as little lambs. Take my advice, act really meek and penitent. Let them think that you fully accept the regime. That way they don't single you out for extra tough treatment and you can still retain a bit of your real self inside, which they don't know about. It's better than trying to act tough, because if you do they will squash your personality like an egg under a steamroller, and you will never be the same again. You will find that we are a pretty tightly bonded year group and that when you have been initiated into the group we are all supportive of each other. There are a few exceptions, teacher's special pets and sneaks and so on, but on the whole we stick together.'

Julie was grateful that Anita was taking the trouble to make her feel better and was just about to question her on the subject of initiation when Anita opened a door to reveal a long room with a floor of bare boards and a row of metal-framed beds down each side. Julie's heart sank because the overall effect was so Spartan, an effect which was emphasised by the plain white walls and barred windows. This initial impression was not lost on Anita.

'Welcome to our beautiful dorm,' said Anita with a huge grin and a mock flourish. 'This is going to be your boudoir for a long time unless you escape and I don't think there is much chance of that. Pigs will fly before anyone gets over the wall from this bloody awful place. So make the most of it. You will soon feel at home.'

9

The Dormitory

Anita showed Julie and Sophie to their metal frame beds which, fortunately, were adjacent. Sitting on Sophie's bed, Anita began to tell them all about the reformatory; which mistresses to be especially afraid of and which ones were more lenient. Julie was most eager to hear all the details of life at Roughton Hall but the combination of lack of sleep at the interrogation centre and the night on the phallic chairs meant that exhaustion quickly overcame the two girls. They both fell into a deep, dreamless sleep despite the thinness of the mattress.

They must have been asleep for a number of hours for when Julie was wakened by a noisy group of her fellow third-formers it was dark outside and a number of bare lightbulbs were illuminating the dormitory. A girl with red hair and freckles, who Julie recognised as Suzy Lodge, was looking down on her with a kindly expression. She spoke with a trace of a Scots accent.

'Wake up, lazybones. How are you feeling? You've been asleep for ages. Welcome to the third form dormitory. We want you and Sophie to be happy and loyal members of the year group. Let me fill you in on the way we organise the dorm and what our basic rules are. Life is tough here, so we stick together with bonds of loyalty like sisters. My name's Suzy and I'm the dorm leader, which means that I take charge to help us do things together and sort things out for the good of us all. Olu and Mandy are my deputies who help add weight to my authority. If there are any disputes between our members, the dorm leader has the authority to make a ruling to solve the dispute. Any girl who offends against the vows of loyalty will be tried by the other members of the dorm who form the jury. I am the judge in such cases and Olu and Mandy assist me on the bench. Witnesses for the defence and prosecution can be called. In addition, the plaintiffs and the accused can be represented by advocates from the dorm if they so wish. I decide the punishment, although pleas for leniency or severity from the jury will be seriously considered. Fortunately, we do not have a trial very often. The last one was early last term when one of our dorm, I will refrain from mentioning names so that painful memories are not reawakened, was judged guilty of informing on one of the other dorm members who had stolen some sherry from the kitchens. That was a particularly serious crime because it breached our code of loyalty and it also resulted in the serious punishment of the girl who stole the booze.'

'I didn't tell anyone, I never did,' shouted a voice from several beds away.

This was followed by an uproar of angry voices shouting, 'Yes you did.'

'You arse-faced teacher's sneak.'

'You got off lightly, so shut your ugly mouth.'

'You admitted it yourself: you owned up to it.'

'No I didn't – well, only after you lot had had me hanging upside down and were doing those things to me for hours which were rotten and cruel.'

'We should have taken turns to do it all night. That's what you deserved.'

'Shut up, all of you,' yelled Suzy. 'I am trying to welcome Julie and Sophie to our dorm. What sort of impression do you think you are giving them? Now, where was I? The dorm leader is elected by the dorm members every year. If there is an equal number of votes

126

for each candidate the winner is decided by a fight in the place known as the mud hole in the woods until one of the candidates submits. The loser is then allowed to be one of the deputies automatically. The next election is not due for six months so nobody is really thinking about it at the moment. Until your new girl status is over you cannot take a full part in the dorm organisation anyway. It's best to get a feel for the way things are done in here before you start saying too much in meetings. For the moment, we have the initiation ceremony to do tonight which is the first step towards full membership of the dorm.'

'What is the initiation ceremony?' enquired Sophie.

'You will know soon enough,' replied Suzy. 'We change the ceremony in some little way every year so that it doesn't become boring. After all, part of the purpose is the entertainment of the dorm. However, it is also to inculcate in new members a serious respect for the rules and our group loyalty. Therefore, the ceremony is designed to be a mixture of the tough and the tender. The tough is to remind us of the power of the dorm so that no girl is tempted to break our code of trust and loyalty. The tender is to remind us of the love and support that our fellow dorm members can give us all, to stay strong and survive our sentences on this bloody awful island. So the ceremony is in two parts and the first part will start now. Jaleel, Lin and Karen, get the rubber sheet and spread it out at the end of the dorm where we had it last time. There is plenty of room there. Hazel, bring out the cooking oil from our secret store.'

Julie and Sophie watched with mounting apprehension as an enormous red rubber sheet, big enough to cover the floor of an average-sized bedroom, was spread on the floor while Hazel emerged from behind a cupboard dragging an industrial-sized plastic container labelled SKEFCO ECONOMY COOKING OIL.

127

'Now the fun really begins,' declared Suzy, and a ripple of giggles circulated around the dorm. 'Heidi, get ready for the bout.' A large, rather Scandinavian-looking girl with blonde hair immediately stepped forward and slipped off the short, transparent night-dress that she was wearing. Julie noticed that the girl had big breasts jutting proudly forward with the whole area of the areola standing proud from the surrounding breast. A trace of blue veins was just visible through the pale, unblemished skin. She was also the owner of a very large bottom, generously endowed with fat, which quivered as she walked and which clearly bore the six maroon and purple lines of the earlier punishment. She had a thick midriff in spite of the reformatory's strict ideas on the desirability of a slim figure.

'Heidi has a slow metabolism,' explained Suzy, as if reading Julie's thoughts. 'She is also the dorm's champion wrestler. Oil her up, please, Hazel.'

'And let me help, please,' shouted a few more voices.

'Okay, Lin and Amy, you can help, too.'

Heidi stepped on to the rubber sheet, her milky-white breasts slowly swinging from side to side, and raised her arms in the air with a sensuous grin. Meanwhile, Hazel, standing astride the giant container, gradually tipped it so that the oil cascaded into the waiting, cupped hands of her eager assistants, much of it overflowing and slowly spreading across the rubber sheet. With their cupped hands full, the girls set about pouring it all over Heidi's body and massaging it into every square inch of pale skin. The girls worked hard to assiduously pummel and stroke every crevice and fold of skin, paying particular attention to the breasts, thighs and bottom. Heidi wore an expression of absolute rapture as Lin concentrated on getting the oil right into the crease of her buttocks. The palm of her hand was pushed right down and under Heidi's widely spread legs so as to emerge over her smoothly-shaven, and now gleaming, pubis. Amy massaged handfuls of oil over Heidi's breasts with firm circular motions until they shone, taking care to lift each one in turn to rub the oil into the area underneath. Meanwhile, Hazel kept herself busy smoothing the oil over each leg and massaging the insides of the thighs.

After many minutes of feverish activity, and the spilling of many pints of oil, Suzy pronounced herself satisfied that Heidi was well and truly greased to perfection. Turning to Julie and Sophie she calmly instructed them to remove their clothes and to step on to the rubber sheet. Plainly, there was no scope for hesitation so Julie and Sophie, both rather sheepishly, stripped as the dorm looked on with keen interest and tentatively stepped on to the glistening rubber. A murmur of excitement rose up and Julie heard one of the girls nearby whisper to her neighbour, 'What lovely kissable titties.' Julie caught several other similar comments but who they referred to was not clear. She could feel that the sheet was now extremely slippery and found it difficult to walk on the surface without sliding about. On reaching the centre of the sheet, Julie heard Suzy command in military style, 'Initiates! Spread your legs and raise your arms. Amy, Hazel and Lin, oil the candidates for initiation.'

Soon, the three girls were working just as hard on Julie and Sophie as they had done on Heidi. Julie braced herself to stop slipping as the oriental girl, Lin, rubbed and pummelled her and worked what seemed like pints of oil into every pore and crevice. The rest of the dorm looked on with glee. At one point, when Lin massaged her buttocks particularly energetically, Julie slipped over and slid across the sheet, slowly rotating as if on ice. The initial feeling of embarrassment soon began to wear off as a warm glow of well-being suffused Julie's body and mind. Lin was seemingly an expert in the oriental arts of whole body massage as she gradually worked her way up the front of Julie's body from her feet to her neck and back down the other side, pausing to give special attention to Julie's perfectly rounded bottom. Here Lin performed firm circular movements with the tips of her fingers which brought Julie to the verge of orgasm. Out of the corner of her eye, Julie could see that Sophie was enjoying the attentions of two girls and was in a similar state of excitement.

'Cease oiling the candidates for the dormitory initiation,' yelled Suzy in her ceremonial voice. 'Dormitory members, remove your night-dresses and gather round, forming an unbroken circle,' she continued. Obediently, the girls quickly stripped and gathered round the area of the giant sheet holding hands as if forming the ropes of a boxing ring. 'Lin! Attach the ten-foot lines, and Olu and Mandy, attach the masks,' ordered Suzy. From behind the circle, Lin stepped out carrying two lengths of thin rope while Olu and Mandy appeared clutching three leather masks. Julie watched with increasing curiosity as Olu, who had removed her night-dress as well, pressed herself against Heidi to attach an elaborate mask which buckled under the chin and behind the head, completely covering her eyes whilst leaving her mouth and nose uncovered. Julie was transfixed by the beautiful sight of Olu's muscular velvety black body pressed against the gleaming white Scandinavian. Lin at the same time tied the end of one rope to Heidi's left wrist and the other end to Sophie's right wrist. She tied the other rope to Heidi's right wrist and attached the other end to Julie's left wrist. Meanwhile, Mandy attached a similar mask to Sophie who swayed slightly as if finding it hard to balance deprived of the power of sight. Olu then turned to Julie and, placing a mask over her head, buckled it in place, her large, rubbery nipples brushing against Julie's own more delicately formed ones. This sent a frisson of excitement through to Julie's engorged clitoris, which was still throbbing with the arousal caused by the oiling process. The absence of visual stimulation seemed to increase Julie's awareness of all the other sensations; the pressure of Olu's squashy breasts sliding against her own, the friction of Olu's nipples rubbing firmly against her own nipples, the smooth feel of the oiled rubber against the soles of her feet, the warm moist aroma of Olu's breath against her cheek, the tight grip of the rope around her wrist and the excited giggles of her surrounding dorm-mates.

'All right, girls, quieten down. The bout will begin soon. This is a twenty-minute, one round contest between the dorm champion, Heidi, and the two new girl initiates, Julie and Sophie. To win, Julie and Sophie must force a submission or two falls on Heidi. For Heidi to win she must gain a submission or two falls over her opponents. If Julie and Sophie win, they can be excused dorm cleaning duty for a whole term. If they lose, they can do double cleaning duties for a whole month plus being general fags and dogsbodies for the dorm committee. Either way, the contest forms the first part of the initiation rites of the dorm. It is a test of the spirit and grit of a new dorm member. Everyone who is forming the ropes of the ring hold your neighbour's hand tightly, we don't want to have the ring broken so that the fighters slide all around the dorm. Are you ready, dorm champion?'

'Yes, Suzy,' shouted Heidi.

'Are you ready, initiates?'

Julie answered in the affirmative, even though she did not particularly feel ready for anything, being blindfolded, stark naked and hardly able to stand on the rubber sheet which was now swimming in oil.

'Let the first and only round begin!' shouted Suzy as someone rang a little bell and a loud cheer went up.

Julie edged backwards, afraid of what might be coming in her direction but soon found that her back was pressed hard against the soft protuberances of

131

naked breasts. Slipping sideways, she was pushed forward by a larger, soft bosom which slid with pneumatic ease across her oily back. Suddenly, she felt an almighty jerk on her left wrist which made her feet slide from under her and caused her to fall face down on to the sheet. As she tried to recover herself, another great tug caused her to slide across the rubber sheet. With an abrupt thud, her face came to rest against a soft body. Immediately, she felt her head gripped between two immensely powerful thighs. Her nose felt smothered by the smoothly shaven pudenda and her mouth tasted the salty taste of a well lubricated vagina. She tried to wrench her head away, but the strong thighs, which Julie assumed belonged to Heidi, redoubled their tight grip.

A smart move, thought Julie, Heidi must have sat down open-legged when the bell rang and just wrenched on the rope. At the same time, Julie felt a hand slide down her side to locate her wrist and then felt her arm wrenched up behind her back, causing her mouth to press even more strongly into Heidi's gaping quim. Struggle as she might, she could not break free. With her mouth and nose pressed so tightly against her tormentor's soft haven, Julie gasped for breath.

Above her, she could hear Heidi repeating over and over, 'Suck, you bitch, suck. Suck harder or I'll pull your arm a bit more. That's right, suck and use your tongue. Harder, you stuck-up, spoilt bitch.' Heidi's thighs quivered as if she was pulling the other rope. Julie felt someone trip over her legs and a fraction of a second later, Sophie had landed on top of her, slid up her back and walloped with a loud slapping noise into Heidi's chest. A grunt emanated from Heidi's direction and, immediately, Julie felt her captor keel over, releasing the grip of her thighs at the same time.

Julie staggered up, but her feet slid apart so that she ended up doing the splits which was very uncomfortable. She tried to get up again, but every time her feet slipped sideways and she sank back down on the floor. Gradually, she managed to stand, using her hands to get extra purchase on the floor, but as she slowly straightened up, another yank of the rope on her left wrist pulled her sprawling and spinning across the sheet. This time, she impacted on to a forest of legs formed by the dorm members' 'ring'. Eager hands grasped her under the armpits and set her back on her feet. Completely disorientated by the darkness of the mask, Julie blundered forward again with hands outstretched, only to find that she had reached the other side of the ring as her hands made contact with a pert pair of breasts. The owner of the pert breasts gave a giggle, span Julie around and pushed her back towards the middle of the sheet. Now Julie could hear the sounds of panting and groaning in front of her and, feeding the rope through her hands, made her way towards Heidi in the hope of rescuing Sophie from her clutches. Moments later, Julie stumbled over the bodies of Heidi and Sophie locked in an oily embrace. As Julie fell on top of them, she also became embroiled in the struggle in which the three bodies, shining with oil and perspiration, were constantly slipping out of each other's grasp like three orange pips. No sooner did Julie get Heidi – or the body that she thought was Heidi – in a hold than she slipped through her arms. Instead, Julie would find that someone else was getting her in a headlock or armlock. The spectators cheered and hooted with joy as the three wrestlers got into more and more ludicrous positions. At one point, Julie found herself in a vicious half-nelson hold and began to call a submission when her opponent cried out, 'Oh God, I didn't know it was you . . . Sorry,' and let go. It was Sophie, who had mistaken Julie for Heidi. A few seconds later, Julie found herself clutched tightly from behind in a crushing bear-hug. She knew that this was Heidi as she could feel her vast, squashy breasts squeezing against her back. Due to the oil, it was an easy matter to twist around to face her opponent. Julie pushed away with all her strength, but Heidi squeezed all the tighter. Julie located Heidi's ears and, with a hand on each ear, dug her nails in and pulled.

Heidi yelped and screeched, 'You little bitch. I'll have you for that,' as she released her hold and blindly unleashed a flurry of slaps, most of which failed to land. Two hard slaps did connect, though; one to Julie's right breast and the other to her cheek. Julie staggered sideways into the back of Sophie. Clutching on to Sophie for support, Julie felt herself grabbed from behind and wrenched away. Again, she wriggled around to face her opponent, when, without warning, Heidi lifted Julie off her feet and dropped her down. Julie's feet slipped from under her and she slid on to her back. In a trice, Heidi dropped down, squatting on Julie's face with her arms pinioned under her knees. For the second time Julie's mouth was enveloped in the warm clamminess of Heidi's quim as the big girl let her whole weight rest on Julie's face. Julie tried to shout out a cry of submission but Heidi's silky-smooth sex lips, almost dripping with love juice, were a very effective gag.

Heidi was laughing and shouted down to Julie, 'Now suck hard, as hard as I want. If you don't I just sit down a bit more. Your face makes a very nice seat for Heidi's big bottom.'

Julie began to panic, worried that she would not be able to breathe. Heidi had obviously thought of that, because every few seconds she would raise herself a couple of millimetres, just enough for Julie to quickly gulp a lungful of air. She tried to twist her head from side to side but Heidi's weight on her face, along with her immovable arms, meant that all she could move was her legs. As if in reply to Julie's vain attempts to extricate herself, Heidi shifted her bottom forward so that her cheeks spread wide and her anal dimple was now pressing down even harder on Julie's mouth. To the accompaniment of cheering, Heidi now began slowly to gyrate, grinding her bottom over the tip of Julie's nose. The intense aroma of sexual arousal and fresh perspiration filled Julie's senses as she gradually succumbed to the sweet sexual excitement of true submission under a more powerful and dominating partner.

Meanwhile Sophie, who had cannoned off the dorm members forming the ring a number of times, found her way by pulling on her wrist rope to the scene of Julie's discomfiture. Groping blindly, she located Heidi and attempted to topple her from her sweet throne. Heidi resisted strongly and, flailing blindly with her palms, quite by luck managed to give Sophie an almighty slap around the face. Sophie was incensed and, groping forward again, dragged her from Julie by the hair. Heidi let out a howl of rage and flew at Sophie but missed by several inches, careering into the human 'ropes' which gave way in a heap under her momentum in one big, slippery mass like a shoal of mackerel tipped on to a trawler's deck.

Julie found that she could barely move for exhaustion, and was slowly dragging herself up when she heard the tinkle of the bell and Suzy's voice announcing that the allotted time for the bout had expired. She then ordered Hazel and Lin to remove the masks and ropes while a great cheer went up, followed by a sustained round of applause. Julie sank back down on the floor, overcome with fatigue. Moments later, she felt someone fiddling with the buckles of the mask and the knots of the rope around her wrist.

As the mask was removed, Julie became aware of Lin's smiling face looking down on her and heard her whisper, 'Well done, you've really got guts. Heidi will be hopping mad until she gets even. Congratulations!' At the far edges of her vision, Julie saw the laughing faces of the human ring as they struggled to find their feet. Heidi was trying to extricate herself from the mass of bodies that were on top of her, but whenever the group was almost all upright, someone would slip over and bring the whole lot of them down again. Other girls went over to help, but since everyone was now thoroughly covered in oil, those trying to tug the flailing limbs free of the pile soon ended up just as helpless as those whom they were trying to assist. Soon the whole rubber sheet was one great mass of slithering, slippery and gleaming bodies. The dormitory echoed with giggles and screams so loud that Suzy, standing on a chair, had to repeatedly bellow for quiet. Gradually the message got through and the sounds of hilarity died away.

'That's better. If that racket had gone on much longer one of the duty prefects would have been along and we would have received another class flogging. We wouldn't want two in one day, would we?' This was received with general murmurs of assent all round and the process of disentanglement continued with greatly muted mirth.

When everybody had precariously regained their footing, Suzy, still standing on the chair, announced, 'Well done everyone. That was a really good bout. Lots of titty-slapping and fanny-eating. I almost joined in myself. Congratulations go to our two new initiates, who have forced a draw from our champion, since Heidi could not make the challengers submit or gain a two fall advantage over each challenger. The judges, myself and Mandy, only registered one fall, which was awarded to Heidi over Julie. Quite an achievement as no other new girl has survived more than ten minutes without submitting totally to Heidi's skill and strength.'

'And fat,' an anonymous voice shouted from the back.

Suzy pretended not to hear and continued, 'Hazel and Lin, please put the sheet and oil back in the hiding place but pour out a mug of oil first because we will need it for the next part. It is now time for the second part of the initiation ceremony, the part which focuses on the tender, sensuous and mutual support side of life here. Right, fellow dorm members, put a towel on your bed to stop the oil from getting on to the bedclothes and lie down with your feet sticking out through the metal bars at the end. Just do it like we did when Lisa Butcher joined us last month. The new initiates will anoint and massage the soles of our feet with their breasts.'

This was received with a few cheers and cries of, 'Wonderful, it's absolute heaven,' and, 'Make sure that their nipples are standing up nice and firm when you do me, please.'

Suzy, Olu and Mandy moved to the end of the rows of beds and indicated that Julie and Sophie should stand with them. Suzy brushed the back of her fingers over Julie and Sophie's nipples, pursed her lips and said, 'It's really important that your nipples are sticking right out, for this part of the ceremony. The effect is just not as good when they are not. Olu will get them hard and pointed, like little thimbles, in no time. Olu has a real talent with nips, don't you, Olly?'

Olu grinned, her white teeth perfectly set off by her ebony skin, bowed with a flourish and pecked Suzy on the cheek. She flexed her fingers and speaking huskily, said, 'Mandy, some oil on the initiates' titties, please.'

Mandy carefully poured a small amount of the golden oil on each breast in turn and, putting the cup down, spread the oil carefully all over, using the tips of her fingers. Olu flexed her fingers again and moved behind Julie. Pressing herself against Julie's back, she cupped a breast in each hand whilst nibbling the girl's ear. Then, with the tips of her fingers, she slowly teased each nipple in long, tugging movements which gradually became harder and more forceful. Each slow, teasing pull brought the nipples further and further out as she increased the pressure. After a couple of minutes she changed her rhythm so that she pulled each nipple alternately and more rapidly. First she would bring one nipple between thumb and index finger and then pull it several inches so that the whole breast stood out like a ripe melon. Then she would slowly let it slip through her fingers so that the breast resumed its normal shape. Without a pause, she would then do the same to the other nipple. Within minutes, Julie's nipples were more sensitised and more prominent than she had ever known them. Each nipple stood out proudly and rock hard, as if straining to grow even more. Julie felt a hot throbbing of lust which began at the tips of her nipples, spread down through her heart, which was beating madly, and ended deep in her yearning quim. She felt a sensation of breathlessness. Waves of surging heat flowed through her body. The hot aching in her quim demanded that she frig her engorged clitoris, which was now standing out proudly like her nipples. Her right hand strayed automatically over her smooth pudenda to stroke her clitoris, just as she would do when half asleep in bed whilst she dreamed erotic dreams. In this state, Julie was unaware of onlookers and the situation that she was in. All her consciousness was taken up by the elemental, animal sensations coursing through her body.

Suzy cast a look of cool appraisal over Julie and announced, 'She's ready now: good work, Olu. You can do the same with Sophie while we get Julie started doing this side of the dorm. When Sophie is ready you can start her on the other side. It's convenient having two initiates together because they only have to do half each. Now come with me, Julie, to the first bed of the row where we have our fellow dorm member, Alison. See what pretty little feet she has? It's your job to give each foot a thorough massage with your breasts.'

Julie looked at Alison who was lying naked on her back, a smile playing on her lips. A towel covered the bedclothes to protect them from the oil which was still evident on Alison's lithe body. Her delicately formed feet protruded from the metal uprights of the iron bedstead and her toes wiggled expectantly.

Suzy guided Julie by the shoulder and said, 'Kneel down here, so that your left boob is touching the sole of Ali's right foot. Mandy, a little more oil on the soles of Ali's feet, please. We don't want Julie's nips to get sore. Good, now hold Ali's foot and slowly rub your left tit up and down the sole, making sure that your lovely, erect nipple is pressed up tight, right from the heel to the tips of Ali's toes. That's right, you are getting the idea already. Up and down, up and down, that's good. Now, circular movements please, around and around as you go up and down. Keep going, each foot needs at least a couple of minutes separately. Now do the same with the right foot and your other boob.'

Julie grasped the right foot and began the same process. She could feel her nipples aching with erotic sensation as her breast squashed and kneaded against the slipperiness of Alison's right foot.

'Now both feet together. Keep a good grip on those ankles and move your whole chest around so those boobies squish and squash against Ali's feet.'

Julie's nipples felt hypersensitive, as in their highly engorged state they slid around every contour of Alison's feet. Before long, Julie was aware that Alison's legs were moving in a rhythmical fashion. In addition, Julie could hear the sound of sighs and heavy breathing.

Julie heard Olu's voice call, 'Sophie's nipples are now ready; sticking out like pokers.'

'Good work, Olu. Get her started doing the other side. And Mandy! Have you got the dorm toothbrush ready?' asked Suzy.

'Yes, would I forget?' Mandy produced from behind her back an electric toothbrush and a tube of toothpaste labelled TINGLEFRESH. Julie wondered why Suzy was concerned with dental hygiene at such a time but did not have long to wait for an explanation.

'The rest of us know the history and lusciousness of the dorm toothbrush but for the benefit of the two initiates let me explain. The dorm electric toothbrush belonged originally to one of the mistresses, but it was "borrowed" by one of our sisters in the dorm. They have given up trying to find out who pinched it now. No names; no pack-drill. The brush part moves at a rate of over ten thousand times per minute or something like that. It moves in two directions, side to side and backwards and forwards. We have taken out the old bristles and glued in some soft sable brushes that we got from the art studio. We call it Eric the Electric Orgasm Machine. Even the most frigid woman in the world could not resist a minute of Eric on her clitty without having a stupendous, howling orgasm. Eric is the most popular member of the dorm, but we only bring him out for special occasions. For one thing we have a hell of a job stealing replacement batteries for him, so Eric has to be rationed. You will get your turn later, when you have finished your foot duties. The toothpaste is a little extra enhancement which some of us go for. It's a strong peppermint flavour. When a little bit is put on the clitty, it makes it tingle like it's hot and cold at the same time. The toothpaste and Eric together have an explosive effect on a girl's erogenous regions. It produces an orgasm so intense that we have to hold a towel to each other's mouths to stop the noise alerting the whole building. That would be disastrous, because for one thing we would all get punished and for another thing, the other dorms would move heaven and earth to steal Eric. Right Julie, now step up the pressure with those boobies. And Mandy, apply Eric to Ali's clit, nice and gently. Olu, get ready with that towel – they don't call Ali "Lassie" for nothing. The last time, I swear they could hear her howling on the mainland.'

Julie stepped up the pressure as she heard the toothbrush click on and start to hum. Within seconds the bed started shaking as if it was the focus of a local earthquake and Suzy grabbed hold of the frame in an attempt to stop it from rattling. A few seconds later a muffled wail that seemed to go on forever emanated from behind the folded towel Olu was holding. Gradually the wail tailed off and the bed stopped shaking.

Suzy leant over, stroked Alison's brow and said, 'That's all for now, Alison. Come on, Julie, on to the next bed now. It's your friend who was so glad to meet you in the refectory. Jaleel, our little Star of India.'

It was at least thirty minutes later that Julie, with Mandy's help, was able to clamber up from her knees, having finished her last breast-to-foot massage. Sophie had worked slightly quicker and had therefore finished at about the same time. Eric the electric toothbrush had worked his magic on every member of the dorm apart from Suzy and Olu. In every case Eric's effect had been virtually instantaneous and vocally explosive. Olu's attendance with the towel to muffle the sounds of orgasm was certainly a necessary precaution. Julie had never before heard such a variety of orgasmic sounds, ranging from plaintive cries to guttural grunts deep in the throat.

Suzy guided Julie and Sophie to their own beds and said in a sultry voice, 'Come along you must be tired. You have worked well. But the ceremony is not yet finished, it is your turn to receive some tender attention. This shows the reciprocity of our support for each other. You have both learnt tonight that you can give pleasure of a deeply sensual kind to your sisters in the dorm. Now you will see that your sisters can do the same for you. Now, that Olu and Mandy have pushed both of your beds together you can both lie on your backs on your beds whilst holding hands. Now wriggle down so that your feet are poking off the ends of the beds and leave the rest to us. Sandra and Amy, you've both got big boobs and firm nipples. You can do Julie and Sophie's feet. Put some more oil on your boobs first, though.'

Sandra knelt at the end of Julie's bed and Amy at Sophie's. Seconds later, Julie felt an exquisite sensation as Sandra grasped her feet and slowly massaged the soles with her breasts. Her firm, pointed nipples pressing hard, describing circles all around the ball and arch of each foot while the fuller softness of the large breasts squashed softly all around. Julie felt Sophie's hand grip more tightly and heard her give a blissful sigh; evidently Amy was working the same magic on Sophie.

Suzy moved to the head of the bed, stroked Julie's brow and said, 'There's more to come isn't there, sisters? We have a girl's satisfaction and pleasure down to a fine art in this place. After all, there is not much else to do at night and there's not one man or boy within fifty miles. Moira and Alison, come over here. You can massage Julie and Sophie's boobs with your fannies, like we did with Lisa. Do the whole chest first and be careful, remember you are not supposed to sit on them.'

Moira, a pert blonde with little pointed breasts skipped over to Julie's bed. Alison followed and quickly climbed astride Sophie, her hands supporting her weight on the bed headrail. Mandy poured a liberal amount of the oil from the cup over the chests of each initiate and then, with a signal from Suzy, Moira and Alison started gliding their smooth quims up and down from belly to nipples and back again. Julie could feel the firm bud of Moira's clitoris, surrounded by the soft sex lips, gliding from navel to nipple, circling each one so that the hard little nubbin caressed the aroused flesh. Meanwhile, Sandra had stepped up her breast massage of Julie's feet and was rubbing both boobs up and down in a regular rhythm. Julie felt Sophie's hand grip even tighter and heard her emit some guttural cries which she found herself almost imitating as she began to feel waves of lust course through her body. Slowly, she became aware of her legs turning to jelly. Then, almost with disbelief, she saw Olu bend over Sophie's quim and lightly flick her proud clitoris with her tongue whilst Mandy, her bottom rubbing against Olu's, bent over and applied her tongue to Julie's clitoris.

Julie was rapidly losing control of her body, her legs bucked and her cries became more urgent and drawn out. She heard a click and a hum and Suzy moved past with the electric toothbrush in her hand saying as she passed, 'Moira, get ready to put your hand over Julie's mouth. We are about to have lift-off.'

Seconds later Julie felt Mandy's tongue withdraw to be replaced by an unbelievable sensation as the sable brush at the tip of the electric toothbrush flicked back and forth across her clitoris hundreds of times per second in a blur of speed. As the sensation heightened, Julie felt a curious warmth and at the same time a strange coldness which resulted in an almost unbearable tingling centred on the tip of her clitoris. She raised her head but a psychedelic shower of burning lights blurred her vision as she just caught sight of Mandy passing the toothpaste tube to Olu. Waves of sensation swept up from between her legs to encompass her whole body. With a brutal suddenness, Julie felt her whole being torn asunder in an orgasm so explosive that she felt as though a bomb of concentrated sexuality had gone off inside her. In vain, as Julie's back arched and trembled, Moira tried to muffle the girl's howl, which threatened to penetrate the furthest reaches of the reformatory. As Julie's climax slowly subsided and she felt a hot blush spread up her chest to her cheeks she became aware that Sophie was reaching an orgasm of similar intensity and was astounded at the loud screams and convulsions that racked her friend's body.

Was I just like that a minute ago? wondered Julie as she tentatively tried to move her legs, which still felt like two trembling jellies.

After an interval of a few minutes, Suzy shouted to the dorm to gather in a large semicircle, holding hands, around the beds of Julie and Sophie who were still clutching each other's hand in mutual exhaustion. Suzy held Julie's free hand and Olu took Sophie's, so that the whole dorm was joined in a circular ceremony of mutuality.

Suzy invoked her most sonorous tones to say, 'We are all gathered here tonight to initiate Julie and Sophie into the warm bosom – and warm bosoms – of our dorm. They have both acquitted themselves honourably at every stage of the initiation ceremony. There is therefore no good reason why they cannot be admitted and fully accepted into the traditions and fellowship of the dorm. The dorm will show loyalty and trust to Julie and Sophie as long as they, in return, demonstrate the same qualities to the dorm. Now, Julie and Sophie, I want you to repeat the oath after me. "I do most faithfully promise to be loyal to the dorm to never split on a fellow dorm member to obey the rules of the dorm to share any cigarettes or chocolate that I may come across to be brave at all times and to keep the activities and conversations of the dorm secret." '

Julie found the little ceremony oddly moving and burst into tears at the end of it, especially when each dorm member in turn kissed Julie and Sophie on the lips. Finally, everyone went to bed thoroughly exhausted.

Suzy helped Olu move the beds of Julie and Sophie back to their proper positions, tucked them up in their starched new sheets and whispered, 'Goodnight, little darlings. Get your sleep now, for tomorrow's early morning swim is not many hours away and you do look tired. You have had a tough day but you have both coped very well. Remember to keep your hands above the bedclothes at all times. It is an offence to put your hands under the sheets at night. If a prefect comes round for a night inspection while you are asleep and finds your hands anywhere but on the top of the sheets you will be set down for a punishment. Goodnight and happy dreams.'

10

The Swimming Pool

The reformatory was on fire. Julie was trying to direct the fire-engine through the grounds of Roughton Hall before the flames engulfed the whole building. Hordes of panicking fellow inmates and stern-faced mistresses were blocking the driveway. The fire-engine was crawling forward at a slow walking pace; it needed to speed up. In a panic, Julie wildly tugged on a rope which operated the fire-engine's bell. Clang, clang, clang!

With a start, Julie woke up. The bell was still ringing. As her head cleared, she saw that her dorm-mates were leaping out of their beds. As soon as their feet hit the floor they began to tuck in their sheets and blankets neatly, so that their beds were made with military precision. Julie shook her head groggily, it felt as lively as damp cotton wool.

'Julie and Sophie! For heaven's sake get up and make your beds. It's the six o'clock alarm bell. The senior prefects will be here to inspect us in one minute's time. Make your bed neatly like mine and stand up straight at the foot of your bed. If you don't hurry, you will be for it.' Julie looked round as she edged a limb out of her warm bed and felt the icy touch of the chilly morning air. Suzy was the source of the advice and was rushing down the centre of the dormitory, her night-dress billowing, as she was speaking. Grabbing Julie and Sophie by the arms, she hauled them out of bed and quickly helped to tuck the bedding and smooth the neatly turned down top sheet so that their beds looked like all the others. Julie copied the other girls and stood stiffly to attention at the foot of her bed. Glancing down the line, Julie observed that everyone wore an identical short and very transparent pink night-dress. Gazing across at the girls opposite, she noticed that the night-dresses were so transparent that they revealed every detail. Looking down, she saw that her firm breasts pushed against the sheer nylon. Her navel and naked sex were also clearly visible. It was a cold morning and everyone's nipples were soon proudly punctuating the flimsy material.

A few seconds later, the door opened and in marched two senior prefects each wearing white blouses, tight black skirts and calf-length black boots. Each had a short plaited leather crop clipped to her belt.

'Dormitory three all present and correct. No offences to report,' shouted out Suzy.

The taller of the two senior prefects fingered her leather crop and slowly stalked her way down the centre of the dormitory, gazing deep into the eyes of each girl as she spoke, 'Not even a hand under the sheets during the night? Think carefully, everyone. Has anyone put their hand under their sheet last night? Has anyone been playing with themselves or put their hands between their thighs? It would be in your best interests to own up if you have. Perhaps someone has had an illicit masturbation session. Perhaps a prefect did an inspection in the middle of the night and gave us the names of the culprits. Perhaps we might let you off lightly if you own up now ... Very well, I'll take your word for it that there has been no illicit behaviour in this dorm last night.' She paused, and sniffed the air. 'There's something odd about this dorm, though. I recognise guilty faces when I see them. You all look as guilty as hell. There's also a slightly odd smell in here. I have detected it before in this room. Almost like a chip shop; a greasy, oily smell. I can't quite put my finger on it, but be warned, if I find evidence of wrongdoing in this dorm you will all be well and truly for the high jump. Perhaps a midnight bottom-warming session followed by a length of the pool and two circuits of the playing fields in the rain would take the spring out of your step. I will be keeping an extra-close eye on you lot. We are in danger of treating you sluts far too softly and letting you get away with too much slack behaviour. So be warned. About turn!'

Julie and Sophie, caught unawares, turned to face the door a fraction of a second behind the rest. Luckily, this went unnoticed.

'Quick march!' shouted the tall senior prefect. Immediately, the two lines of girls proceeded to march out of the dormitory, keeping in close step with each other. Staying in their two lines, the pupils marched down the wide staircase to a corridor leading to the rear courtyard. Marching along the corridor, Julie saw that they were now in a long procession with the lower forms in front and the higher forms following behind. The whole procedure was conducted with military precision by the prefects and senior prefects, who marched alongside, occasionally cracking their crops and shouting imprecations at anyone who fell out of step or who spoilt the strict symmetry of the two lines. Eventually, the corridor terminated in a large foyer with double doors leading outside to a wide flight of steps. Without any pause the twin columns passed out of the relatively warm building and into the chill wind as they descended the steps.

As the cold blast lifted Julie's night-dress her skin erupted in goose-pimples and a spasm of shivers started her teeth chattering. Cynthia, the girl next to Julie, whispering very quietly under her breath, said, 'Awful, isn't it? Don't worry, you'll get more used to it. Summer is on its way; it's not so bad, then. How do you think the first and second formers feel?'

In answer to this rhetorical question, Julie focused her eyes on the figures at the front of the procession and saw through the gloomy half-light that they were completely naked. The march continued down a wide avenue bordered by formal gardens, populated by stone statues of naked nymphs. Geometric shapes and animal sculptures formed by privet and box topiary surrounded each statue. The avenue was at least one hundred yards long and Julie felt increasing discomfort as the cold wind swirled around her flimsy night-dress and the gravel path caused her to walk as gingerly as was possible. At the end of the avenue they passed under a high stone arch complete with Doric columns and Latin inscriptions. On reaching the far side, Julie saw that the front of the procession had come to a halt and had formed up into formation like a military inspection on a parade ground. In the middle of the area there was a large swimming pool. Julie's dormitory quickly formed up line abreast behind the lower forms with the efficiency that daily routine brings. The higher forms took their places behind.

After a long pause, a young-looking mistress with long blonde hair, climbed on to a high podium beside the pool and announced, 'Let us pray.'

Immediately, the assembly put their hands together, bowed their heads and began intoning a dirge which Julie was not familiar with. In order not to incur the wrath of the senior prefects, she pretended to pray and hoped that nobody would notice. Julie tried to follow vaguely the words that she could hear Cynthia saying, which consisted of phrases such as, 'Please drive the evil from our unworthy bodies and cleanse us through our suffering,' and, 'We beseech you to give the mistresses strength to purge the corruption and depravity from us, and may we be truly thankful for everything that we receive.'

Following the 'Amen,' the mistress barked, 'Night-dresses off!' The flimsy garments were cast aside and in seconds, the whole reformatory stood stark naked, shivering in the half-light. 'Position two for illicit hair inspection on the count of three ... One, two three,' continued the mistress. With military precision the whole assembly adopted position two, with their legs apart and hands clasped behind their heads. For the next five minutes senior prefects moved down the lines, inspecting under the arms and between the legs of each girl to check that they were completely hairless. When in doubt, due to the poor light, the senior prefects would shine a powerful torch to make doubly sure that no hair or stubble was evident. Occasionally, a senior prefect would detect a millimetre of growth and would then shout out the name of the miscreant to be put on report for later punishment.

Eventually, the inspection was concluded. The mistress then set a large wooden metronome on the podium and set it ticking slowly.

'The morning physical training will now commence. In time with the metronome, please. Begin as usual, with twenty push-ups,' she announced. Immediately, the whole assembly commenced vigorous push-ups, one per beat of the metronome. After a minute, the exercise was changed to sit-ups and then it was knee-bends. The morning light slowly grew stronger and Julie became more aware of the rather bizarre sight of over a hundred pairs of breasts and bottoms all wobbling in time with each other as the metronome ticked. The last exercise was to bend from the waist to touch the toes. Julie smiled to herself as on the way down, she saw such a great mass of bottoms so blatantly revealed. The view from the back row must be even more spectacular, she thought.

This programme, in which every exercise was included, continued for about 25 minutes, after which Julie felt totally exhausted. At last the mistress shouted,

'That concludes this morning's exercise. Stand to attention until it is your dorm's turn for the pool. First year dormitory, step forward.'

Immediately the front two rows of girls stepped up smartly to the edge of the pool, their bodies glistening with perspiration in spite of the cold air temperature and strong wind which whipped the grey surface of the water into little waves.

'First row, get ready – and dive!' ordered the mistress. With one huge splash, the first row dived into the pool and began swimming to the far end. When they were halfway across, the mistress shouted, 'Second row, get ready – and dive!' at which point the remainder of the first year dived with another huge splash. Seconds later, the first swimmers reached the far side and hauled themselves, dripping and shivering out on to the concrete apron. Julie could see a senior prefect at the far end shouting and waving her leather strap so that soon the girls were organised again into rows and were running on the spot with their hands on their heads. This process continued, until before long, Julie's row were on the edge of the pool.

Cynthia pretended to sneeze, and covering her mouth with her hand, whispered, 'Prepare yourself for a hell of a shock. The pool is not heated, and it's bloody freezing even in summer.'

'Form three, first row, get ready – dive!' shouted the mistress. Sixteen naked bodies hit the water simultaneously. The shock took Julie's breath clean away and she came up to the surface gasping and stunned. The water really felt as if it was not far above freezing point. The strength seemed to leave her limbs and she floundered for a couple of seconds as the others swam away from her. With an enormous effort, Julie ordered her limbs to obey her. Gradually they responded and she began to manage a slow crawl towards the far end. Almost defeated by the cold, she just made it to the end

151

but did not have the strength to haul herself out of the pool.

'You two. Help get her out. Grab her arms. And you, get your hand under her bum and lift,' shouted the senior prefect to those nearest Julie. Soon Julie's dormitory companions had hauled her out of the water and set her on her feet.

'You'll soon get used to it. We have to do it every morning and more often, if it is part of a punishment,' whispered Sandra Berry as she loosened her grip on Julie's arm. Julie staggered into line and began to run on the spot in time with the rest of the group. Sophie was in the next batch across the pool, and Julie saw that she had similar difficulties, coughing and sputtering all the way across the pool. A freezing early-morning swim was obviously something that took some getting used to.

The cold wind on Julie's wet skin brought on a rash of goose pimples and made her breasts tingle as her nipples hardened like ripe strawberries. The running on the spot was, however, one way of keeping the circulation going and keeping a modicum of warmth in the core of the body. Before long, the last of the forms had completed their length of the pool and had assembled on the far side to run on the spot. The mistress then commanded each form in turn to run back to the reformatory in double file, picking up their night-dresses on the way, where appropriate.

Julie ran back with her classmates, her night-dress clutched in her hand and her breath exhaling in great clouds in the damp air. The gravel path did not seem quite so painful now as Julie seemed gradually to be becoming resistant to physical hardship. Reaching the stairs, the girls ran up at top speed, breasts swinging outrageously as the senior prefects shouted at the slower ones and occasionally cracked their straps across quivering buttocks. Back in the dormitory, they just had time to towel off any remaining wetness, brush their hair and put on their uniforms before they once again had to be in position standing at the ends of their beds for inspection.

Within a few minutes, the same two senior prefects appeared and slowly sauntered down the line of beds, closely scrutinising each member of the dormitory. It soon became apparent to Julie that these particular senior prefects were extremely difficult to please, since several girls who appeared to be perfectly well turned out managed to incur their displeasure. The taller of the two senior prefects, who was called Lucinda, seemed to be especially vindictive and would pick on the smallest detail in order to make life hell for the quaking pupils. After closely inspecting Karen Philips, she lifted Karen's skirt and gasped as if in mortal horror and shouted, 'Karen Philips! What is the meaning of this? One of your suspender straps is twisted. Come to my study at end of school today. Don't think that you can get away with such slovenliness while I am the senior prefect assigned to this dorm. I'll soon teach you to have some respect for the uniform.'

Seconds later, it was the turn of Lin Tsang, whose beautiful oriental complexion turned pale when Lucinda bent down to examine the girl's shoes and then bellowed, 'I thought as much. A scuff mark on the heel. It's your responsibility to keep your shoes polished at all times. You know that, and yet you insist on going back to your old lazy habits. Well, you will not get away with it. I'll see to it that you regret your laziness and wish that you had never been born. You see if I don't. You can also come to my study after school. Wait in the queue outside my door and have your knickers removed, I want to see them clutched in your hot little hand. I don't want to waste time. And don't be late. I've got other lazy pupils to see, apart from you. And make sure that your shoes are clean tonight or it will be a double dose of the same medicine. And not before time,

153

I might add. You seem to be just the sort of candidate for a grade two senior prefect's meeting. Carry on like this, with your scruffy ways, and that is what you will get. I've been watching you lately and I seem to be detecting an air of insolence. Well, let's see how insolent you feel after tonight.'

The two senior prefects strutted out of the dormitory and a sigh of relief was clearly audible around the room.

'Let's go, girls,' shouted Olu, 'otherwise there will be precious little porridge left for us. We are already a bit late. The second formers had half our share yesterday and I'm damned if I can last until lunch on just a quarter of a bowl again.'

The girls raced out of the dormitory, along the corridor and down the stairs, only slowing down to a brisk walking pace when they neared the refectory and came in view of the prefects patrolling outside. Hearing Olu's enthusiasm for the breakfast, Julie was expecting a pleasant surprise and was sorely disappointed when she received a small bowl of barely warm and very lumpy porridge. As with every meal, breakfast was conducted in absolute silence. It was only when the bell went for assembly and they all filed down the corridors to the main hall that Julie managed to whisper to Amy, 'What's so bloody good about breakfast? Why was Olu so keen to get there early? That porridge was disgusting puke. Surely they don't dish that rubbish up every day?'

Amy waited until they were well clear of a prefect who was scrutinising the girls as they passed, and replied under her breath, 'That's all we get every morning, year in and year out. Sometimes it's completely cold. At least it was warm this morning. Sometimes we get it for dinner as well. None of us likes it, including Olu, but we feel hungry most of the time because they are not over-generous with the food in this place. If you miss your portion of porridge in the morning, you feel extra hungry all day.'

Miss Spenser, surrounded by most of the mistresses, took the assembly, speaking from a lectern on the platform. The main hall was an impressive beamed and vaulted structure with walnut panels and a matching walnut grand piano. The prefects and senior prefects were stationed at the end of each row, on the lookout for whispering or inattention. Much of the assembly reminded Julie of the ones at her previous school, a mixture of hymns, prayers, lectures on morality and dire warnings about wrongdoing, the only difference being that at Roughton Hall, the wrongdoings were mere details and the warnings were more dire. It took a turn for the worst at the conclusion, when Miss Spenser read out a list of routine announcements. Sandwiched in with lists of pupils on report, lists of merit marks and demerit marks, and rosters for rolling the playing fields and scrubbing the corridors, was the announcement that Sophie and Julie were welcomed as new girls and would receive their official Welcome in ten days time along with another new girl, who was due to arrive within a couple of days.

After assembly, the rest of the day consisted of a succession of lessons taught by mistresses who seemed every bit as strict as Miss Hedges and Miss Davies of the previous day. Lunch was exactly the same as the day before as well. Julie had been under the impression that the stew of the previous day had been tepid because she was late for lunch, but she soon realised that it was served up at that temperature as a matter of course. Sophie was even less happy to receive another plate of dry bread and lettuce, which completely failed to satiate her increasing hunger pangs. There was one big improvement, though, in that no one in Julie's class was punished by the mistresses that day.

Resting on their beds after the school day, Julie and Sophie recollected the description of the Welcome that Miss Spenser had enthused about during her introduction to the reformatory. Sophie was unclipping the nylons from her suspender straps and rolling them down her legs, revealing the whiteness of her thighs. Her face looked serious as she became absorbed in her task, ensuring that no careless move would snag them.

'I'll never get used to wearing suspenders and stockings; tights were so much more practical. I'm terrified of catching them on a fingernail, and getting punished for laddering them,' she muttered. She delicately pulled each stocking from her toes, curling them slightly to avoid catching the nylon.

Apprehensively, Julie called Anita over, to shed some light on the Welcome ceremony. Anita sat on the edge of Julie's bed but was somewhat reluctant to supply much information about the ceremony. Julie pressed Anita to explain in more detail, but she rose to go, saying defensively, 'Look, I had my Welcome a year ago and I am trying my best to forget it. It really is best if you just wait and take it as it comes. The whole thing doesn't take more than half an hour but it's a pretty tight thrashing. You are allowed to eat your meals standing up for the next five days if you want to. I was able to sit down after two: I hated everyone looking at me. Everybody in the place has had to go through the same thing. They say that is the whole point of it. Everyone who comes out of the reformatory system has had at least one decent thrashing for definite, however much they toe the line. When we come out to the outside world, people will be able to look at you and say, "I know that you have had at least one good whipping, because everybody gets at least one at a reformatory. It's probably exactly what you deserved. I hope it did you good." Anyway, it's too early to start worrying about it at the moment. It won't be for ten days yet. You have to go out and gather the birch twigs yourself, and then they have to be soaked in brine for 24 hours to help stop them splintering. So you will know

all the details well in advance. Cheer up, everyone here
will look after you both afterwards. Come on, lie face
down on the bed and I will give you a massage to help
you relax. You look absolutely exhausted. Everyone
feels like that for the first few days. The trauma of being
sent here, the tough discipline, the early-morning swim
and so on knocks everyone for six until they get used to
it. Moira can give Sophie a massage. You do a first-class
massage, don't you, Moira? I get moist just thinking of
Moira's magic little fingers.'

Julie reluctantly turned over and rested her chin on
her arms. It was true, she did feel particularly weary.
Anita straddled Julie and began to rhythmically knead
her shoulders with powerful fingers. Julie could feel the
warmth of Anita's bottom on the small of her back, as
it pressed and moved with the rhythm, pressing her on
to the mattress. She could feel her breasts and pudenda
rubbing gently backwards and forwards on the soft
surface and a lazy warmth spread throughout her whole
body. Soon, Julie wafted away into a very deep sleep
untroubled by nightmares.

She pictured herself totally naked, speeding along
astride a racing bicycle. She was surrounded on all sides
by hundreds of other girls also naked and riding bi-
cycles. They were sweeping at high speed through a
village in Southern France on a beautiful, hot summer's
day. The roadside was crammed with thousands of
spectators all cheering and waving. The houses and
lamp posts were decorated with great wreaths of bunt-
ing and banners. Pennants were strung across the road
from the upper windows. Television cameramen riding
pillion on motorcycles and police cars with flashing
lights escorted the phalanx of riders. Coming out of the
village, they reached a steep hill and soon every rider
was standing on her pedals straining every muscle to
reach the top. From her position halfway down the
field, Julie could see a long stream of hundreds of

straining backs and quivering, tight-muscled bottoms stretching into the distance. A helicopter with television cameras protruding swept low over the long stream of riders; so low that Julie could feel the cooling effect of the wind from its chattering blades. After a long, strenuous climb, she reached the summit. Now it was downhill for miles of sweeping curves until the seaside Riviera resort was reached. Julie sunk back on to the saddle, feeling the firm leather work its way between her sex lips. As the bicycle gathered pace, the hard racing tyres transmitted a strong vibration through the frame and up through the saddle. Julie applied more pressure to the pedals and felt the saddle dig deeper as she shifted her body from side to side. The vibration on her clitoris and the effects of the hot sun and warm rushing breeze all combined to make her feel on top of the world. Shifting up to top gear, Julie hurtled downhill, the strong slipstream drying the perspiration from her back. Feeling a new surge of energy, she bent low over the drop handlebars and, with a superhuman burst of strength, sped by scores of other competitors. Her voluptuous breasts hung down, trembling, as the bicycle shook and the hot summer air buffeted and gusted against her. Looking around her, Julie saw that all the other girls had beautifully tanned, athletic bodies and that their breasts were also wobbling wildly as they bent over the handlebars and strained at the pedals. In front of her, there were still hundreds of naked cyclists, buttocks squashed against the saddles, all trying to beat her to the finishing line.

Soon the town came into view. The outskirts were thronged with cheering crowds pressed up against crash barriers and straw bales. Every window of the offices and flats was a sea of faces and every balcony groaned under the weight of jostling spectators. Cordons of police, sweltering in their uniforms, fought to restrain the over-enthusiastic fans from spilling on to the road.

The crackling public address system urged the crowds to show restraint and not to throw streamers. As the riders swept round every corner, a chorus of shutter clicks accompanied the cheers. Everyone had a camera and wanted a record of the grand occasion. Some intrepid enthusiasts had climbed up on to statues or bus shelters for a better view, and some had even set up tripods on top, in order to pan their video cameras smoothly.

As Julie came in sight of the winning line, at the end of a grand tree-lined avenue, the roar of the crowd became deafening. She was almost neck and neck with the race leader. The other girl had an all-over, golden tan and a stunningly beautiful figure. Julie gazed in admiration at her pert breasts, narrow waist and slim, rounded buttocks working hard on the saddle. With only a hundred yards to go, both girls rose up to stand on the pedals for that last extra effort. With their heads down over the handlebars and buttocks high in the air, the cycles gyrated from side to side as every last ounce of energy was thrust into the pedals. The cheers rose to a crescendo and every camera lens zoomed in on the two leaders and their desperate bid for first place. Straining every sinew, Julie edged in front, inches from the ribbon stretched across the road, to claim a narrow victory. The crowd went wild and officials with stop watches and clipboards moved forward to congratulate her.

Julie sank down on to the saddle as well-wishers gathered round, hugging her, patting and stroking her behind and offering garlands of flowers. Julie felt a frisson of sensual well-being as the pressure of the saddle massaged her clitoris and many hands massaged the aches from her legs and buttocks. The warmth of the sun on her naked skin and the abundance of affection offered by the friendly crowd combined to make Julie feel blissfully at one with the world.

When she woke up, she realised that it was the middle of the night. The dormitory was in darkness and she was in bed. A barely discernible figure was sitting on the edge of the bed and a hand was resting between her thighs. Squinting slightly, in an attempt to make out the identity of her visitor in the darkness, Julie could just perceive that the figure was wearing a white blouse, just like those the mistresses usually wore.

'Who are you?' whispered Julie.

In reply, the hand was withdrawn from the girl's moist sex, and a finger bearing her own aroma was laid gently across her lips. Julie was also able to discern another, strangely familiar scent. A voice, the timbre of which also seemed familiar, whispered, 'Courage, little Julie. Be true to the cause and Fightback will look after you.'

The figure, shrouded in darkness, arose with a rustle of skirts, and abruptly disappeared into the night.

11

The Welcome Ceremony

Julie, Sophie and the new girl in form two, Jasmine, had been waiting outside Miss Davies' study for over half an hour. Jasmine had only arrived on the island three days ago, and her young face perpetually registered a state of puzzlement and confusion. If anything, her reformatory haircut had been even more severe than Julie and Sophie's and she had the appearance of a lost waif. Dressed in their PE uniform, which consisted of tight black Lycra shorts, a white singlet and plimsolls, they were waiting nervously for Miss Davies to escort them to the woods bordering the Roughton Hall estate. When they had knocked timidly on Miss Davies' door she had tartly told them to wait in silence in the corridor until she was ready. All three wanted to compare experiences and reassure each other. However, fear of Miss Davies prevented them all from uttering a single word in case she chose just that moment to exit her study. Julie tried shifting her weight from one leg to the other but whenever she moved, the polished oak floorboards creaked alarmingly, and so Julie felt obliged to stand motionless, watching the hands of the grandfather clock at the end of the passage slowly move around the dial.

Julie was just wondering whether to risk a few words to Jasmine, when the door opened and Miss Davies, wearing a silk kimono, appeared in front of them with hands on hips. Smoothing the patterned silk over her bosom, she snapped, 'Stop slouching! You may enter and help me dress, seeing as you are here. I have just had a bath and am not too pleased to have to escort you to the woods on such a cold day. However, since I am regarded as something of an authority on the selection of birch twigs for correction purposes, Miss Spenser insists that I supervise on these occasions. We have got all morning, if necessary, so we can make sure that the birches are of the top quality before you have to go back to your lessons.' Miss Davies closed the door behind them and gathering up an assortment of glass-bottled toiletries from the desk, returned them to the bathroom. To the accompaniment of chinking glass as she arranged them in the bathroom cabinet, Miss Davies' disembodied voice continued, 'It's picking the right branches in the first place that is important. If there is not enough sap in the twigs or if the branch is too old or too young you will never get the correct amount of whip and flick in the birch rod, however well you make them up. I should know, I have been selecting birch twigs since the reformatory opened.'

Miss Davies reappeared from the bathroom, a faraway look in her eyes, and continued, 'Ah, there's nothing to beat a good, well-made, freshly budded birch rod to put a warm glow on a young bottom. Of course, the early Spring is the ideal time for the best buds and young sap. The swish through the air and the dry splashing noise as it impacts across the arse-cheeks; that's the sound I love most in the world. It's so much more musical than the sharp crack of the cane or the loud slap of the tawse. And so much more effective, in my opinion. I should know, I have been correcting young women for longer than most in this reformatory. I have thoroughly tested every implement of correction that can be found anywhere in the world, even Russian knouts, South African sjamboks and the Scottish Lochelly tawse and I can say without a shadow of a doubt that the birch is the implement *par excellence*. It's not just the sound, of course. It's also a much more beautiful sight, as the birch raises its thousands of tiny speckles on the skin. It's much more attractive than the simple straight lines inflicted by the cane. It must be said, though, that not everyone has the necessary knack of applying the birch correctly. I sincerely hope that Miss Spenser selects me to be the right-hander for your ceremony. It will be Miss Perry, no doubt, birching from the other side, as she is the only left-hander on the staff.'

Julie gazed around the room and was surprised to see that it was almost bare of ornaments and decoration. A Bedouin rug covered the floorboards and a large book-case, containing leather-bound volumes, dominated the far end of the room. A *chaise-longue*, a desk and a chair were the only other pieces of furniture. A coal fire flickered in the fireplace, set below a cast-iron mantel-piece. The bedroom led off from the study and the mistress directed the trembling girls to follow her into it. The bedroom was slightly larger than the study and its centre-piece was a double bed covered with a pure white duvet. A collection of teddy bears sat in line across the pillows and on top of the chest of drawers. Next to the door was an antique umbrella-stand festooned with an assortment of canes, tawses and riding crops and topped by just one umbrella.

'I have a mind to be dressed by you three. Why should I do it myself when the place is crawling with idle sluts all needing to be taught their place? After my warm, relaxing bath, I feel the need to be waited on,' grumbled Miss Davies, preening her blonde hair languidly. 'The clothes that I want to wear for this expedition are all laid out on the chair next to the wardrobe. I will direct you, and you will jump to my commands. Firstly, Julie, you can slip my kimono off me, while Sophie brings over my talcum powder puff and pats me all over with the talc. Don't put any on my legs or neck though; just my body. Be sure to put plenty on my cunt. I have just finished depilating it and I am most particular that it is silky smooth. And don't look at me like that, you insolent girl. There is nothing wrong with the word "cunt". It is a fine Anglo-Saxon word. It is one of the few words that is not some sort of apologetic medical term. I will tolerate no alternative expression in my presence. Now get to it.' Julie quickly untied the kimono belt and slipped the garment off, leaving Miss Davies standing stark naked. Sophie stood by, ready with a large circular box of talcum and a fluffy powder puff which she used to gently dab the talcum powder all over Miss Davies' well-toned body.

What a perfect physique, mused Julie. What pert breasts, and such a slim waist. Her back is so beautifully muscular and her ribs show that there is not an ounce of spare fat on her. I wonder what keeps her in such good shape?

Soon Miss Davies' suntan had disappeared and was replaced by a soft whiteness.

'Yes, my body is superb, isn't it? I can see the looks on your faces. I know what the three of you are thinking. I can see you admiring my firm breasts and peach of a bottom. Well, there's no harm in that. It's only natural that you should want to gaze on such an unusually well-defined muscle-tone. Exercise and cold swims are the things to tone a lazy body up. Of course, it does depend to some extent on what you start off with, but you three don't look too bad. After a few months here, you should be in much trimmer physical shape than you are now. Some people spend thousands of pounds to go to health farms which are not much different from what they would get here. Well, apart from the obvious differences, naturally.'

'Permission to speak, please, Miss Davies,' whispered Sophie.

'Very well, what is it, you ugly trollop?' replied Miss Davies frostily.

164

'I can't get the powder under your, erm – cunt, Miss Davies. Your legs are together and they need to be apart.'

'Quite so, trollop. I got carried away, thinking of the invigorating effects of birching a row of burning buttocks. You were right to speak. There, you can get that powder puff right underneath now. Make sure that every square inch is covered; I want to feel the silkiness as the tops of my thighs rub together. Jasmine, fetch my black G-string teddy, and put it on me.' Jasmine returned with the teddy and struggled to put it on Miss Davies. The soft, stretchy material moulded itself to her bosom as Jasmine drew the string at the back between Miss Davies' buttocks and fastened the poppers at the crotch. 'Julie, get the black seamed nylons hanging over the chair and put them on me. Make sure that the seams are absolutely straight. If they are any more than a half-inch off-centre, I will take great pleasure in arranging for you to join the two o'clock in the morning swimming detail, every night for the next fortnight.'

Julie's fingers trembled, the thought of having to endure an extra swim in that freezing pool in the middle of the night was a nightmare. I would rather have a quick six of the cane, she thought.

The suspender straps dangled from the teddy and Julie tried hard to attach them at the correct points of the stocking tops to ensure that the seams were straight. From her position on her knees, Julie's face was inches from Miss Davies' gleaming white buttocks and pudenda, which looked even more perfectly formed at such close range.

When the stockings were finally fitted to perfection, Miss Davies posed in front of the wardrobe mirror and slowly rotated, viewing the seams critically.

'Good, the stockings are satisfactory. I will let you off the night swims. Now, Sophie, bring over my long black skirt and my white blouse. And Jasmine, you can bring over my riding boots and coat. You two can finish my ensemble, between you.'

Minutes later, Miss Davies was fully dressed and ready to go. Pausing in front of her umbrella stand, she perused the selection of tawses and canes. Her hand hovered over a three-tailed tawse but then darted decisively to pick up a short riding crop which she tucked into her belt.

'Oh, just one more detail,' said Miss Davies, and, reaching into her coat pocket, extracted a handful of small leather loops, each one with its own intricate fastener. 'Turn around, Sophie, and put your hands behind your back, while I put these thumb-cuffs on you. I am going to thumb-cuff all of you, since we are going quite a long distance from the reformatory and you are having your Welcome tomorrow morning. I wouldn't want any of you to get any odd ideas about running off and hiding. One deluded girl tried it a couple of years ago. The dogs only took twenty minutes to find her, and, of course, she regretted it later. If I remember correctly, Miss Spenser sentenced her to a double Welcome followed by a week in solitary and a visit to her study at the end of the week. A rather unpleasant week, no doubt.'

Julie watched as Miss Davies looped the leather band around Sophie's thumbs, drew it tight and clipped the fastener. Next it was Jasmine's turn, before, finally, Julie had to place her hands behind her back to have the leather loop tightened around her thumbs.

'Handy little things, these thumb-cuffs; so much more convenient to carry, and almost as effective as hand-cuffs,' muttered Miss Davies to no one in particular.

The mistress opened the door and they all walked in single file through the complex of corridors, out from a side door and across the playing fields. The three girls walked in front and Miss Davies directed them from the rear. Julie walked behind Jasmine and could not help

166

noticing that Jasmine's boyishly slim bottom, clad in the skin-tight shorts looked most delectable. Julie wondered what they would look like tomorrow, though, after the birch had done its work. The whole school would soon know, she supposed. She found herself wondering if Miss Sullivan would be watching, and whether the mistress would feel sorry for her. A public birching – it sounded so medieval, and she wondered if she would be able to bear it. Then again, it would be no more than what all the others had gone through, and they were all still alive. Julie's eyes continued to follow Jasmine's gyrating bottom.

After crossing a rickety wooden bridge over a muddy stream they came into a large area of woodland. Miss Davies surveyed the scene and announced, 'Here we are. The best birch trees are just here. There are also some lime trees, which we also need. You see, one of the reasons why I am best at selecting the birch twigs is that I mix in some lime twigs which strengthen the birch rod and increase the whip of the twigs.' Miss Davies walked up to a birch tree and inspected it closely. 'You see, this is a good example of *Betula pendula*, commonly known as the silver birch. See how the twigs hang down. A good birch rod has a few twigs from this sort of birch but also some from this sort over here.' Miss Davies pointed to another tree and continued, 'Observe this tree. It is an example of *Betula purpurea*. Notice how the twigs have a purple tinge. These twigs are a lot more whippy and we will take some twigs from this tree in a minute. Now, look over here; I want to show you something else.' Miss Davies marched some distance, the three girls stumbling behind. Finally, she stopped at a taller type of tree and announced, 'Now, this is a lime tree, *Tilia petiolaris*. Of course, the type you get in this cold climate doesn't bear lime fruit. A few long twigs from this tree mixed in with the birch twigs really will make a good birching rod. In fact, I always aim for two long twigs from each of the three types of tree, tightly bound together. A birch like that, laid on by an expert, always makes a girl sing even after only a couple of strokes. It is a mistake to have too many twigs in a birch rod, the idea is not to produce something suitable for sweeping garden leaves. Now, Jasmine, you can make your two birch rods first. We always make two each, one for the right-hand flogger and one for the left-hand flogger. It's also in case one splinters before the allotted number of strokes has been applied.'

Miss Davies unfastened Jasmine's thumb-cuffs and produced a pair of secateurs from her pocket. Giving them to Jasmine, she instructed, 'Let's start with this lime tree. Climb up and cut four straight twigs about forty inches in length each. Those ones over to your left look about the right length and thickness. We can cut off the side shoots that we don't want when you get down.'

Half an hour later, all three girls had cut their own twigs from each of the three types of tree and had gathered them into piles on the ground. Producing some long strands of leather lacing from her pocket, Miss Davies said, 'Now I will show you how to bind the twigs together very firmly over one third of their length so that they are turned into a formidable instrument of correction.' She then picked a combination of twigs and bound them together tightly. Soon each girl had made her own two birch rods and had written her initials on the sides. Miss Davies then marched them back to the reformatory, carrying their two birches tucked under their arms. Crossing the playing fields, they had to pass a class playing hockey and were forced to endure a barrage of jokes about the use to which the birches would be put, until Miss Davies silenced them with just one disapproving look.

On reaching the reformatory, Miss Davies removed the thumb-cuffs and took the birch rods from the trio.

'I must hurry and put them in the brine bucket. A good overnight soak keeps them supple and helps to prevent splitting and splintering. They will be ready in good time for tomorrow morning's ceremony. Now run along, back to your lessons. I will look forward to testing the quality of these birch rods against your bottoms tomorrow. I think that you will be quite surprised at how effective your handiwork will be in tomorrow's ceremony.'

That night Julie tossed and turned, barely able to get any sleep at all, in spite of having had another stress-relieving massage from Anita. She could hear that Sophie was also having a restless night and whispered some words of encouragement to her at intervals. Finally, the early-morning alarm bell sounded and the normal routine of the naked physical exercises, followed by the swim, inspection and breakfast took place. The only differences were that a fine drizzle of rain made the exercise session more unpleasant than ever and that everything seemed to happen much faster than usual. Julie and Sophie's apprehension was not helped when, during inspection, Senior Prefect Lucinda made a whole series of unfunny jokes about the Welcome ceremony and birch twigs.

Julie could hardly swallow her cold porridge at breakfast, so bad were the butterflies in her stomach. Sophie appeared to be in the same state, gazing into space, her spoon halfway to her mouth. The lettuce and dry bread regime had been lifted only the day before, Sophie having reached the approved weight, but still she had no appetite. When the bell for assembly rang Julie and Sophie marched down the long corridor, into the assembly hall, seemingly in a trance.

The hall was crowded with all the inmates of the reformatory and all the members of staff. For this occasion, all the mistresses wore the same formal

169

uniform of a white blouse with a ruched neck and a long, black skirt. Miss Sullivan, looking pensive, was standing next to Miss Pengelly who, in contrast, looked eager and excited. It was a widely held belief that Welcome ceremonies brought her almost to the point of orgasm. Julie found herself studying Miss Sullivan's face, trying to divine the mistress' feelings. Suddenly their eyes met. A slight blush rose to Miss Sullivan's cheeks and she immediately looked away and started to engage Miss Pengelly in hushed conversation.

The rain and clouds had now cleared and it was a gloriously sunny morning. The rays from the low sun slanted diagonally across the hall, striping the walnut panelling and illuminating the specks of dust drifting in the air. Set up ominously across the stage, about three feet apart, were three birching blocks. These were similar to, although not as elaborate as the flogging horse in Miss Spenser's study. Julie noticed that they all had a small label on the front with the name of one of the victims. She could just about see that her block was the one in the middle. They had a padded leather ledge to kneel on, a padded, domed top over which the victim would be bent, and leather straps to hold the ankles, waist, knees and wrists. At each corner of the base there were rope handles to facilitate the carrying of such a heavy item of furniture. To the left of each block there was a tall earthenware vase with the initialled birch rods, soaking in brine, each one now adorned by a pink ribbon.

Julie found it increasingly difficult to concentrate on the hymns and prayers as the assembly dragged on. Finally, at the conclusion of the last hymn, the moment that she had been dreading was suddenly upon her. Miss Spenser turned to Senior Prefect Greta and commanded, 'Senior Prefect Greta, bring forth the Roughton Hall punishment book.'

On cue, Senior Prefect Greta stepped forward, a large

black book resting on her outstretched hands. Stepping up to the lectern, she placed it on the top and opened the page where a broad ribbon kept the place. Smartly turning, she curtseyed to Miss Spenser and resumed her place. Miss Spenser ran her finger down the page and then announced, 'The Welcome ceremony will now commence, and as laid down in the Handbook of the Righteous Sisters, the new inmates to be Welcomed shall first be brought to the centre of the stage for the recitation of the Roughton Hall punishment prayer. Therefore, I now call on Senior Prefects Candice, Tammy and Gemma to lead forth the candidates, Julie Semple, Sophie Adams and Jasmine Henderson, for acceptance into the reformatory, whereby, over time, they will be transformed into worthwhile citizens.'

Julie's tongue stuck to the roof of her dry mouth and she felt her hands grow clammy. A moment later Senior Prefect Candice made her way between the rows and, leading Julie by the hand, brought her on to the stage. Meanwhile, the other two also arrived at the centre of the stage so that the trio were standing in a line across the stage, each one in front of their designated block. Julie felt hundreds of eyes looking at her and wished that she could sink into the ground.

'The new girls will now remove their skirts and blouses and give the articles to Senior Prefect Candice,' ordered Miss Spenser. There was no option but to strip in front of the whole assembly. Julie blushed with embarrassment as she quickly stripped to her shoes, stockings and suspenders, although having Sophie and Jasmine either side of her in a similar predicament did help to allay her feelings slightly.

'Let us now pray the punishment prayer of the Righteous Sisters.' The whole reformatory then recited a prayer similar to the one that Julie had heard days before in Miss Spenser's study. Julie looked out over the large mass of inmates and staff through her half-closed eyes and trembled as she thought of them watching her humiliation. Julie's skin seemed to become super-sensitised and she acutely felt every movement of air across her bare body.

The prayer came to an end all too soon and as Julie opened her eyes, Miss Spenser's voice rang out with the instruction, 'New girls, turn around, kneel on the blocks and bend over.' Julie turned around, knelt on the leather padded ledge and bent right over the padded curved top, conscious of the hundreds of eyes on her well-parted bottom cheeks and pouting labia.

'Senior prefects, secure the new girls. Pull the ankle, knee, wrist and waist straps tight and then buckle them up.' Immediately, Julie was aware that Senior Prefect Candice was pulling her arms down, in order to attach the wrist straps at the front of the block. Having done so, she then moved behind Julie and attached the other straps so that Julie could hardly move a muscle. The tightest strap was a broad belt that went across her waist, squashing her tightly to the top of the block and forcing her buttocks to jut out proudly. Seconds later, Miss Spenser's voice rang out again.

'Senior prefects, adjust the new girls' undergarments. Unclip the suspenders from the stockings, roll the stock-ings down and tuck the suspender straps under the suspender belt. Matron, stand by with the smelling salts. As laid down, each girl will receive 24 strokes in six doses of four. Each dose will consist of two strokes from Miss Davies on the right and two from Miss Perry on the left. In accordance with our traditions, the blocks will be rotated to face the assembly after twelve strokes. Clenching of the bottom during a birching is not allowed under any circumstances. Any stroke falling on clenched buttocks will be repeated and may merit an additional punishment stroke. Miss Davies and Miss Perry, take your positions, please, and prepare to birch Jasmine Henderson. Apply the birch with your customary zeal but take your time, please.'

Julie felt Candice fiddling with the clips of the suspenders and then rolling each stocking down to the knees. Julie next heard the sound of the birch rods rustling as they were being withdrawn from the vase next to Jasmine's block, and the sound of the brine dripping on to the floor.

'In your own time please, Miss Davies and Miss Perry. Do your duty.' A profound silence gripped the assembly as if no one dared to breathe. Julie strained her ears to detect what was happening but all she could hear was a faint rustle as the mistresses moved the birch rods and the sound of their heels on the wooden stage as they adjusted their stance. The silence was rudely broken by a loud swish and a splashing noise as if someone had thrown a bucketful of water. Julie felt a movement of air across her naked skin and then a fraction of a second later there was a repeat of the same noise and a gasp from Jasmine.

'Two strokes, both satisfactory,' called out Gemma.

Julie twisted her head slightly and was just able to see the grimace on Jasmine's face. The silence seemed to intensify as many seconds ticked by without Julie hearing any movement. It was a torture of frustration, not being able to see what the mistresses were doing. Julie sneaked another look at Jasmine and saw that her eyes were tightly shut and her jaw was clenched. As Julie turned her head back, the second double stroke was administered and Julie heard a louder gasp and a muted squeal from Jasmine.

'Clenching during the second stroke, Headmistress,' shouted Senior Prefect Gemma.

'Very well, repeat the second stroke, please, Miss Perry,' replied Miss Spenser, 'and add another one, off the record, as punishment for clenching.'

After a pause, another two strokes resounded across the hall and Julie once again heard the gasp and a much louder cry from Jasmine. Miss Spenser, in strict and measured tones then added, 'Gemma, please record four strokes satisfactorily administered to Jasmine Henderson. The birching of Julie Semple may now commence.'

Oh God, it's my turn now, thought Julie. Whatever I do, I must not clench my bum cheeks. 24 strokes is bad enough without having more added. I must try not to cry out as well, especially with all these girls watching me. They probably expect me to be tough and stoical.

Julie tried to shift slightly but found that the straps were very effective at preventing all but the slightest movement. She heard the mistresses click across the stage to her block and the rustle of the birches being withdrawn from the vase. More sounds of the mistresses shifting their positions and their long, formal skirts sweeping the ground registered on Julie's heightened consciousness. Julie held her breath and shut her eyes. It must be coming soon, she thought. Oh, please let it all be over quickly. As if in answer to her prayer, the first of the double strokes landed, taking Julie's breath clean away and shattering her consciousness. An instant later the second stroke fell, this one from Miss Perry, doubling the effect of the first stroke. She heard herself emit a strangled cry with the shock of the impact and then felt a searing sensation spread outwards from her buttocks. Bloody hell, two is enough. How can I take another 22 like that thought Julie.

'Two strokes, Headmistress,' reported Candice.

Seconds passed, and the burning subsided slightly, to be replaced by a fiery tingling sensation. As Julie concentrated on her determination not to cry out, the second pair of strokes fell, building on the intensity of the infernal throbbing and causing her to emit a loud screech. Her whole body felt the urge to writhe and squirm but the tried and tested design of the birching block efficiently prevented any movement and Julie had to remain entirely motionless.

Through a fiery mist, Julie heard Candice report, 'Four strokes, all satisfactory, Headmistress.'

'Candice, please log four strokes, satisfactorily applied. Miss Perry and Miss Davies, please commence the birching of Sophie Adams,' replied the headmistress.

And so the ceremony continued. This process was repeated three times. Each girl was given four strokes in turn until all had received twelve strokes. Each time the mistresses came round the birch did its work more effectively and the cries of the three victims became more urgent. Julie's whole bottom seemed to be ablaze right from one side to the other. In her torment, a riot of thoughts and emotions raced through her mind. That Miss Davies is a sadistic bitch. She was hitting the tops of her thighs as well. Now she knew why they had a right-hander and a left-hander; there was not a square inch of her bum that had not been flayed by those bloody twigs. And to think that she had chosen them herself, just as she had chosen to submit herself to the reformatory's ways.

After the twelfth stroke there was a long pause until Miss Spenser announced, 'Duty prefects, make your way to the stage and gather four to each block.' Julie heard a lot of shuffling around as the legs of two duty prefects came into her restricted field of vision. 'One to each rope handle, please. Lift on the count of three. One, two, three – lift.' Julie felt the block rise an inch off the ground and wobble uncertainly in the air. 'On the count of three, rotate. One two, three – rotate.'

Slowly the room began to spin and for a few moments Julie was treated to the view of Jasmine's glowing red bottom as all three birching blocks were spun round. The block came to a halt and, with a feeling of horror, Julie found herself looking directly at the whole assembly. With a bump, the heavy wooden block was lowered to the floor and once again Miss Spenser directed the ceremony.

'As it is laid down in the handbook, the Welcome ceremony is to be instructive for the spectators as well as the new girls. When the rear view of the new girls is on show, the assembly can see how well the birchers do their duty. We can all see the sin being beaten out of the evil flesh and the way in which the buttocks cringe as if in rebellion. We can also see how the birch casts its fiery glow upon the flesh, as if it is burning out the sin with a cleansing fire. However, when the faces of the girls who are to be reformed are on show, as they are now, we can see how arrogance and pride, once natural instincts to these criminals, are transformed into the pathetic whinges, tears and cries that are now so obviously displayed. What better way to start the whole process of reforming the character? With no shred of pride left, the reformatory can start its work of rebuilding a decent character on the blank page that is left after the Welcome ceremony. Here, we beat out the old criminal character in order to make way for the new reformed one. Before the second half of the strokes are applied, cast your mind back to the day when you yourselves were in the position of these pathetic, whimpering sluts you see before you. Remember how you felt, but remember, also, that, painful as it undoubtedly was, it was the start of your journey on the long road of recovery to moral fitness. Please think carefully about these serious aspects as you witness the rest of the Welcome ceremony. Watch the faces of these young trollops as they are being soundly birched and consider whether they will be tempted to go back to their misguided ways when they are released from the reformatory. And as you watch them cry out with each stroke of the birch, consider, also, whether you want to be in that position again. For you surely will if you re-offend when you are released. As you know, the police keep a specially close watch on ex-offenders.

'Very well, Miss Davies and Miss Perry have rested their birching arms so the ceremony can continue.

Gemma, Candice and Tammy, check the birches, please.' One by one the senior prefects reported that the birch rods were still in serviceable condition and so, with a quick nod, Miss Spenser called out, 'In your own time, please, Miss Davies and Miss Perry.'

The next fifteen minutes were ones that Julie only ever brought to mind when at the virtual pinnacle of an intense orgasm. The shame and abject humiliation of the trio facing the whole school whilst babbling and screeching as the birch rods methodically lashed down was an experience so intense that Julie blocked it from her mind most of the time.

When the allotted number of strokes had been dealt, Miss Spenser made a final announcement, 'These three girls, Sophie Adams, Julie Semple and Jasmine Henderson, are now officially full members of the reformatory. They have been fully Welcomed and can look forward to a long but fruitful process of moral healing. I would like to thank Miss Perry and Miss Davies for their sterling skills in applying the birches. The senior prefects will now carry the blocks to the exit doors, so that all members of the reformatory may gaze on the results of this morning's work and may fully consider what awaits them if they re-offend and are ever committed to Roughton Hall again. Senior prefects, do your duty.'

As her mind reeled in the aftermath of the birching, Julie became aware that the block had been lifted again and that four senior prefects were carrying her down the centre of the assembly hall. Julie looked at the faces gazing at her and registered the fact that some had expressions of sympathy whilst others smirked or leered. The birching block was dropped with a jarring bump at the hall exit and was soon joined by the other two in a neat line. Julie craned her head sideways and made eye contact with Sophie, whose tear-stained face flushed with embarrassment as the whole reformatory started to file past slowly. It took a further ten minutes for the last of the pupils to leave by which time Julie's feeling of utter humiliation was complete.

Within four days, Jasmine, Julie and Sophie were able to eat their porridge sitting down and daily life at Roughton Hall became almost routine. Even after several weeks, however, it was still not possible to get fully accustomed to the daily cold swim, in spite of the fact that the weather was getting warmer as Spring approached. Julie was gradually able to make some progress with the important tasks assigned to her by Fightback. Sophie and Julie had disclosed to one another one evening that they were both committed Fightback agents, as it now seemed safe to do so. Jack had wanted each agent to be a totally self-contained cell until the rebellion was more fully developed but the two girls trusted each other completely and found that it was easier to work together. It was clear that almost all of the third form would eagerly support an insurrection if it was effectively organised. The main problem was the ever present fear of informers and double-agents. Julie and Sophie found that they had to tread very carefully to avoid giving their rôles away and found that it was best to wait until others discussed their dislike of the system before making subtle hints about the possibility of an uprising. After ten weeks from the date of their arrival on the island, Julie and Sophie were allowed to wear the plain white bra and white thong panties that comprised the regulation third form underwear. Although Julie had become rather used to the sensations of going bra-less and pantie-less, it was nevertheless more comfortable when her heavy bosom was firmly supported. All in all, thought Julie as she lay in bed one night, it's the first two weeks that are the worst. If you can survive the first two weeks, you can survive the whole stretch – that is, unless things get worse.

12

The Contact

Yolanda's arm ached as though it was going to drop off but she did not dare stop turning the oaken handle of the hand-mill until the counter set in the top read two thousand. The hand-mill was a device once common in English prisons and, like the treadmill, was designed to keep prisoners in a state of exhaustion and therefore unlikely to revolt against the system. It was also a device of punishment since turning the handle for hours was laborious and tedious. It consisted of a sealed wooden box from which a crank protruded, bolted to a heavy table. Every revolution of the handle caused a counter to advance one digit. The box was half filled with sand and as the crank rotated two cups inside alternately scooped up sand and then tipped it out again. Yolanda was using both hands on the handle as she gasped and strained to reach the allotted target of two thousand revolutions.

'God, I've been in this poky cell for three sodding days and I can't stand another four days in this lousy solitary confinement,' she grunted under her breath as her back ached and her blistered hands throbbed. A rivulet of perspiration trickled down her neck, past her collar bone and channelled its way down the deep furrow of her cleavage to add to the dampness of her thin white bra, turning it partially transparent. This had the effect of emphasising the large, dark areolae of her generous breasts, which stretched the material taut as they wobbled with the exertion of turning the handle. Yolanda wore only one other item of clothing, which was a pair of white knickers cut high on the leg and with a thong back revealing a firm, feminine bottom unusual only in the fact that it had six yellow and blue lines etched across it. Yolanda's crudely cropped dark hair could not obscure the fact that she was a pretty girl with large blue eyes set in an innocent looking, slightly freckled face. The cell in question was large and clean with a barred window set high up on one wall. Apart from the table the cell contained a bed, a rowing machine, an exercise bicycle and a chamber pot. On the wall above the bed there was a wipe-clean notice board which had neatly written on it:

CELL: 6
NAME: YOLANDA MARESZ
FORM: 4
OFFENCE: INSUBORDINATION (MISS LADD)
SENTENCE: 7 DAYS
HANDMILL: 2000 TURNS PER DAY
ROWING MACHINE: 385 STROKES PER DAY
BICYCLE: 25 MILES PER DAY
PENALTIES: DAY 2. 6 STROKES/INTERMEDIATE CANE,
   HALF RATIONS.

Yolanda glanced quickly at the clock face set into the wall above the door and a wave of panic flooded through her. The counter only read 1733 and it was almost ten o'clock in the evening, the time when the duty prefects did their rounds of the eight solitary confinement cells to check if the inmates had completed their allotted tasks and to administer any necessary punishments.

Blast those sadistic bitches, she thought. She had been only five miles short on the bloody bike and they had still given her the standard six strokes and half rations for today. It might only be lousy stale bread and water, but she was famished having to do all this back-breaking exercise all day. The previous evening's scene flashed through Yolanda's mind. Two overbearing prefects had dragged her out of the cell into the corridor to join two other girls, both attractively petite second formers wearing only their panties, who had not fulfilled their quota of tasks. They had had to line up standing to attention in front of the punishment table that was arranged in the centre of the corridor. This heavy oak table had a pillory section attached to one of the longer sides and a bench attached to the other. Being last in the queue Yolanda had to watch each girl in turn kneel on the bench and gingerly lower herself to lie across the table with her bottom pertly raised at the edge of the table and her breasts squashed against the wooden surface. One of the two prefects would then lower the hinged part of the pillory so that the unfortunate girl's head and wrists were firmly held in place. The other prefect would then deliver six bottom-shuddering strokes of the cane at full strength while the poor girl yelled and begged for mercy. As Yolanda watched the other two being caned her mouth dried up and a nervous tremble ran through her legs. She resolved not to utter any sound at all when it came to her turn, however much it hurt, so as to deprive the prefects of any satisfaction that they may feel. When it finally came to her turn to lie across the table, Yolanda noticed that the surface was polished smooth with years of contact with the squirming, sweating bodies of punished girls and was now warm from the contact of her two prede-cessors, both now in floods of tears behind her. The top section of the pillory snapped shut and Yolanda's head and wrists were securely gripped, her breasts squashed and bulging to each side and the material of her panties cutting into her bottom as it was thrust up by the edge of the table. Unfortunately, after just two strokes

Yolanda found that she could not help making just as much noise as the others had done. Her knees rattled on the bench as her bottom swayed to escape the cane and, on being released from the table, she writhed, danced and clutched her bottom just as they had moments earlier.

Yolanda glanced again at the clock. It was now ten exactly. She looked up in alarm. Yes, that was the sound of the key in the outer door and the creaking as it swung open. Damn, what did the counter show? Only 1744. She might just have time if they visited all the other cells first. The prefects were allowed to wear stiletto heels in the evening and Yolanda heard the clicking of the heels on the stone flagged floor getting nearer and nearer. She strained every sinew to complete the last few turns needed. Please let them check the other cells first, she thought, I can't take another day of half rations and another six of the cane. Just then the footsteps halted and the spy-hole cover moved aside in Yolanda's cell door. Yolanda strained even harder even though she knew that it was a futile effort. She was well short of the allotted number and would not be able to avoid another dose of punishment. She tensed, waiting for the sound of the key in the lock. Another ten turns of the handle and still the cell door had not opened. Yolanda glanced over her shoulder towards the door. It was still shut, there were no duty prefects standing in the doorway gleeful with cruelty and insolent power. What was going on? Why had the prefects not checked her numbers? It was then she noticed a slip of paper that had been pushed under the door. Yolanda walked over and picked it up, although even this small effort increased the aches in her shoulders and arms. Her heart was pounding with excitement. Whenever Fightback communicated with her it was always done in an anonymous way. She could never give away the names of her contacts because she did not know who they were as yet.

Surely it would not be one of the duty prefects who had so cruelly caned her the previous night. There was no way of knowing. It could not be discounted. After all, the mystery agent would have to ensure that she did not arouse suspicion and besides she had probably been picked, like Yolanda, for her sadistic or masochistic potential. Turning the paper over revealed the following message:

Make contact with Julie Semple and Sophie Adams. Third Form. They will help organise year three. Tell them to wait for instructions from you. Our numbers are increasing and the time for revolt is getting closer. I will be able to make myself known to you soon. Eat this message immediately.

Yolanda's hands trembled with anticipation as she quickly tore the note into four pieces and stuffed the paper into her mouth, desperately trying to chew as the paper dried up her saliva. She breathed a sigh of relief and set about thinking of ways in which to make contact with Julie and Sophie. It would not be easy. First she would have to finish this sentence of solitary confinement and then she would have to find a way of approaching the girls in private without arousing undue attention. Yolanda uttered a heartfelt sigh. Solitary was bad enough, but now it was ten times worse, knowing that she had a job to do but being unable to make any progress at it. Once again, Yolanda bent her efforts to the hand-mill as she chewed the remains of the note. It was still possible that the prefects would be round, albeit late, and insist on inspecting the counters set in the machines. Suddenly, the door crashed open. Yolanda's heart leapt into her mouth. Miss Spenser, Miss Chapel and two senior prefects were standing in the doorway.

13

The Summons

Of all the prefects' rituals, grade three senior prefects' meetings carried the most trappings of tradition and ceremony. If the mistresses agreed to a certain pupil undergoing a grade three senior prefects' meeting they did not interfere in any way, even to the extent of not enquiring about the outcome of it. Normally the prefects' meetings were convened by the prefects if they felt that a girl was getting above herself, but had been clever or lucky enough not to attract the attention of the mistresses. After putting their case to the deputy headmistress the senior prefects would be told whether permission was granted to hold the meeting. Unfortunately for Julie, permission had been given and the notice was given at the end of the previous day's morning assembly when the roll call of correction was read out. Julie had heard the rumour and could not understand why she was being picked out, but there it was, announced in the unemotional voice of the headmistress.

'And now for the correction roll call: Jane Wilby, Jumana Nwhiga, Charlotte White, Alice Pereira, Carina Trent to the gym at six o'clock. Miss Pengelly will supervise you. Do not take your P.E. kit, plimsolls only.' Everyone knew what that meant. Miss Pengelly was renowned for making a squad of girls on report do a three-mile cross-country run through the coppiced woodland full of saplings, brambles and nettles, wearing nothing but plimsolls and carrying a two-pound dumb-bell in each hand. Having to hold the dumbbells that were attached to each wrist by a chain helped to make it difficult to push the whippy branches, nettles and brambles out of the way. On making it back to the gym, bruised, covered in scratches and exhausted, the first to return would receive a mere four strokes while secured over the vaulting horse. However, the second back would get six and so on. The slowest runner would be likely to receive a good twelve strokes from Miss Pengelly's three-tailed tawse and be put on report to repeat the run a week later with heavier dumbbells. Julie looked across to Charlotte Wright, a pretty freckled girl with auburn hair who was standing a few yards away, and saw her visibly shudder.

Poor Charlotte, thought Julie, she is constantly picked on by Miss Pengelly. She gave her a ferocious caning only a few days ago in the maths lesson. The roll call went on.

'Zeva Patel, report to Miss Davies' study at 6.30, Briony Barrington, report to Miss Taylor's study at 6.30 and Gail Bowditch, Susan Dowse and Deborah Marshall, report to Miss Hedges' study at 8.30. In addition, Julie Semple is to attend a grade three senior prefect's meeting tomorrow and Sangita Khan a grade one at midday Saturday. You are all dismissed except for form one, who are to remain here, strip naked, stand to attention and wait for me to return. Miss Willard and I will discover who set off the fire alarm yesterday even if we have to flog the whole lot of you. In fact, we shall probably flog you all as accessories to the culprits, anyway. Gemma, Karen, Lucy and Anna, when you are undressed set up the three birching blocks in the centre of the hall as soon as the other forms have finished filing out. And whoever that is whimpering at the back, pipe down immediately or it is a double dose for the whole back row.'

Julie looked at the terrified faces of the young girls in

form one. Wearing their shapeless, rough cotton smocks some of them looked very guilty indeed and they were clearly already in mortal terror of the headmistress in spite of the fact that they had not been at Roughton Hall for long. Being first years, they were still learning the hard way about the disciplined regime that was designed to eradicate their waywardness. A faint smile tinged with sympathy stole across Julie's face as she imagined the chorus of soprano cries that would echo across the assembly hall within the next hour.

The day passed very slowly. Every hour seemed like two hours and as time passed Julie became more and more nervous, anticipating the ritual that would take place that evening. Concentrating on the lessons was difficult as she wondered how severely she would be dealt with. In the geography lesson, Miss Davies observed her gazing absent-mindedly out of the window, watching the rain lash the courtyard, but decided to let it go for the moment. Without a doubt, Miss Davies mused, it would be most pleasant to set aside a whole evening in order to correct Julie in the privacy and luxury of her own quarters. She made a note to herself to have a word with Miss Sullivan; Julie, despite having been at the reformatory for only a short time, seemed already to have become a favourite of Miss Sullivan's, and, in Miss Davies' opinion, the other mistress was getting a little too possessive of the girl.

It was, nevertheless, to Miss Sullivan's study that Julie was summoned after tea. Recently the mistress had acquired a text book on the art of massage and had picked Julie as a suitable guinea-pig on whom to practise her techniques. A few weeks' study of the subject had turned Miss Sullivan from a clumsy beginner into an accomplished masseuse. At first, Julie had dreaded the rough pummelling, but now she luxuriated in the mistress' expert touch. On entering Miss Sullivan's

186

study, Julie automatically stripped, folded her uniform neatly and climbed on to the silk covered massage table. Miss Sullivan removed her blouse and skirt, as she usually did to give herself freedom of movement. Julie noticed that today the mistress was wearing a matching black bra and G-string knickers, with embroidered lace-and-pearl insets between the bulging bra cups and where the thong emerged from between the cheeks of her bottom. Miss Sullivan took the stopper from an ornate glass bottle, poured a liberal amount of rose-scented oil over Julie's back and commenced a series of firm, stroking movements whilst intermittently referring to her instruction book. The mistress' taut stomach pressed against Julie's body as she gradually increased the pressure, and Julie found herself melting away into deep relaxation. Miss Sullivan's fingers eventually found their way into all of Julie's most sensitive spots and a gentle languor washed slowly over the girl.

As usual, the time went far too quickly and it seemed like no time at all before Miss Sullivan slapped Julie smartly on the bottom and said, 'That's all I have time for today, you can get along to your dormitory now. I may want you for more practice tomorrow.' She paused. 'No, on second thoughts you are going to be whipped tonight, if I remember correctly. The weals will get in the way and it will spoil my technique. I'll get someone else for the next few days. That's all, you are dismissed.'

Julie trotted to the dormitory, a glow exuding from her face, in spite of her coming ordeal.

'Another session with Miss Sullivan, I suppose?' enquired Sophie somewhat tartly. 'You must be getting tired of her using you for her experiments.'

'Too right,' replied Julie, the glow receding from her face, 'I can do without her pummelling and slapping. I wish she would pick on someone else for a change.'

Sophie let the subject drop.

* * *

Prefects' meetings were traditionally timetabled at ten o'clock on Friday or Saturday evenings. Just before the appointed hour, Julie heard the footsteps approaching the dormitory door and the whispers of encouragement from her dorm mates. The door opened letting in a shaft of tungsten yellow light from the hall. Silhouetted in the light stood two prefect monitors. These girls could always be relied on to fulfil their tasks with zeal as being efficient in helping the senior prefects was the key to eventually becoming a prefect yourself.

The prefect monitors strode up to Julie's bed. Julie saw that they were wearing the customary bizarre garb for the occasion, namely a very short pleated tennis skirt, sandals with ankle straps and a black velvet neck choker. They were both topless as, for some reason known only to those familiar with the Righteous Sisters' handbook, monitors were required to be naked from the waist up when attending any kind of prefects' meeting. They each carried a leather punishment strap and a shoulder bag. Julie immediately recognised them as Pippa Sanderson and Lavinia Emberly, two particularly odious, snide and overbearing girls, both intent on achieving prefect status when they reached the sixth form. Pippa was tall, blonde, willowy and barely had breasts at all. Her large nipples jutted out an unnaturally long way, and her short cropped hair gave her a boyish, ingenuous aspect. It gave Julie a fleeting sense of glee that Pippa was probably envious of her own large breasts. Lavinia however, was of more average proportions. She had long, mousy hair, a rather plump, rounded bottom and quite big, slightly droopy breasts that swayed and wobbled as she moved. Pippa spoke first and a pang of apprehension shot through Julie.

'Julie Semple, stand by your bed.' Julie quickly stood to attention by the bed; to hesitate even for a fraction of a second meant extra punishment. Julie saw out of the corner of her eye the other girls of the dormitory, furtively watching the proceedings, peeping above the bedclothes in the subdued glow of the dormitory night light.

'Strip!' barked Lavinia. In one movement Julie tore off the transparent night-dress and regained her stiff pose. Lavinia and Pippa circled around Julie as if inspecting a sculpture or an example of prize livestock.

'Position two, legs apart, hands behind head,' Lavinia instructed. Julie felt Lavinia's fingers probing between her legs from behind.

'Now bend over and grasp your ankles, in position one,' Pippa snapped. Julie soon felt both monitors stroking and kneading her pouting labia and her buttocks as she struggled to maintain her balance. After a short while she felt a warm sensation spreading through her body and her legs began to twitch involuntarily. Lavinia slid two fingers deep between Julie's sex lips and moved them back and forth so that the slippery wetness bathed her clitoris. Then, tweaking the clitoris between thumb and forefinger, she repeatedly made it slide between her fingers, playing with it like a slippery orange pip.

'Ooh, Pippa,' squeaked Lavinia. 'I do believe this dirty little bitch is enjoying this; it is certainly getting rather slippery down here.'

'Yes, she must be a very dirty-minded little bitch who needs a good flogging on her fat, bare arse to make her think purer thoughts. This fine bum feels like it could easily take a couple of dozen of the birch. Now, stand up and go to the centre of the dorm,' shouted Pippa.

'Now, what are you?' barked Lavinia.

'I am a dirty-minded bitch who needs a good flogging on my fat arse.' Julie knew better than to demur in any way.

'That's not good enough,' yelled Pippa. 'You left some vital words out and they could not hear you at the end of the dorm, so louder this time, much louder.'

'I am a dirty-minded bitch who needs a good flogging on my fat, bare arse.'

'It is still not loud enough,' growled Pippa. 'And you have still left some words out. Let me remind you. You are a very dirty-minded little bitch who needs a good flogging on her fat, bare arse to make her think purer thoughts. Now say it, and make it even louder this time.' Stifling back the tears, Julie shouted the words out at the top of her voice. Pippa paced to the end of the dorm.

'Stand by your beds, girls.' In an instant all of the girls were standing to attention by their beds. 'I want you to tell me what Julie is, and it's six strokes for anyone who gets it wrong.'

Dutifully the girls piped up in unison, 'Julie is a very dirty-minded little bitch who needs a good flogging on her fat, bare arse to make her think purer thoughts.'

Julie could see through a mist of tears her dorm mates looking at her and she knew that each of them was thanking God it was her and not them this was happening to.

'Okay, you miserable third formers,' said Lavinia menacingly. 'You seem to be word perfect. Let's make it a little more difficult. One of you is going to feel the strap before we are finished.'

Lavinia sauntered up to Julie, leant over and whispered in her ear, 'You are a filthy-minded, ugly little bitch with a fat arse and fat, wobbly tits and you would be grateful for a severe caning by your superiors. Now say it nice and loud so that everyone can hear.' A tide of humiliation swept through Julie as she managed to shout the words out correctly.

'Well done, ugly bitch,' said Pippa.

'Now let's hear if you pathetic little lot have been concentrating,' Lavinia bellowed to the assembled girls. 'What is Julie?'

'She is a filthy-minded, ugly little bitch with a fat arse

and fat, wobbly tits and would be grateful for a severe caning by her superiors,' chanted the pupils dutifully.

'Well done, dorm,' said Lavinia. 'But I think one of you was not putting her heart into it.' Quickly she wheeled to face Cynthia Flowers, a thin, nervous girl with a pale complexion who shuddered and whimpered as Lavinia grasped her by the ear.

'Stand here in the middle, remove your night-dress and prostrate yourself in a position three but with your hands behind your head,' shouted Lavinia. Cynthia, shaking with nerves struggled with the night-dress to obey as quickly as possible. Pulling it over her head, her narrow, conical little breasts shivered as the night-dress slid past the tiny, erect nipples. Soon she lay naked on the floor with her hands clasped behind her head and her mouth pressed to the floor in the approved manner. Tremors of fear ran through her whole body and her pale, boyish buttocks twitched in anticipation.

'Now, what is Julie, Cynthia?' Lavinia asked in her most menacing manner. The tremors increased and some muffled words could be heard from Cynthia's mouth pressed as it was on the floor. 'Not good enough. Not good enough at all. You obviously want me to punish you severely and I will be happy to oblige,' snarled Lavinia. 'Spread your legs wide, Cynthia. I am now going to apply my strap to the inside of your upper thighs, three on each thigh, and afterwards you will thank me most effusively. If you don't thank me enough I will have to do it again. Do you understand?' A muffled sob and further tremors indicated that Cynthia did understand, and reluctantly her legs parted wide to reveal her milky white inner thighs.

'Moira and Christina, hold on to her ankles and pull them further apart. Heidi, you are a great, heavy lump: sit on her back,' barked Lavinia. The girls rushed to obey and in a moment had pinned the hapless Cynthia motionless. Lavinia unhooked the strap from her belt and ran it through her hands; eighteen inches of stiffened yet supple leather that narrowed to a six inch, leather-covered handle. Handled by an expert, this instrument – relatively mild though it was, by the standards of Roughton Hall – could be excruciating, and Lavinia, in the six months that she had been a prefect monitor, had rapidly become an expert. Pippa, on the other hand, was not at all well co-ordinated and found wielding the strap accurately to be quite a problem. However, she had started to practise on an old cushion in the prefect monitors' common room and was rapidly improving. She was hoping that if they allowed her to join the ranks of the prefecture next year that she would manage to apply the cane better. It would be hard to command the correct degree of respect otherwise.

Lavinia strode over to stand beside Cynthia, 'I want you to count the strokes and thank me for each one, Cynthia. Understand?'

A muffled, 'Yes,' and a sob from Cynthia could just be heard. Lavinia measured the strap against the inside of Cynthia's inner left thigh, slowly raised it over her shoulder, and brought it down with a resounding crack like a pistol shot against the quivering thigh.

Cynthia's whole body jerked in spite of the efforts of the three girls holding her, a gasped sob and a cry of, 'One thank you, Prefect Monitor Lavinia,' could be heard from the ground. A livid red stripe rapidly stood out against the creamy whiteness of Cynthia's inner thigh and her legs renewed their shaking with increased vigour.

'Moira and Christina, you are not pulling hard enough, her legs are shaking like a jelly. How can I concentrate on my aim if you do not keep them absolutely still? If you do not do better I will give you a dose of the same treatment, and don't think that I won't.' The two girls redoubled their efforts and soon poor

Cynthia's legs were at maximum stretch and virtually motionless, apart from a slight trembling. Lavinia crossed to the other side of the prostrate pupil, again measured the strap against the other inner thigh and then raised the strap high above her head.

Another pistol crack and a spasm from Cynthia announced the next stroke. A high-pitched squeal and a sobbed, 'Two, thank you, Prefect Monitor Lavinia,' rapidly followed. Now the right inner thigh matched the left one with a perfectly positioned stripe running across it three inches below the crotch.

'Please Lavinia, no more, please. I beg you, it's too awful. Please, mercy, please,' Cynthia intoned in a ghastly wail. Four more strokes followed, at half-minute intervals, two on each thigh alternately. As each one fell Cynthia's sobs, squeals and counting grew more frantic and the three girls holding her had an increasingly difficult task holding her down despite her thin, weak build. A bead of perspiration ran down her back as the red stripes merged into one scarlet patch on each thigh. At a command from Pippa, the three pupils let go of Cynthia and returned to their places. Cynthia, meanwhile, was writhing like a cut worm, clutching her thighs and sobbing uncontrollably.

'Shut up, girl,' sneered Lavinia. 'Get on your knees and thank me. And don't stop until I tell you.'

Gradually, Cynthia rose to her knees and clasped Lavinia's legs for support. Her voice shaking she wailed between the sobs, 'Thank you, Prefect Monitor Lavinia for a well-deserved punishment. I am most grateful to you for spending the time to correct me in such an effective way. I am really not worthy of your kind attention and superb skill with the strap. I am truly penitent and will try much harder in future to behave correctly.'

'That's enough, you stupid girl,' yelled Lavinia. 'Take your night-dress and go back to bed, and that goes for the rest of you, too.' Cynthia hobbled back to her bed whimpering. Rather more quickly the other girls scuttled back to their beds leaving Julie standing in the middle of the dormitory.

'Right, you have been told the drill, so let's not have any messing about. We are already late. Hold still while I put this on you,' said Pippa, producing a collar and lead from her bag. 'Now on your knees and crawl.' Julie did as she was bid and was soon crawling down the corridor, led by Pippa holding the lead and spurred on by Lavinia, who wielded the strap across Julie's bottom at intervals.

'Since you are our little doggy, Julie, I think you can bark like a dog whenever you feel my strap,' ordered Lavinia.

Pippa giggled and whispered gleefully, 'Being a certain mistress' little pet won't help you now. In fact there are one or two others, far prettier than you, who are in love with – shall we say "Mistress S".

Julie blushed.

'Oh dear,' Pippa continued, her tone mocking and sarcastic, 'I meant to say "Mistress X" – the two letters sound so similar don't they? Obviously a slip of the tongue. Anyway, some of those girls want you to be taught a lesson – and a very painful one, I hope.'

By the time they reached the door of the senior prefects' common room, which was down several long corridors, Julie was trying hard to fight back the tears from the combination of the events in the dorm, the pain of the strap, the ache in her knees and the humiliating necessity to shout 'woof-woof' every few yards. Indeed, Lavinia and Pippa knew that if Julie had not been in such a state they would be punished themselves and possibly demoted from their prefect monitor status.

I know why they act in this sadistic way, thought Julie, it's to soften up the poor victim, so that they are less able to psychologically resist the senior prefects in the meeting. They will only be satisfied when all the rebellion in a girl's character is eradicated and true submission is instilled. They are not satisfied with people pretending to submit, they want everyone to come out of here, truly and permanently submissive.

Finally, at the end of the last corridor they came to a door marked, SENIOR PREFECTS' COMMON ROOM. Underneath, a piece of card bearing the instructions, KNOCK ONCE AND WAIT was attached to the door with drawing pins. Julie gulped and her stomach tied itself into a knot. What horrors awaited her, on the other side of this door?

14

The Senior Prefects' Common Room

Pippa knocked three times on the door. There was a long pause and then the sound of a muffled voice. Julie caught the command, 'Enter.' Pippa opened the door and Lavinia led Julie in, still crawling on her hands and knees. Julie saw that the senior prefects' common room was very large and mainly in semi-darkness. Thick velvet curtains hung down over the tall windows, and large oil paintings and portraits were recessed in gloom. Antique furniture and classical busts from Roughton Hall's historical heritage littered the room, all carefully illuminated with subdued downlighters. An enormous circular oak table stood at the far end of the room around which eleven senior prefects, wearing white blouses, short pleated skirts and black stockings, sat on ornate chairs festooned with carvings and barleycorn twists.

'Julie Semple,' announced Pippa. 'We are sorry to be late but she resisted rather violently.'

Julie fought hard to suppress the urge to call Pippa a liar.

'Bring the slut over here,' ordered Vanessa Smith, who was the head senior prefect. Vanessa's unmistakable form was standing at the far end of the room, away from the other senior prefects. Julie could see her jet-black pageboy cut, atop her six-foot athletic frame. Her haughty features carried an imperious sneer. Pippa led Julie over towards the table. As she slowly crawled across the huge expanse of carpet she saw the prefects each turn their chair around so that the back was against the table. Each prefect then knelt on her chair facing the high back, arched her bottom and lifted her skirt. None of them was wearing panties and so Julie was presented with a view of a row of pert and not so pert bottoms.

'You know what to do,' stated Vanessa. 'And make sure you kiss our arses thoroughly. Get that tongue working, and don't stop until I tell you to go on to the next. You can start right here with me.' Julie crawled to Vanessa's chair, raised herself on her knees, grasped the front of Vanessa's thighs and buried her head in the proffered bottom, licking and kissing as far up as she could.

'Deeper, you useless girl,' shouted Vanessa. 'You will get more strokes later if you don't put more effort in. Now, pull my bottom cheeks apart slightly. I really want to feel that tongue.' Julie did as she was bid, pressing her head into Vanessa's soft bottom cheeks and smelling the scent of sex and sweat.

'Enough girl, do the same for Senior Prefect Greta, and make sure that you put just as much effort in. I'll be watching just to make sure that you do,' ordered Vanessa after Julie had kissed and tongued the girl's bottom for what had seemed like an eternity. Julie shuffled on her knees to the next chair on which Greta was kneeling. Greta had a rather large bottom and slightly plump thighs, so that the suspender belt straps and stocking tops were indented into her soft flesh. Julie pressed her mouth to Greta's bottom and began kissing it. Suddenly, she felt Vanessa's belly pressing against the back of her head and realised that she was encircling the two of them with her arms and squeezing them tightly together. Her nose and tongue were thrust hard up Greta's bottom and Julie luxuriated in the soft, all-enveloping, silky flesh. A minute later the pressure eased.

Vanessa stepped back and said calmly, 'Okay, now do the same for Senior Prefect Theresa and put your heart into it a bit more this time, otherwise I'll have to help you again.' So saying, she grasped Julie by the ear and hauled her to the next chair where Senior Prefect Theresa was kneeling, her bottom thrust out. Julie applied her tongue with redoubled zeal, not wanting to be squashed and nearly asphyxiated again. She was rewarded for her extra effort after some minutes when Vanessa praised her and commented that her technique seemed to be improving. Senior Prefect Gemma was next. She possessed the most beautifully smooth, pert bottom that Julie had ever seen, it was a pleasure to attend to it so closely. Julie kissed it lovingly with unfeigned passion. It took another fifteen minutes before Julie had finally finished tonguing the bottoms of all twelve senior prefects and by that time her tongue and neck were well and truly aching. She felt keenly the total humiliation of her predicament and tears rolled down her cheeks while a libidinous fire of submissive bliss surged through her.

'Position two,' ordered Vanessa. Julie obeyed with alacrity and stood facing the twelve senior prefects at attention with her hands on her head. The senior prefects now lounged in their seats, a couple of them smoking, whilst looking her up and down, their eyes roving over her nakedness. Julie felt particularly conscious of her smoothly shaven pudenda that made her feel all the more naked.

'What shall we do with this little minx?' enquired Vanessa. A flurry of proposals was immediately shouted out. Each senior prefect seemed to have her own favourite punishments and rituals.

'She needs to lose a little weight,' shouted Senior Prefect Gemma. 'She needs to lose at least half a stone, look at the way those tits shake about. Third formers should be forced to be really thin.' The others laughed. 'Put her on the running machine for twenty minutes, that will shake the fat off her. And then put her through our patented fat girl's exercise routine on the table. Remember we did it to that ginger-haired girl a couple of months ago – what was her name?'

'It was Leonora Whittle,' answered Vanessa. 'Didn't we put a ginger suppository up her arse as well? That certainly made her move about a bit. Pippa, get the ginger suppositories. Lavinia, take Julie over to the running machine and cuff her hands to the rails.' Lavinia walked over to Julie, gazing contemptuously into her eyes and picked up the loop of the leash where it trailed on the floor.

'Crawl like a snake on your belly!' shouted Greta, to the amusement of the others. It took Julie a full minute to squirm over to the running machine, the friction of the carpet on her nipples making them stand out like little corks. It also made them rather sore. Any attempt to raise her body at all to make the passage easier was rewarded by a stinging cut of Lavinia's strap across her buttocks or thighs. Meanwhile Pippa had obtained the ginger suppository and was standing at the running machine, waiting for Vanessa's instructions.

'Now Julie,' said Vanessa, 'bend right over and touch your toes whilst Pippa inserts the run-faster suppository.' Julie bent right over touching her toes and felt Pippa pulling her bottom cheeks apart and then gently rubbing some lubricant oil deep into the dimple of her bottom. After a pause of some seconds Julie felt something pressing hard against her bottom. There was a sharp penetrating sensation and she felt Pippa's finger push something deep into her.

'You can stand up now and step on to the machine,' ordered Vanessa tartly.

When Julie had stepped on to the running machine, Lavinia took the wrist cuffs that were attached to the handrails at each side of the machine and attached them to each of the girl's wrists. Julie was now powerless to move from her position standing on the platform of the machine. The senior prefects all gathered around the machine, delighting in Julie's predicament.

'Right, Lavinia, switch on. I think a brisk jogging speed will do to start with.' Lavinia adjusted the controls and with a slight jerk the running platform began to move. Julie started running as the speedometer and the mileometer on the dashboard in front began to register. The room was rather hot, the pace was certainly brisk and within a minute Julie had broken out into a sweat. A few seconds later, she became acutely aware of a burning sensation deep in her bottom. She wriggled her bottom and clenched her cheeks but this only seemed to make the burning worse. By now the perspiration was pouring off her forehead and running in rivulets down her back and down her cleavage. The further she ran, and the more she wriggled, the more her bottom felt as if it were on fire. The burning heat from the suppository was spreading up from her bottom across her whole body and up to her breasts, which were swinging from side to side in front of her. Her nipples, already sensitive from the belly crawl across the carpet, were protruding further than she had ever seen them protrude before and were a deep scarlet. They felt as if they were going to explode with the heat.

'Look at the bitch sweat,' chortled Senior Prefect Tammy. 'Can we turn the pace up, Vanessa?'

'Everyone, look at that bottom wobbling,' laughed Greta.

'Never mind the bottom,' squealed Theresa. 'Look at those tits swinging. Oh, we are so cruel. With jugs that size we should have let her wear her bra.' This led to renewed gales of laughter all round.

'With her nipples standing out like that, she wouldn't have been able to get it on,' spluttered Sabina in a fit of giggles. Vanessa studied Julie's face. She was panting hard with the exertion, her mouth hanging open, sweat was pouring off her face and tears were running down her cheeks. The burning sensation was now all over her body although the centre of it was in her bottom. She had now run almost half a mile according to the dashboard and her legs felt as if they were going to drop off. Her breathing was coming in tortured gasps and she felt that she could not go much further.

'Increase the speed one notch, please, Pippa,' said Vanessa with a cruel smile and Julie felt the machine speed up slightly. She was determined not to cry out but after five more minutes at the higher speed she heard herself begging amid the tears for the machine to be turned off.

'Please, please Vanessa, I can't run any further. My legs won't move, I can't do it any more. Please, Vanessa, I beg you, please turn it off,' she panted.

'Oh, I don't know what to decide,' pondered Vanessa with mock seriousness. 'I'll have to give the matter some careful consideration.' Julie's head began to loll and her legs turned to jelly; she knew that she could barely manage another step. 'I know,' cried Vanessa as if some brainwave had occurred to her. 'Switch off the machine and Julie can have a couple of minutes rest.'

Pippa turned off the machine and Julie collapsed on to her knees gasping for breath. Every part of her body was racked with exertion. Her bottom stung from the ginger suppository, her lungs ached as she gasped for breath, her legs hurt and her breasts ached from swinging so much with the running. On top of that she could still feel the smarting from the cuts of Lavinia's strap. Gradually, Julie felt the crisis in her breathing and legs ease off slightly and became at the same time aware of the ache in her wrists as the weight of her arms pulled against the cuffs attached to the side rails.

'Your two minutes are up, my girl,' said Vanessa.

201

'Get on your feet and start running. Pippa, adjust it to a steady jog, please.'

Julie slowly and shakily rose to her feet. 'Permission to speak, please, Senior Prefect Vanessa,' piped up Pippa.

'All right, what is it, and it had better be good.'

'Could we use the ball gag on her? That way, we wouldn't have to listen to her dripping on as soon as it gets a little bit tiring. I could give her some smart cuts with the strap as soon as she starts getting lazy and we wouldn't have to listen to any soppy crying.' Vanessa considered the idea for a second and then, with a great show of indulging Pippa said, 'Oh, I suppose so. Get the red ball gag, that's size number three, and strap it on her. Make sure that it's tight.'

Pippa strode over to a large, ornate cupboard decorated in the Japanese style with black and gold lacquered panels, set against the far wall. She opened the door to reveal a cornucopia of gags, saddles, back braces, dildoes, vibrators, handcuffs, hoods, whips, tawses, canes, birches and every other type of correctional device that could possibly be imagined. All were neatly laid out in separate sections. Pippa surveyed the collection for a moment and then reached in to retrieve a gag with black leather straps and a bright red ball. She turned and strode back across the enormous expanse of carpet, the gag in her hand, her minuscule breasts quivering and a mischievous trace of a grin on her face. Julie watched in nervous anticipation and noticed that Pippa's nipples were noticeably erect. Bet she's enjoying every minute of this, the sadistic bitch, she thought. She was, however, simultaneously glad of the extra time to rest her legs and capture her breath. Her body was still drenched in sweat and her breathing was laboured but she felt better than she had done before the rest period that Vanessa had allowed her. Pippa ordered Julie to open her mouth wide and soon had the ball gag firmly inserted and tightly strapped in place. It was a large ball and Julie's jaws immediately started to ache as her mouth was stretched almost unnaturally wide. She had the typical look of astonishment that all those who wear a ball gag exhibit; staring eyes and a gaping mouth. The ball in her mouth and the tight straps around her head made Julie feel like a prize racehorse, bitted and bridled for her run on the machine.

'Oh, Pippa, go back and get the nipple clamps and some weights, the three ounce ones with the little bells on will be quite adequate, I think,' said Vanessa as an afterthought. Dutifully Pippa hurried back to the lacquered cupboard and returned with the clamps and lead weights and began to attach them to Julie's nipples. The weights pulled down rather heavily on Julie's engorged teats and she knew that it would feel a lot worse when she started running.

'Now you can start the machine,' Vanessa commanded. Pippa turned the dial, the platform shuddered into life with a whine and Julie had to start running. The machine was set to a brisk jog again and soon Julie was gasping for air, especially as the ball gag made breathing a lot more difficult. In addition, the nipple clamps and weights were tugging hard as they swung wildly, the little bells tinkling merrily, stretching her already sore nipples out to an astonishing degree. The heat of the ginger suppository had still not subsided and her legs were again turning to jelly. When the mileometer showed another quarter of a mile, Julie tried to beg for mercy but the ball gag was totally effective, only a faint mewling sound escaped from her mouth.

'She's starting to lag,' shouted Pippa. 'May I apply the strap please, Senior Prefect Vanessa?'

'Yes, half a dozen strokes across the buttocks, please, Pippa, and lay them on well. Remember the flick of the wrist.' Pippa smiled with ill-disguised glee, moved to one side, adjusted her stance, brought her strap right back in a wide sweep and lashed it forward with all her strength culminating with a final flick of the wrist. The strap impacted centrally across Julie's bottom with a resounding crack, sending ripples of shock fleetingly across the fatty tissue. A searing sensation shot through Julie as she tried vainly to increase her stride. Five more strokes followed at ten-second intervals, each one building on the throbbing pain of the one before. Julie's instinct to cry out was effectively prevented by the ball gag and so she bore the strokes with an unnatural silence. She urged her body to supply every last ounce of energy so that she would not falter in her stride and incur more strokes, but the energy was not there. Great streams of perspiration ran down her body and dripped on to the base of the machine as she staggered to keep running. Each lash seemed harder than the one before and seemed to actually drain her strength. Eventually, she found herself on the point of collapsing, with the moving platform jerking her backwards against the wrist cuffs attached to the rails.

'Switch off the machine. Release the wrist cuffs and remove the nipple clamps, Lavinia,' bellowed Vanessa and a second later the platform ground to a halt. Julie lay half hanging from her wrists, half kneeling on the platform, her head hanging down as she fought for breath. As the cuffs were undone, Julie sank down, her body heaving with exhaustion and sobbing, although the ball gag ensured that it was all completely silent. Her nipples, once Lavinia had removed the clamps, had stretched to virtually half an inch in length and were glowing scarlet like twin volcanos.

'Stand up you lazy slut,' ordered Vanessa. Hard as she tried, Julie could not haul herself to her feet; her legs just would not support her. 'Lavinia, Pippa!' Vanessa shouted. 'Help the stupid girl to her feet and take the ball gag off, if you please.' The two monitors grabbed Julie by the arms and set her upright, holding on to her as she swayed and threatened to sink back down. Julie's skin glistened with perspiration so that Pippa and Lavinia had to hold on quite tightly to get a grip on her slippery body. After a few seconds of fumbling with the buckles, Pippa released Julie from the tight embrace of the hated gag. Now Julie could inhale great gasps of air into her lungs and she soon felt some strength returning to her limbs and the ache easing from her strained jaws. Gradually, the trembling in her legs diminished and she could stand without the support of the two monitors.

'Stop whimpering, girl, and stand up straight. Hands by your sides,' barked Vanessa. Julie did her best to obey but sniffs and sobs continued to break out every few seconds. Yet, paradoxically, she had never felt more alive in all her life. Complete and utter domination was what she had always craved and now she was getting it in abundance.

'I think you are in the right condition to answer our questions and account for your rebellious attitude. We will hold our meeting as usual around the table and you, Julie, as the pupil under investigation will stand on the two stools as tradition dictates for this category of meeting.' Vanessa signalled to Lavinia, who fetched two tall, science laboratory stools and placed them about twelve inches apart in the centre on top of the large circular table. Meanwhile, the twelve senior prefects took their seats around the table. Pippa took Julie by the arm and led her to the table. Julie clambered up on the table and gingerly climbed up to stand on the stools with one foot on each stool as she had been directed. Standing so high above the floor made her feel unsafe and slightly vertiginous. Vanessa took her seat directly in front of Julie, switched on her anglepoise lamp and directed the light glaringly towards the girl. With the two stools spaced as they were, Julie had to stand with her legs apart making her feel ashamed and vulnerable. The circle of faces all around and below, looking up, seemed to devour every inch of her exposed body as she blinked in the dazzling beam of light. It seemed to Julie that her smoothly shaven quim and freshly whipped bottom were the focus of everyone's attention.

'Hands clasped behind head and keep your eyes directed straight ahead,' ordered Vanessa. 'We want answers to our questions. Any hesitation will be rewarded with extra strokes when we come to sentence you.'

What followed put Julie's mind in a whirl. For the next twenty minutes, questions were fired at her from all directions, without any pause. The senior prefects were sitting all around the table, so the questions came from in front, from behind and from the sides. What upset Julie even more was that most of the questions were of a very embarrassing, personal nature. Not being allowed to hesitate served to make it impossible to dissemble or lie. Questions about relationships with her fellow pupils, about her feelings towards the mistresses, about masturbation, about her body, about her thoughts towards the senior prefects and about her reactions to being punished were all fired in rapid succession and made Julie's head reel. As the tears welled from her eyes she did her best to answer, but it was a losing battle; the events of the evening had effectively worn her down and her resistance was shattered. Gradually her answers became more incoherent and the sobbing took over.

'That's enough, we have heard too much blubbering and not enough truth,' snapped Vanessa. 'The wretched girl is obviously trying to hide the truth. All this sobbing and stammering is a sure sign of mental confusion brought on by lying. What we need is something to distract the little trollop from her calculated evasiveness so that she can't help but tell the truth. Pippa, fetch the saddle belt that goes with the vibrating dildo and put it on her.'

This instruction was well received by the assembly of

senior prefects who Julie heard murmuring, 'This will be fun,' and, 'I love watching them when they've got that up them.'

A moment later, Pippa returned and clambered up on to the table.

'Make sure that it is as tight as possible up between her fanny lips,' commanded Vanessa, flicking the ash from her cigarette. Pippa buckled the leather belt of the saddle around Julie's waist, pulling with all her might to get it as tight as it would go before fastening the back buckle. Julie felt as if she was being cut in half but she knew that the worst bit was still to come. Like a conventional Roughton Hall saddle this one had a strap that passed from the back of the belt between the buttocks and up between the legs to the front of the belt. Being pulled up tight made walking or any kind of movement a sheer torment. However, this particular saddle had a large, black, vibrating dildo attached to the strap that passed between the legs. Pippa smeared some lubricant jelly on to the tip of the dildo and slowly inserted it right up into Julie as far as it would go. She then pulled the strap up tight and buckled it to the front of the belt. Julie grimaced as she felt the fat rubbery dildo filling her up as if it would split her and the leather straps of the saddle biting into her.

'Switch it on now, Pippa, and let's see if she can stop herself dancing and gasping,' said Vanessa. Pippa reached between Julie's legs and fumbled with the base of the dildo. With a click, a low hum started up and Julie was aware of a fast vibration deep within her. Vanessa and the others resumed the questioning, but, within two minutes, Julie was blurting out whatever confessions came into her head as waves of orgasmic sensation flooded through her. Her legs began to shake uncontrollably and involuntary gasps and whimpers merged with her confessions. She soon became insensible to the comments and peals of laughter coming from her audience and was only aware of the waves of erotic ecstasy rippling and surging continuously through every nerve fibre. A hot flush spread from her cheeks down over her chest and beads of perspiration stood out on her forehead. As the shaking became more frenzied, it became apparent that Julie would soon fall off the stools.

'Lavinia and Pippa, I want you to carry the little trollop down off the table before she does herself an injury. Get the wrist cuffs, put them on her and attach them to the ceiling chain. I want you to hoist her up so that her toes are just touching the carpet. Do you understand?'

'Yes, Senior Prefect Vanessa,' chorused the two monitors and immediately bent their efforts to the task in hand. They soon had Julie down from the stools although it was not without some difficulty as the vibrator was still humming and she could not help writhing and jerking spasmodically. With practised efficiency, the cuffs were snapped shut on Julie's wrists and clipped to the chain which dangled down from a rope over a pulley on the ceiling.

Lavinia strode to the far wall where a cranked handle and ratcheted drum controlled the rope. Slowly, Lavinia cranked the handle which hauled up the rope and made the ratchet emit a loud clicking. Gradually, Julie felt her wrists being raised up, then her arms. As she was hauled to her feet she could see the muscles of Lavinia's naked back clearly defined with the exertion of turning the crank. Up and up rose the chain until Julie was standing on her toes with her hands high above her head. Lavinia stopped turning the handle and wiped her brow. This new position seemed to force the vibrator further into Julie, which intensified the sensations. Spasms shook her body as she climaxed, loudly screaming and gasping. This caused untold amusement amongst the senior prefects, especially as the orgasm was prolonged and vocal. As the sensations subsided, Julie hung her head in exhaustion and embarrassment. Within seconds though, she realised that the dildo was still vibrating and the pleasure was beginning to build up again.

'Please, Senior Prefect Vanessa, I can't take any more. Please switch it off.'

'Impertinent girl, a little slut like you should be grateful. Three strokes are added to your sentence for cheek. Now don't say another word unless you are first given permission,' replied Vanessa.

'Besides, it gives us a good show, watching the little sex kitten shout the house down,' added Senior Prefect Candice. Slowly the sensations intensified and, after a few minutes, they were so strong that Julie could no longer feel the ache in her arms and wrists. Gradually, her eyes closed and little animal-like cries escaped from her lips. Her limbs writhed and twisted. The sensations were so intense that they were actually painful and she climaxed again in a long, shuddering explosion that went on and on. A loud howl came from deep within her and diminished into breathless sobs. She felt herself sliding into unconsciousness as the vibrator still buzzed relentlessly inside her. The next thing that Julie was conscious of was being jerked into awareness by a bottle of strong smelling salts held under her nose.

'Thank you, Lavinia. Take the bottle away now,' said Vanessa. Julie realised that she had probably only been unconscious for a few moments and that the vibrator was still in motion. She hung limply from her wrist cuffs totally worn out, but the vibrations were powerful and unrelenting. Ten minutes later Julie orgasmed again more violently and intensely than before, her legs thrashing and her vocal chords gasping hoarsely. Again she momentarily lost consciousness and was brought round by the application of the smelling salts. Hanging limply from the chain, she presented a picture of total exhaustion as Pippa unbuckled the saddle and removed the still-vibrating dildo.

Slowly, Julie regained her composure and lifted her head. She became dimly aware of the senior prefects standing in a semi-circle in front of her with Vanessa to the fore, holding the senior prefects' punishment book.

'Ah, good, I see that you have finally come to your senses, Julie. Whilst you were coming round, we discussed your case and have given careful consideration to your demeanour and behaviour. We have also taken into account your co-operation tonight and the humility that you seem to be showing now. We think that tonight's experience has probably taught you a lesson and that you will not want to repeat it in a hurry. However, be under no illusions, we will ask permission to call you to another meeting, which will be more severe than this one, if we feel that you are forgetting your lowly position. Remember, you must remain as totally submissive as you appear to be at the moment at all times, if you are to avoid more corrective treatment. It is after all, for your own good. Taking all these things into consideration, we have decided that the flogging sentence, which, as you know, always concludes a grade three senior prefects' meeting, can be relatively lenient. I don't need to remind you that our normal practice is to order a sentence of a healthy number of strokes of the senior cane on the bare and a good birching to finish off, positioned over our birching horse.'

Julie glanced over to the leather horse with its place to kneel and the plethora of straps hanging from every corner, over at the far end of the room in the window bay and shuddered. Only a fortnight ago, Amanda Rigg from Julie's dormitory had received a sentence of a dozen strokes of the senior cane followed by a dozen strokes of the birch all delivered by Senior Prefect Theresa who was the school tennis captain. A full minute was timed between each stroke so that Theresa did not tire and so that the full effect of each stroke was fully appreciated. Amanda had lost all control by the tenth stroke of the birch. When she was finally able to stand up and had finished thanking Theresa for her punishment, she had to don a punishment skirt which had the back cut away to reveal her bottom. This, she was ordered to wear for the rest of the week, so that the evidence of her punishment was revealed for everyone to witness.

'Therefore,' Vanessa continued, glancing at the senior prefects' punishment book, 'we have generously decided to award a sentence of a mere eight strokes, plus the three specified earlier for speaking out of turn, making a total of eleven strokes. These eleven will be applied to the buttocks and the back of the thighs. You will remain in the hoisted position. The chosen instrument of correction will be the thirty-inch, fibreglass switch. You will count each stroke and thank us for each one. You will endeavour to keep still so that the strokes are applied accurately and you will endeavour to refrain from screaming. You may, however, cry out if necessary, as long as it is not so loud that it wakes the girls in the dorms. If you do make too much noise we will employ the gag and apply three extra penalty strokes. Each of the senior prefects here tonight with the exception of myself will deliver one stroke. If you fail to co-operate fully, the number of strokes will be increased by a margin of not less than double. Do you understand?'

Julie raised her head slightly and without meeting Vanessa's eyes, said with all the enthusiasm that she could muster, 'Yes, Senior Prefect Vanessa, thank you very much.' Julie inwardly reflected that the sentence could have been far worse, from what she had heard from other girls. Besides, her wrists, arms and legs were aching terribly from the strain of being hoisted up on her toes. It would be a relief to get it all over with, even though the pain would undoubtedly be horrible.

'Lavinia, one more notch on the ratchet if you will. Pippa, get the 24-inch leg-spreader and put it on her,' commanded Vanessa. Pippa ran to the lacquered cabinet and returned with the leg-spreader, a long metal bar with shackles for the ankles at each end. This was intended to prevent the victim kicking and jerking her legs about. Pippa knelt at Julie's ankles and quickly attached each one to the opposite ends of the bar. Now her legs were spread wide. Lavinia, straining at the crank, turned it a fraction of a turn so that it emitted one click and Julie felt herself raised a couple of millimetres so that only the very tips of her two big toes were now touching the carpet. The strain of being stretched out for so long and with legs spread wide was now becoming extremely uncomfortable. Every muscle was at full stretch. It would be pretty hard not to co-operate strung up in this position, mused Julie to herself.

'Pippa, get the appointed instrument of correction,' instructed Vanessa. Pippa returned seconds later. She held a tasselled cushion on which lay a slender switch tapering to a fraction of a millimetre at one end whilst the other end was thicker and wrapped in a lattice of leather plaits. Julie had not seen this implement before, although she had heard it mentioned by the others. She thought that it looked like a short fishing rod and surmised that the thin, whippy tip would sting sharply. Pippa turned to Vanessa and, with a deep curtsey, presented the switch to her. Vanessa held it at each end and effortlessly bent it in a big curve so that the two ends met. She then let go of the thin end, which sprang in the air with a quiet whistle and shook. Julie's stomach turned with fear as Vanessa held the quivering switch in front of her face. To her surprise, Vanessa reached out with her other hand and began stroking the side of her face. Gently, she lifted Julie's chin with the tip of her finger and looked deep into her eyes. She then let her hand slowly fall and in doing so, brushed her fingertips over the still-stiffened nipple of Julie's left breast, sending ripples of excitement down Julie's spine.

'Pippa, put *Pomp and Circumstance* on the player. I like to whip these hussies to patriotic music so that they know that we are making Great Britain strong again,' Vanessa instructed. Soon the martial strains of the military bands reverberated around the room.

Vanessa inclined her head slightly towards Julie's ear and breathed very softly the words, 'That's better, they can't hear me now. Some of them are with us and some of them are not. Everyone has their own rôle in the rebellion. Yours is to suffer and show total submission in order to allay all suspicion. When the time comes, nobody will suspect you of leading the insurrection on the year three corridor. That will be your main task. Sophie will help you, plus others whose names you will be told in due course. The time is not far off now, there are more of us here than you think. As the day gets closer all the members of Fightback will be revealed to each other. Even I don't know the names of all of them. Some time ago, I got a message via one of our members in year four, Yolanda. She had a message for you but could not deliver it. The poor girl's cover has been blown and they have kept her in solitary ever since. I have also had a coded message smuggled in from Jack. He says that this rôle is what you want more than anything. I can see in your eyes that this is true.'

This half-inaudible message put Julie's mind in fresh turmoil. So was this all a ruse, then? But did she hear it right? Could it be a trick? The mention of Jack suggested that it was not. The puzzle was immediately put out of her head as Vanessa announced, 'Senior Prefect Gemma will commence the punishment. Remember you are only getting one stroke each, so make it count.'

Vanessa placed the switch back on to the cushion which Pippa held in her outstretched hands and stepped to one side. Gemma, blonde and extremely buxom so that the buttons of the white blouse always looked as if they were about to ping off, stepped smartly forward and, with a curtsey, took the switch from the cushion. Looking into Julie's eyes as she moved to a position behind her, she seemed to be saying, 'Wait till you feel this, my girl.' There was a pause. Julie's stomach tightened into a knot and she tried to clench her buttock muscles to minimise the pain. But she knew that clenching was not allowed and that Gemma would wait till she relaxed her bottom, so she slumped and just shut her eyes, waiting for the stroke to fall. The wait felt like an eternity; she sensed Gemma moving around behind her, adjusting her footing, and then she heard a sharp whistle. Julie bit her lip and braced herself for the pain but it did not come. It was obviously a practice swing to get the feel of the whip of the switch. Oh, the cruelty of it, thought Julie, this waiting, not knowing when the stroke will come, is sheer torture. Without warning there was a much louder, higher-pitched whistle, a loud crack and a searing impact across the back of her left thigh. The impact knocked Julie forward. An involuntary howl broke from her lips and her legs tried to raise themselves up as the left leg rose up slightly, pulling the other one attached by the leg-spreader. This was virtually impossible, and her toes were soon resting back on the carpet. Through the throbbing sting, Julie then realised why the leg spreader had been used. If it had not been for that device, her legs would be kicking in all directions, her knees would probably now be under her chin and the punishment would be delayed for ages between each stroke. Through a red haze, Julie saw Gemma replace the switch on the cushion and step smartly back to the rank of senior prefects standing in front of her.

'One, thank you, Senior Prefect Gemma,' Julie managed to gasp out just in time to avoid incurring a penalty for disobedience.

'Senior Prefect Theresa,' announced Vanessa. Julie's heart sank. An accomplished tennis player, Senior Prefect Theresa was said to wield a whip with twice the power of any of the others. This rumour was undoubtedly true, any of the other third formers who had experienced Theresa's floggings quailed at the thought of another one. Theresa stepped forward, curtseyed and picked up the switch. Her wrists were thick like a man's and she had a broad back and big shoulders. Her face was rosy-cheeked, exuding health, her large bust and equally large bottom contrasted with the slimmer frames of most of the other senior prefects. It was said that she had been brought up on a sheep and cattle farm before being sent to the reformatory and that the hard physical work there had built up her physique. Purposefully, she strode behind Julie, who now felt an uncontrollable trembling begin in her legs. She did not have to wait long for the next stroke. A sudden movement behind her, a loud swish and an even louder crack and Julie felt the sting of a thousand wasps impact right across the full width of her buttocks. As she swung back from the impact that drove her forward, the sting leapt like an electric shock right through her body and she shrieked out loud. Her mouth was dry and her tongue felt as though it were glued to the roof of her mouth as she croaked, 'Two, thank you Senior Prefect Theresa.' All strength to resist now had deserted her and her head hung limply. She had only had two strokes and feared she could not stand another nine.

'Senior Prefect Lucinda,' announced Vanessa. Lucinda was considered to be an outstanding beauty by most of the pupils and many had a crush on her. She was tall and aristocratic with high cheek bones and classic features. Her honey blonde hair, arranged in curls, bounced as she walked, as did her petite breasts, supported only by a quarter-cup bra, which Julie could clearly make out through the white blouse. Her slim body moved with feline grace as she curtseyed, picked up the switch and flexed it in her hands. Without a pause she took up her position behind Julie. Julie's stomach tensed up again and she gritted her teeth. A few seconds of nervous anticipation and then, swish-crack, the switch landed again, this time right at the top of the right thigh where the bottom cheeks began to swell.

'Oh, no, mercy,' cried Julie as the pain erupted and her toes danced on the floor. As the sensation diffused through her body she just managed to squeak, 'Three, thank you, Senior Prefect Lucinda.' Lucinda turned and smiled at Julie as she replaced the switch on the cushion.

'Look at the state she's in, and she's not halfway through yet,' Julie heard someone whisper.

'I still prefer them strapped to the horse,' someone else replied. 'This allows them too much movement.'

'Senior Prefect Sabina,' called out Vanessa. Sabina was also tall but more angular than Lucinda. She had short hair, freckles and a very slim figure. It had been rumoured, earlier that term, that she and Lucinda had enjoyed a lesbian relationship for many months but had been forced to recant after the tutors had discovered it and made each one punish the other. This was the custom when uncondoned lesbianism was discovered. Julie noticed as Sabina walked forward that her bosom was unsupported by a bra, as her small breasts jiggled tremulously and her nipples could be clearly seen, pert and rubbing against the thin material of the blouse. Her long legs and short skirt caused her stocking tops and suspender clips to show with every stride. Julie also noticed that Lucinda's eyes were fixated on those very obvious nipples. She realised in a flash of intuition that the rumours concerning Lucinda and Sabina were undoubtedly true. Sabina took an eternity to deliver her stroke, having to test the flex of the switch in her hands and place her feet just so. At one point, for a brief moment, Julie felt Sabina's hand gently moving over the raised weals of her bottom and assumed that the prefect was checking to see which part to lay the switch across next. As the tension mounted in Julie, the stroke came, positioned perfectly horizontally across the upper part of the buttocks. The tip landed on the left cheek. Sabina was noted for the accuracy and power of her backhand stroke. The cut was ferociously whippy and again Julie could not restrain a loud cry, followed a good few seconds later by, 'Four, thank you Senior Prefect Sabina.'

By now her whole bottom felt on fire and Julie could not help beginning to sob, but, mindful of Vanessa's warning, tried to keep it as quiet as possible. Sabina sauntered back to Pippa, laid the switch on the cushion and, like Lucinda before her, glanced back at Julie with a smile as she did so.

'Senior Prefect Tammy,' called out Vanessa. Tammy was short and petite with beautiful large eyes and brown hair arranged in two long bunches. Her slender wrists and light frame implied that a flogging from her would not be half as bad as one from Theresa. Indeed, she had the reputation of being very lenient and soft-hearted. Some questioned why she was accorded senior prefect status since she did not seem to be cut out for it. The answer seemed to lie in the strong rumour that she was summoned to Vanessa's bedroom every night. Everyone in Julie's dormitory wondered why the tutors turned a blind eye to it. Tammy curtseyed delicately, picked up the switch and took up her position. A few moments later the stroke came whistling across the centre of Julie's buttocks and landed diagonally across one of the earlier weals.

Although Tammy was not a hard flogger, this cut on top of the other one drove another squeal of pain from Julie's lips. As she gasped, 'Five, thank you, Senior Prefect Tammy,' Julie's mind reeled and she wondered how on earth she'd be able to last out. All her consciousness seemed directed to the throbbing waves of pain spreading outwards from her vividly wealed bottom. The sweat dripped from her body as she writhed and squirmed in her bonds, making the metal links of the leg-spreader and ceiling chain rattle.

The next in turn was Senior Prefect Veronica. Julie raised her head and, through a mist of tears, saw Veronica take the switch and advance towards her. Veronica was the most studious looking of all the senior prefects. She was of above average height and sported her auburn hair in a tight bun held in place with a silver clip. Wire-framed glasses perched on her nose, her nylons were seamed and her high-heeled shoes were the type that also had a strap around the ankle.

'She's quite a cry baby,' Julie heard Theresa whisper.

'Another one with a low pain threshold,' someone replied.

'No, she's putting it on. Quite a little actress, I would say,' said Theresa.

'Well, she did have quite a few strokes earlier on the running machine,' commented Greta.

'And a fairly long session on the tall stools,' added Lucinda under her breath.

'Come off it,' retorted Theresa. 'If I had my way she would be strapped to the horse for a dozen of the cane and two dozen of the birch to finish off. Between you and me, I think that Vanessa has been far too lenient with her. Why, I can't imagine. Last Monday, she gave that poor little second former with the freckles a dozen with the strap, half a dozen with the senior cane and a full dozen with a fresh birch. You should have heard her howl. But this one she lets off very lightly.'

'How is it looking, Veronica?' enquired Vanessa.

'Well, I think the strap from earlier has made the whole area from the middle of the thighs upwards very red and speckled. And then the strokes from the switch on top have raised some rather impressive weals. The tip of the switch must have curled around the side a couple of times because there are two scarlet lines on the edge of one thigh and another one high up on the hip.'

'Very good, Veronica, you may continue,' replied Vanessa. Ten seconds passed and then Julie heard a shuffle, a whirr and then felt the explosion of the impact as Veronica cracked the switch across and around the lower portion of her bottom.

'No please, mercy! Six, thank you, Senior Prefect Veronica,' Julie heard herself crying. As much as she tried to stop wailing she found that she could not. Great shrieks and gasps shook her frame, interspersed with imprecations for mercy. She had tried to be brave but now all reserve had given way like the walls of a dam and floods of tears were pouring out.

'Good God,' shouted Theresa. 'Give her a double dose penalty for waking the dorms – she was warned. Double eleven makes it a total of 22. I'll gladly lay them on myself.'

An angry expression passed over Vanessa's face and, raising her voice, she interrupted, 'Silence! Senior Prefect Theresa, you are not head senior prefect yet. You will come to my room tomorrow evening at eight.'

'Yes,' replied Theresa. 'I'm sorry, Senior Prefect Vanessa.'

'This squealing and screeching is far too loud,' announced Vanessa. 'Pippa, get the leather hood and horse-bit gag, I don't want the girls in the dorms kept awake. Now, Julie, raise your head up and listen to me. One of the aims of Roughton Hall is to instil discipline. I could understand all this fuss if you were receiving three dozen of the birch. You must try harder in future to take your punishments like a Roughton Hall girl, I don't think you are trying quite hard enough at the moment. For the rest of the strokes you will wear the mask and gag. I am adding another three strokes to the allotted punishment, making a total of fourteen strokes on account of this lack of discipline and the trouble that you are putting me to. Do you understand?'

'Yes, Senior Prefect Vanessa. I'm very sorry,' Julie replied.

'So how many strokes does that leave, Julie?'

'Um, eight, thank you, Senior Prefect Vanessa.'

The next moment, Pippa was fitting the tight, black, leather mask over Julie's head. It was a close fit all round and had laces at the back to secure it like a glove over the head. Julie could feel the firm breasts and erect nipples of Pippa's body pressing against her back, as she fastened the laces. It had apertures for all the orifices of the head which could be covered by snap-on leather patches.

'Put on the ear and eye sections, Pippa,' ordered Vanessa. Soon Julie's eyes and ears were covered by the soft leather; only her mouth and nose were left exposed. Now in total darkness and with muffled hearing, Julie felt more helpless than ever before. Next she felt Pippa's fingers opening her mouth and inserting the bar of the horse bit deep into her mouth. Pippa moved behind her, and again she felt the girl's hard nipples sliding across her sweaty back and pressing hard as she tightened the buckles of the horse-bit gag. Now Julie could see nothing, hear very little, say nothing and barely move, stretched upwards as she was. Her clitoris, standing proud, tingled with undiluted sexual excitement. She could not understand what made her react in this way. It was a state of bliss that went right to the heart of her soul. She could never be satisfied with anything less – she knew that only through this suffering could she achieve complete fulfilment.

The last eight strokes passed in the haze of a fiery dream. Due to the mask, each one would come without any warning. As they fell across her thighs and buttocks the throbbing heat mounted continuously, and on two occasions the smelling salts were administered as she slumped as if ready to faint. She tried to scream but the horse bit, cruelly pulling into her mouth, prevented any cries and only a very faint gasp or gurgle could be heard from Julie as each stroke fell. Such was her frenzy, that she completely lost count of the number of strokes and was only aware that the allotted number had been administered when, after a pause, she felt Pippa's breasts pressing against her own as the eye patches were taken off, followed by the ear patches. Blinking with the sudden light, Julie saw Vanessa replacing the switch on the cushion and wondered if that was who had given her the extra three strokes.

Vanessa ordered Lavinia to lower Julie down, and as the prefect turned the ratchet Julie sank to her knees. Meanwhile, Pippa efficiently bustled around, removing the leg-spreader, the gag and finally the wrist cuffs. Freed, at last, from her bondage, Julie writhed on the floor and frantically rubbed her burning thighs and buttocks. She could clearly feel the sharply defined lines etched across her skin. As her arms came down the relief had been immense and Julie rubbed her aching arms and wrists in turn as she rolled on the carpet.

After some moments, Vanessa said, 'That's enough. Get back on your knees and express what is no doubt your enormous gratitude for tonight's correction.'

Slowly, Julie raised herself to her knees with her arms at her sides and, pausing between sobs, said, 'Thank you for my punishment, senior prefects.'

Moving close to Julie, Vanessa said, 'You are now dismissed, and don't forget this lesson. I do not want to see you back here for a senior prefects' meeting for a long time. Remember the rules of obedience and humility at all times. I am sure that this punishment, lenient as it was, will do you a lot of good. You can spend the rest of the night on the post-punishment bed so that you will not be distracted by your dorm mates and can reflect on the lessons of tonight instead of sleeping the whole time. It will also prevent you from rubbing that bottom. Stand up and turn to face the door. Pippa and Lavinia, take her to the post-punishment bedroom next to Matron's quarters. When you get there, replace the eye and ear patches on the hood so that Julie is not distracted from the sensations of the chastisement and from her thoughts of self-improvement. Now, be on your way.'

15

The Night in the Post-Punishment Bedroom

Pippa and Lavinia grasped Julie by each arm and half carried, half propelled her through the door and along the maze of semi-darkened corridors. Julie found it difficult to walk as fast as the prefect monitors since the hoisted position and the switching had taken the power from her legs. In addition, she could not completely stifle her sobs. Pippa and Lavinia, however, were not inclined to show much sympathy.

'Shut up, you soppy mare. Grade threes are usually a lot tougher than that. You were let off lightly. Sharon Jarvest got twice what you got, and she's half your size,' Pippa remarked.

'That's right,' agreed Lavinia. 'I've never seen Vanessa so soft before. I can't understand it. But still, if Vanessa leaves or gets demoted from head senior prefect, Theresa will get the position without a doubt. Then we will see to it that anyone who steps out of line, in particular anyone jammy like you, will get the full treatment. And then you will know the meaning of respect. Theresa knows how to get results, there's no softness there. I think I would rather die than get on the wrong side of Theresa.'

At last they reached the area of Roughton Hall known as Matron's quarters which Julie remembered from the traumatic first day at the reformatory. Apart from Matron's own living quarters there were other rooms leading off the lengthy corridor. These all had their own brass plate to indicate that they were the sick room, the dispensary, the isolation room, the padded room and the enema room amongst others. Pippa opened the door of the room labelled the POST-PUNISH-MENT BEDROOM and guided Julie in. The room was sparsely furnished, containing only two chairs, a table with a jar of cold cream on top, a chamber pot and a bed. The bed, however, was of the most unusual design. Instead of having a mattress it had a polished wooden surface for lying on. But the strangest feature was that the wooden surface had two holes cut into it, positioned next to each other and about a third of the way down. Instead of having a headboard, it had the upper part of a pillory with holes for the neck and wrists. At the other end it had a similar arrangement for the ankles, like medieval stocks, with about 18 inches between the holes. Julie quickly realised that she would not be getting much sleep that night, or what was left of it.

'Here we are,' said Lavinia. 'What a cosy bedroom.' Pippa chuckled mirthlessly as she produced the eye and ear covers of the leather mask. Pressing herself against Julie, she snapped them all into position. Deprived of sight and hearing, Julie once again felt a keen pang of fear surge through her.

A finger pulled at one ear patch and Pippa's voice at close range bellowed through the thick leather, 'You can perform on the chamber pot first.'

Julie felt herself being pushed across the room and then forced down to squat on the chamber pot. At first, the strangeness of the situation and the embarrassment prevented the flow but after a while she felt the relief as the waters gushed out. She then felt herself guided on to the bed and turned to lay face down. Her legs were drawn apart and secured by the ankles in the stocks. Next, she faintly heard the hinge of the pillory board squeak and her wrists were drawn forward and the placement of her head adjusted. Another faint squeak and she felt the upper part come down to secure her head and wrists in place. So far, it was not too uncomfortable, especially as there was a padded cushion for her to rest her chin on. However, Julie realised that, as the night went on, the hard surface and the inability to move would prove to be a torment. It was at this point that Julie realised the function of the two circular holes – her breasts were hanging straight down through them. Presumably the holes meant that if the breasts were sore through punishment they would not rub on the surface. Julie's nipples were still slightly tender from the episode with the nipple clamps, but, having large breasts, she soon felt more discomfort from the weight of them hanging down unsupported. In addition, the sensations blazing across her bottom made Julie yearn to rub her tender parts but the cruel design of the post-punishment bed made it impossible to move. She had no idea whether the two prefect monitors had left the room or not. She could not hear them, but then the all-enveloping nature of the leather mask meant that only very loud or very close sounds penetrated the leather. As far as Julie was concerned, all that she could hear was her own breathing. The eye patches meant that there was no way of telling whether the light was on or off because all was total darkness inside the mask. Julie soon lost all track of time. Had she been on the bed for three minutes or half an hour? It was very hard to estimate. Julie tried counting her heartbeats in order to gauge the passage of time, but gave up within seconds because the pain and discomfort made it difficult to concentrate.

The minutes crawled by tediously. Julie knew that she would not be able to get any sleep, the discomfort of the strange bed and the hot sensations across her thoroughly whipped bottom were too intense. Not being able to move a muscle or rub the painful area exacerbated the sensations greatly and Julie marvelled at the ingenuity of the nuns of the Ancient Order who could devise such fiendish refinements to the art of chastisement. The sightless and silent world inside the hood only served to make Julie more aware of the throbbing of her bottom and the memories of the evening's events.

Suddenly and without any warning, Julie felt finger-tips gently caressing the ridges imprinted across her bottom. Startled she stuttered, 'Who is it?' but the silence inside the hood was not broken. 'Please, tell me, who you are,' Julie pleaded, but there was no reply.

A cool, soothing sensation was now spreading over her buttocks and Julie realised that cold cream was being massaged into her sore behind and thighs. 'Who are you? Please tell me your name,' she repeated but still there was no sound or indication of the identity of her visitor. 'Please take off the hood or even just the ear covers and speak to me,' she begged, but the silence remained.

The gentle visitor obviously wanted to remain anonymous. The massage continued; gentle fingers palpated Julie's bum cheeks, rubbing the cream deep into her skin. Sometimes the fingers would be drawn in a straight line, slowly sliding down the contours of Julie's bottom to her thighs. Sometimes the movement would be in the opposite direction, with the palm of the hand and thumbs pressing gently down and the stroke ending in the small of the back. Sometimes the hands would describe a circular motion with the hands pushing the bum cheeks together or pulling them apart according to the direction of movement. Gradually a dreamy languor crept over Julie and she felt the ache of her punishment slipping away.

After what seemed an eternity, the mystery hands slowly worked their way down to Julie's hot, glistening sex lips. With her ankles held some distance apart by the placement of the holes of the stocks, Julie could do nothing to deny access to her most intimate places. With an electrifying jolt of pleasure, she felt the tip of an index finger tenderly trace its way upwards over her quivering clitoris and back between her legs, over the dimple of her anus and continue upwards between her cheeks and up to her waist. The finger lifted and Julie felt an agonising few seconds of frustration as the sensation of the soothing contact vanished. The wait was a short one, as almost immediately the finger started the identical journey again. Time and time again the exact same path was repeated, always starting at the same place on the swollen tip of the clitoris, now bathed in slippery juices, and tracing its way back via the sensitive crater of the anus and up through the cleavage of Julie's bottom. The motion of the finger did not falter, hesitate or deviate in any way from the exact route that it had traced in the beginning. Julie had no idea of how many times the slow teasing movement had been repeated but imagined that it must have continued for almost half an hour. Her thoughts were not very clear, however, as the sensation gradually built up to a monumental, tantalising weight of frustration. Her whole body ached for the release of an orgasm but still the finger did not change its pace or motion. Julie realised with a sudden shock of awareness that her breath was coming in urgent pants interspersed with little cries and gasps which gradually increased in frequency. Julie's knees began to rattle on the hard wooden board of the bed. The mother of all orgasms was about to be unleashed. She had never known such a slow build up of erotic tension before and now she knew that she was on the verge of exploding with pent up passion.

Abruptly the stroking stopped. Julie could not believe it. There she was on the verge of a passionate eruption and now the finger had disappeared. Julie's whimpers and cries turned to desperate pleadings but still the stroking did not return. She wondered whether this was some new form of torture, to bring a girl to the brink of unimaginable ecstasy and then let her down. Some minutes elapsed and Julie strained her ears to detect whether her mystery visitor had departed, but the hood was most effective in blocking out all but the loudest sounds. The overwhelming sense of frustration was unbearable and Julie pleaded into the darkness for her unknown lover to finish her off, so that the tension would be released. Just when she was giving up all hope and was resigned to a night of trying to squirm her throbbing sex against the wood, in a vain attempt to release the orgasm that was so tormentingly close, she felt the fingers again. This time they were teasing her nipples, which were exposed due to her breasts hanging down through the holes in the board. Her guest must have moved to a position lying beneath the bed. Now the fingers stopped pulling and squeezing her nipples and began to brush them lightly backwards and forwards from side to side. At first, Julie was only conscious that they were still sore from the nipple clamps but gradually she felt them stiffen as they became increasingly aroused. Again, the fingers did not vary their motion but just continued in the same motion without a pause. The touch was so light that the weight of Julie's breasts hanging down was not relieved and they hardly even swung from side to side. The caressing continued for minute after minute and showed no sign of ceasing. It could have been continuously for three quarters of an hour for all Julie knew. She was only aware that she was once again on the verge of a stupendous orgasm, something that she had not known was possible from the mere stroking of nipples. Her panting grew more urgent and she could feel the waves of pre-orgasmic electricity surging through her breasts and down to her toes.

And then it stopped again. Whoever it was in the room knew exactly, to within a fraction of a second, when to stop. It was like being pushed right to the edge of a cliff, with toes curled over the extreme edge; any further and the consequences would be unstoppable. Julie felt as if she would either die or go insane with frustration; her body seemed like a vast balloon inflated with erotic pressure that urgently needed to be released. 'Oh, no,' she wailed. 'Please don't stop. I beg you. Please let me come, whoever you are.'

And then it happened. Having moved back to the rear of the bed, Julie's visitor squeezed the bud of the girl's engorged clitoris, pulling it and letting it slide back between moistened, slippery fingertips. Julie's whole body seemed to explode in a rapturous frenzy. The room resonated with a banshee howl that Julie only later realised was her own voice. Uncontrollable spasms shook her body and strained at the rigid bonds of the restraining pillory and stocks whilst her knees played a staccato flamenco on the hard surface. The orgasm seemed to continue endlessly with an almost painful intensity and when at last it subsided, Julie felt an utter exhaustion and helplessness, as if she were coming out of a demented fit. As her composure gradually returned, she became aware of the tip of a tongue running lightly over the livid, raised weals of her bottom and finally a smouldering kiss first on one bottom cheek and then on the other.

'Who are you?' Julie cried. 'My tormentor or my lover? Please speak to me. How can you be so cruel?'

There was still only a deep silence. A draught of cooler air, scented with the merest trace of sandalwood perfume, played for a moment on Julie's bare skin, indicating that the intruder had now left the room. Within minutes, Julie had fallen, exhausted, into a deep sleep, still desperately wondering if she would ever discover the identity of her nocturnal visitor, and whether she could ever experience such a shattering orgasmic explosion again.

16

The Uprising

It was an unnaturally warm summer. The heat was stifling, which was most unusual so far north of the mainland. Two teachers, Miss Hedges and Miss Jackson, were even conducting some of their classes outdoors, on the lawns where the breeze gave some relief from the clammy heat of the classrooms. Julie always enjoyed these lessons, sitting on the parched grass under the shade of a huge oak tree, while Miss Hedges would indulge her interest in Shakespeare and enthuse about *The Tempest* or *A Midsummer Night's Dream*, for most of the afternoon. Julie was now completely accustomed to life at the reformatory and had soon adapted to the iron discipline and utter submission required of her. In fact, for once in her life she felt completely fulfilled and at ease with herself. Going to the front of the class or a mistress' study for punishments were aspects of reformatory life that Julie bore with fortitude. Those who struggled and wailed, Julie regarded with contempt. The necessity to help organise the rebellion was, of course, a priority, but Julie found some of the secret meetings and the clandestine retrieval of secret messages a trifle irksome. However, this almost imperceptible dimming of her enthusiasm for the donkey work of organising the uprising was something that she paid little heed to.

One sweltering, airless night, Julie was woken by Sophie tapping her on the elbow.

'Julie, are you awake?' she whispered.

'I am, now. What do you want?'

'Julie, I've had a brilliant idea. I must tell you now.'

'Well, hurry up, I want to get some sleep. It's difficult enough to sleep in this heat without being woken up by people wanting to have a chat.'

'It's not for a chat and it's too important to wait. I've worked out a way of getting into the kitchens at night without getting caught. We can get some utensils that won't be missed and use them as weapons when the big day comes. I've worked out how we can get past the duty prefect patrols. It's really quite easy, I don't know how we didn't think of it before.'

'Look, I don't want to seem rude,' replied Julie, 'but I don't see why you couldn't have waited until tomorrow to tell me all this. And if it's merely some stupid scheme to get into the kitchens, you can forget it pronto.'

'Why do you say it's a stupid scheme? You haven't even heard it yet,' answered Sophie testily.

'It's totally stupid, because firstly we have not been asked to break into the kitchens. For all we know, some other Fightback members have already been assigned to do it. Secondly, it's far too risky. There is no way that we could guarantee getting away with it. And if we got caught, it would probably blow the secrecy of the whole operation and set back the uprising for months, even years. Now go back to sleep; the heat has obviously addled your brain.'

'That's right, reject the plan before you have even heard it. I'm not surprised: I almost expected it,' replied Sophie.

'What do you mean?' retorted Julie angrily.

'I'll tell you what I mean. The regime here's turning you soft, isn't it? You're not angry any more and you have lost your nerve, too. If you ask me, you are getting sucked into the system.'

'Shut up, you silly cow,' hissed Julie.

'No, I will not shut up,' retorted Sophie. 'You're the silly cow, not me. Do you really think I haven't noticed that something's going on between you and Miss Sullivan?'

'I have no idea what you are referring to,' countered Julie. 'It's not my fault if she calls me to her study. She invites lots of other girls there, too. It's only to act as her skivvy; making tea, waiting on her, reading to her, helping her cane some of the first formers and so on. You don't think that I actually want to spend the whole evening and half the night in her study, do you? I don't know why she picks on me so much. I would much rather she left me alone. Why are you blaming me? If she calls me to her study, I have to go. It isn't as if I've got any choice in the matter. You're jealous, aren't you? That's it. I realise now why you're getting at me. It's because you're jealous. You're green with envy. You're sore because you think that she fancies me and doesn't even look at you.' Julie's voice was now beginning to rise.

'Keep it down, for heaven's sake,' whispered Sophie. 'You're getting so uptight because I've hit on the truth, haven't I? We have been through so much together that I can read you like a book. I think that you're soft on Miss Sullivan and she's soft on you. And you're going soft on the whole reformatory system and not pulling your weight organising for Fightback. Of course I'm not jealous. How could I be? I hate the whole damn lot of them and their political masters. No, I'm worried about you. I'm worried about what you're getting yourself into. You'll live to regret it if you are not careful,' whispered Sophie.

'Shut up, just shut up,' croaked Julie vehemently and, feeling close to tears, she dived under the sheets with her hands over her ears. She lay there in the darkness, feeling uncomfortable in the still heat of the night, as her emotions swirled in her mind. Am I in love with Miss Sullivan? Julie asked herself. No, of course not. How could I be, she's on the other side. Julie cast her mind back to the day Miss Sullivan had first asked her to attend her study in the evening and relived the flash of pleasure she had felt, knowing that Miss Sullivan had noticed her. That night, Miss Sullivan had wanted Julie to assist in the process of caning a dozen first formers. Julie had merely had to ensure that each pupil kept her hands outstretched while Miss Sullivan lashed each flinching palm with the cane. Not a very difficult task, but Julie had felt a glow of pride as Miss Sullivan had sent the last pupil on her way and had invited Julie to share a glass of sherry as a treat for having been a good assistant. She had even given Julie a wink and a broad grin as she had poured out the sherry.

Miss Sullivan had then decided that she needed a bath to unwind and she ordered Julie to soap her down thoroughly. Julie had felt a frisson of excitement as she had carefully soaped Miss Sullivan's lean yet curvy body, and then worked up a lather with the sponge. And all the while, Miss Sullivan had lain back in the bath, with a look of pure bliss on her face.

Since then, Julie had been summoned to Miss Sullivan's study on an increasingly regular basis. Helping Miss Sullivan to hone her skills at massage had merely been the thin end of the wedge; more and more often Julie would be called upon to assist the mistress when she took a bath, to fan her while she read a book, to act as a human footstool, or to assist in the arrangements for group punishments. And even now, with Sophie's accusations of disloyalty to Fightback still ringing in her ears, Julie could not help but feel a pang of eager expectation, at the prospect of being summoned, yet again, to Miss Sullivan's study.

These muddled thoughts were keeping Julie from sleeping. She tried again to analyse her feelings. It was true enough to say that she loved being with Miss Sullivan – the mistress was so strong and yet, at the same time, she was so kind. But was that necessarily the same as being in love with her? Of course it wasn't. Why did she keep thinking such things? And who the hell did Sophie think she was, casting aspersions like that? She'd have to have it out with her tomorrow.

Gradually, however, Julie's eyelids drooped and she drifted back into sleep, albeit it was a fitful and troubled sleep.

So physically and mentally exhausted was Julie the next day, that she felt unable to face the issue of the previous evening's row with Sophie. This was just as well since at tea time, a first-former strode up to Julie and put a note in her hand. Julie unfolded it with eager anticipation, and found her heart skipping beats when she read the message.

Julie Semple – Come to my study at eight o'clock for a Greek and Roman evening – Miss Sullivan.

At eight o'clock sharp, Julie knocked at Miss Sullivan's door. After a short interval Miss Sullivan opened the door and smiled when she saw Julie standing there, hands clasped behind her back.

'Julie, your punctuality is as good as ever. Come in and remove your clothes, I want you naked straight away. Put them on the chair. Going naked is more of a treat than normal in this baking hot weather. Now, stand under the lamp, I want a good look at your naked body.' Julie undid the last suspender clip, carefully rolled down the remaining stocking and gaily stepped over to the standard lamp that was casting a wide pool of light.

'A little straighter please, young lady. I think that you could get those shoulders back a little bit more. That's better. Now, let's have a really good look at you. I want to see if you have toned up and lost those few ounces of pudginess that you had when I first saw you on the boat to the island.' Miss Sullivan circled around Julie, running the palms of her hands all over the girl's smooth skin like a blind person examining a sculpture. Carefully feeling Julie's ribs, Miss Sullivan remarked, 'Your weight is absolutely right now. I like the ribcage to be well defined even when a girl is standing normally. Now, breathe in deeply and hold your breath. Excellent, I can see and feel each rib in fine detail. Now, your buttocks.' Julie remained motionless, as Miss Sullivan palpated each cheek and then slightly lifted each one as if looking for signs of slackness. 'Very nice cheeks, pert and round. Not boyish, but not fat either. One of the best bottoms in the third year, possibly.'

The mistress moved round and ran her palms up from Julie's navel and cupped each breast in turn. 'I thought that these were your best assets when I inspected you on the boat. At the time, I remember that your friend Sophie's were a little firmer, but now you have definitely caught up. The strict diet and daily cold swims have really toned them up, taken the fatness out and made those nipples point up a bit more. Now, part your legs; I want to check that your quim is completely smooth.' Miss Sullivan reached over and directed the light from her halogen reading lamp on to Julie's pudenda. Stooping slightly, she ran her fingers lightly over the whole area and then parted Julie's sex lips and teased the slightly stiffened clitoris. 'Now, turn around and bend over – keep your legs apart. I hope that I won't find any little hairs here, either. Some girls are a little remiss and think that what they can't see doesn't matter. They soon realise that it does matter when Miss Spenser punishes them.' Julie quickly complied and grasped her ankles. Miss Sullivan adjusted the lamp for a thorough inspection. The mistress then pulled Julie's cheeks apart and began probing with her finger which she lubricated by rubbing the girl's rapidly lubricating vagina. Miss Sullivan toyed with Julie's clitoris and anal dimple alternately for many minutes until Julie's head became giddy with the combination of the posture and the mounting sexual stimulation.

'Excellent, completely smooth,' Miss Sullivan enthused, 'pouting and slippery wet. Lovely! You can stand up now and turn around. I have put you on my "Beautiful Body" list, and with good reason. Your body complies with all the requirements of feminine beauty that I regard as essential. Only a few girls from each year group have what it takes to get on to my list. Not everyone has my taste, of course, but I think that mine is rather well informed. I have admired and studied the female form for a long time and know what makes for classic elegance. In fact, that brings me to the main reason for your invitation tonight. I have decided to have a classical evening. I have been reading Ovid, Euripides and Theocritus for the past three weeks and am in the mood for some ancient culture. Be my footstool, while I leaf through the book for a suitable goddess for you to be tonight. Chop, chop; I want to put my feet up now, not next week.'

Having been Miss Sullivan's 'footstool' on previous occasions, Julie knew what was required. Facing away from the mistress' armchair, she knelt on all fours with her head on the floor between her elbows. Julie also knew what would come next, once Miss Sullivan had settled her stocking-clad feet on her back and had started reading. A few minutes wait and – there it was. Miss Sullivan's big toe slid its way slowly down Julie's back, the fine mesh of the nylon chafing Julie's skin, down the crease of her buttocks and into her moist sex. As if absent-minded, the mistress slowly wiggled her toe while turning the pages of her book. A voluptuous shudder surged through Julie as she revelled in the sensation of the rough nylon against her smooth, delicate sex lips. As Miss Sullivan continued to read, Julie found it more and more difficult to hold back her mounting arousal. She was just starting to gently rotate her bottom when Miss Sullivan shut the book with a thud and exclaimed, 'That's it, you can be Artemis, the huntress – Diana, to the Romans. I fancy evoking the scene where Artemis rescues the virgin sacrifice, Iphigenia.' She leapt to her feet and pulled the sash of the bell-pull beside the fireplace. Within seconds a duty prefect appeared at the door with a deep curtsey.

'Yes, Miss Sullivan.'

'Bring me Dominique Butler, at once.'

'Yes, Miss Sullivan.'

The mistress disappeared into the bathroom and returned a minute later with a large container of talcum powder just as there was a timid knock at the door. On entering, Dominique Butler was informed to her evident surprise that she was to pose as a Greek statue of Iphigenia and was therefore required to take off all her clothes. She looked even more surprised when Miss Sullivan told her that she was to be completely covered in talcum powder in order to take on the appearance of stone or marble. Julie watched fascinated as Dominique, a petite and delicately pretty first year girl, removed her clothes, still with a hint of shyness. Miss Sullivan set about covering both girls including their hair, in liberal amount of the powder so that they really did look like alabaster or marble.

'Now, Artemis is rescuing Iphigenia from being sacrificed. So, Iphegenia – that's you Dominique – lie down on the floor and raise one arm up as if in supplication. Julie, you put one foot on Iphegenia's breast and raise one arm and pull the other one back as if you are aiming an imaginary bow. You see, Artemis was a huntress with a bow and arrow. Good, that looks about right. Now, hold that pose perfectly still while I listen to the opera. You do look beautiful, both of you.'

Miss Sullivan adjusted her music system and seconds later the sounds of classical opera boomed out. As she reclined in her armchair with a large glass of sherry, a look of pure rapture stole over the mistress' face. She tapped her foot and gazed at the living statues in front of her. Julie found the pose hard to maintain and, after half an hour, Dominique also showed signs of discomfort. However, the main torment was the operatic music, which Julie found excruciating to listen to. Fortunately, over the course of the evening Miss Sullivan directed the statues to adopt new poses which reduced the fatigue to manageable proportions. For the last pose, Julie was directed to cup Dominique's apple-sized left breast whilst kissing her on the lips. The young girl's eyes widened in surprise when Miss Sullivan described the pose but, after some minutes of the enforced embrace, she seemed to relax and enjoy the experience. When Miss Sullivan eventually tired of her cultural experiment, she helped them wash the talcum powder off each other in the bath and then sent the two girls on their way, saying, 'You'd better get some sleep, you'll be needing it.'

How typical of Miss Sullivan, thought Julie as she trotted back to the dormitory; she really does care about the welfare of the girls here. She is not at all cruel and heartless like the others.

That night, Julie went to bed with all her limbs aching, being a statue was not as easy as it sounded. But she also had another ache which she could no longer deny to herself. Julie lay in bed, gazing at the shadows on the ceiling, while all around the snores and sighs of the dormitory inmates provided a comforting background of noise. It was no good trying to fall asleep: Julie was in a state of agitation. What am I going to do, she pondered, I can't stop thinking about Miss Sullivan. If she doesn't call me to her study, I worry that someone else is taking my place. I can't stop thinking about her

238

all day and when she touches me I feel like I am going to die with pleasure. I can't betray the rebellion, yet I can't kid myself any more that I'm not in love with Miss Sullivan, I know I am. And neither can I bear the thought of her coming to any harm.

Julie felt torn. She was being so disloyal to Sophie, Jack and all the Fightback agents, yet at the same time she knew that she could not help falling in love. It would be so unfair if Miss Sullivan was hurt in the uprising; she was the kindest and fairest of all the mistresses. Julie let out a deep sigh and scrunched up the pillow. It was no good thinking like that, she was here to fight the system. She had to be true to her principles. She was here to help overthrow the state so that a world could be created where people could be happy and free. Consideration of just one person must not be allowed to stand in the way of the revolution. Yet, she was happier than she had ever been, precisely because she was not free. Destroying the reformatory and seeing Miss Sullivan mistreated would make her very unhappy, but, though she wished she knew the answer, there was nobody she felt that she could turn to, now, not even Sophie.

Julie's fretting was brought to an abrupt halt when she noticed that the door at the end of the dormitory had silently opened, letting in a pencil-thin shaft of light. A shadowy figure glided quickly up the centre of the room and halted between Julie and Sophie's beds.

'Both of you, wake up. Julie and Sophie, are you listening? It's Joanne, the fourth year organiser. The big day has finally come, Vanessa heard from Fightback yesterday. It's going to be tonight at three o'clock when the duty prefects on patrol duty have dozed off. One of them is in Fightback anyway and she is going to let us know when it's all clear. Get some sleep in the meantime – it's going to be a busy day tomorrow. I'm looking forward to seeing those bitches get a taste of their own medicine. I've been promised first turn with the birch on Miss Chapel, and I can't wait. I won't let up until she's howling for mercy. Well, anyway, back to business. I'll be back here at three to make sure that you are awake and to help you organise this lot. This third year dorm has got the task of taking over Matron's quarters and the prefect monitors' common room. It shouldn't be too difficult, the prefect monitors are just pathetic little wimps. It will be fun thinking up some suitable revenge for them as well. Right, I'm off now. I've got to get along to the second formers without being seen. It's a pity that it's such a bright moon tonight; it makes sneaking around a lot more risky. There's so much light coming in the windows, it's like daylight in the corridors. Luckily, the duty prefects seem to be keeping mainly in their common room tonight. See you later.'

'Our big day – or should I say big night, at last,' whispered Sophie. 'I'm really looking forward to thinking up some suitable punishments for those bitches. I think that we could start by making them crawl up the driveway on their hands and knees, over all that gravel, like they did to us when we first arrived. Except I would make them crawl the whole half-mile and birch them all the way. Isn't it exciting? I'm going to try to get some sleep now, because once we get going at three o'clock there will probably not be much chance of any sleep for quite a while.'

Julie gripped the edge of the sheet, screwing it into a tight ball. Her mind was in turmoil at the news. What could she do? She wanted to fight the system and help Fightback strike a blow against the corrupt political system, but she could not bear to see Miss Sullivan ill-treated. She was the only mistress who did her best to make life at the reformatory a bit more bearable. The others were all complete sadists and deserved their come-uppance, but it wouldn't be fair if she was made to suffer, too. But, were Miss Sullivan warned of the plan, might she be likely to raise the alarm and ruin everything? Julie racked her brains. Maybe she could persuade Miss Sullivan to slip quietly away into the woods, to take Julie with her, even. Then the uprising could go ahead without the mistress getting hurt. Later, Julie could slip back and say that she was knocked out or something and had lost her memory. Then they would not suspect her of anything. They would wonder where Miss Sullivan was, but in all the excitement they would not bother looking too hard for her. Julie tossed and turned in a fever of perturbation, her mind racing to come up with a solution. An hour later her mind was made up.

Julie knocked timidly on the door. She was not really expecting Miss Sullivan to be awake to answer. I'll just wait a second and then go in and wake her, thought Julie. She will obviously be pretty alarmed, but then she will see how lucky she is to be tipped off. She will probably be really grateful and give me a big hug and a kiss. Julie had just put her hand on the door handle when she was surprised to hear Miss Sullivan call, 'Enter.'

Julie edged into the room. The room was in darkness but Julie was surprised to see that Miss Sullivan was not in her bedroom but was standing silhouetted in her silk night-dress against the window, looking out at the moonlit lawns. There was a trace of cigarette smoke in the air which was puzzling, as Julie was not aware that Miss Sullivan or any of the mistresses smoked.

Miss Sullivan turned her head and observed Julie quizzically. 'Ah, Julie. You know that this is not allowed. What is it?'

'Miss Sullivan, I just had to warn you. The pupils are going to rebel against the reformatory in a few hours' time. You are all going to be attacked and held hostage. Fightback, that's the name of the organisation at the bottom of it, is going to hold you hostage and inflict terrible punishments on you all, until the authorities send a boat so that all the pupils can escape from the island. Fightback's main aim, though, is to get the government to agree to the broadcast of the PPA's alternative manifesto and a denunciation of the conditions in the reformatories and prisons. It could be ages before they give in to those demands and all the time you would be suffering unspeakable humiliation. You must get away. Hide in the woods or something. You could take me with you if you like. You don't stand a chance if you stay here, you must get away quickly. Please don't raise the alarm, Fightback and all the others will think that I am a traitor to them. Fightback can operate without me, I am just a small cog. There's loads of them in it, the whole place has been completely infiltrated. Even some of the prefects and senior prefects are in it. Even the head senior prefect, Vanessa Smith, is a Fightback agent.'

'That's right, I am in Fightback, and I don't like traitors,' came a voice like splintering ice from the shadows. Julie froze in mid-flow, the breath knocked out of her as if she had been hit in the stomach. Out of the shadows and into a pool of moonlight emerged the tall figure of Vanessa, her eyes flashing daggers and her voice rising with passion. 'And let me introduce you to the leader of our operational cell, Miss Sullivan, who doesn't like traitors either. Especially ones that she has taken the trouble to be kind to. And to think that I felt so guilty after the grade three meeting that I woke Miss Sullivan and suggested that she might caress your pain away in the post-punishment bedroom. Well, you may have tried to defeat our plans but you have failed, as you will find to your cost. We have special ways of dealing with traitors.'

Miss Sullivan walked past Julie, her eyes accusing and cold, and turned the key in the lock. Vanessa approached slowly like a cat that had found a mouse in the middle of a room. In her hand she held a coil of rope and a gag.

'I – I didn't mean to betray the movement. I just wanted to save Miss Sullivan. I am not really a traitor. I'm sorry. I'm on your side really, I always have been. I –' Julie's stuttering was finally extinguished by the ball gag.

Julie spent an extremely uncomfortable night gagged and trussed like a chicken, lying on top of Miss Sullivan's shoes and bags at the bottom of her locked wardrobe, whilst listening to the shouts and crashes of the rebellion. The next day was not to prove any the more comfortable.

After a victory address by Miss Sullivan to the jubilant pupils an impromptu courtroom was set up in the assembly hall. The chief 'enemies of the people' were arraigned to hear the charges against them. It was an odd experience to see the once so powerful mistresses and most of the senior prefects brought in one at a time, hands bound with rope, naked and shamefaced, to hear the sentence that had been decided for each. Some bore cut lips and bruises, evidence of the night's conflict. It was decided that each of the prisoners would be awarded a number of strokes of the birch according to how hated they were, and that all the birchings would be carried out that morning. Miss Spenser turned pale when she heard that she was to receive the heaviest sentence of a mighty five dozen strokes. Julie hung her head in shame when it was her turn to stand naked in front of the assembly to hear the charges against her. She was surprised and touched to hear Sophie speak eloquently in her defence describing her as 'misguided' rather than 'evil'. After a prolonged argument it was decided that Julie could be spared the birching but would have to take her share of any other penalties awarded to the prisoners. The afternoon was set aside for what was described as 'a programme of entertainment' to be provided by the prisoners. It was deemed fitting that Miss Spenser, as headmistress, should be the first to taste the birch and that she could telephone the mainland directly after, whilst still feeling the effects, to ask that the demands of the rebels be met. It was unanimously felt that this would add sincerity to her requests.

Yolanda, having spent so long in the solitary confinement cell, was awarded the honour of being the one to flog Miss Spenser, and was itching to get started. Flexing her muscles, Yolanda claimed that, due to the exercise regime inflicted on her while in solitary, her right arm was the strongest in the reformatory. Miss Spenser sullenly allowed herself to be strapped to the birching block without a struggle, knowing that it would be in vain. Julie and the other captives who were waiting for their turn stood nervously on the stage, watching the proceedings. With a cheer and a round of applause from the expectant pupils, Yolanda put all her pent-up anger into the first stroke, which sent a great shudder through the headmistress. Miss Spenser was obviously determined to keep a dignified demeanour and remained unstruggling and silent for the first 18 strokes. Everyone was marvelling at her fortitude when, on the following stroke, she let out a banshee wail and did not stop until she was led from the room ten minutes later, dancing and clutching her burning buttocks.

It was the long hot afternoon that was worse for Julie. It started off with the mistresses and some prefects and senior prefects having to act as human horses racing up the burning gravel driveway on their hands and knees with members of Fightback and other pupils riding on them. Imaginary bets had been placed on each 'horse' so that the jockeys applied their riding crops with gusto to encourage their naked mounts to reach the front door first. Heidi had asked especially to be Julie's rider and so Julie suffered under a heavier than average weight. The shimmering afternoon heat, the sharp stones and the long crawl brought Julie and many of the other prisoners to the verge of collapse. However, on seeing this Vanessa organised the first form pupils to bring buckets of cold water to throw over the panting 'horses'.

Julie had barely time to recover when the second item in the entertainment programme was organised. The two one-ton playing-field rollers had both been fitted with a number of long chains connected to wide leather belts. The mistresses were all harnessed like draught horses to one roller whilst the senior prefects were all harnessed to the other. Julie had been put in with the senior prefects' team. Miss Sullivan explained that this was to be a race to see which team could pull their roller to the other side of the playing field first, the winners would be rewarded and the losers would be punished.

When the rollers had been aligned exactly level, Miss Sullivan dropped her handkerchief and shouted, 'Go!' Julie strained against the broad leather waist belt, leaning forward and grunting with the exertion. To each side of her, the senior prefects strained every muscle, their faces crimson with effort, and perspiration dripping off their naked bodies. The roller did not move an inch. Julie looked across to the other team, the mistresses were grunting and heaving but their roller was also immobile. The crowd of jeering pupils whistled and hooted in contempt.

'First formers,' called out Vanessa. 'Come over here and encourage the two teams. They need a bit more persuasion to strain a bit harder.' At this request, a group of first formers in their shapeless smocks came on to the playing field, each carrying a tawse or riding crop. A great cheer went up as the girls set about lashing the legs and backs of the straining teams and the air was alive with screeches and groans. All of a sudden, super-human strength was possessed by the teams and the rollers began to slowly shift, gathering pace as the panting beasts of burden strained every sinew. Progress was very slow and it was many minutes before the teams had reached even halfway across the playing field. The first formers had not tired of applying their tawses and others had reappeared with more buckets of water to hurl at the overheated teams.

Julie's team was beginning to lose ground when the shouts of glee from the crowd turned into shouts of horror. Seconds later, the air pulsated with the sound of aeroplane engines, and the sky darkened with a mass of red and white parachutes.

'Oh damn,' someone shouted. 'It's the airborne riot squad. We haven't got a hope in hell against them.'

'On the contrary,' shouted Miss Sullivan striding up to the collapsing teams of mistresses and senior prefects. 'We have the hostages. Quick, let's get them into Roughton Hall before the parachute boys reach the ground. And we also have something else in our ar-moury, something rather obvious –' Miss Sullivan's face registered a seductive leer. '– Those lads who are drop-ping down spend most of their lives training in their barracks. They are young and frustrated. I doubt any of them has touched a woman in weeks. Most of you have not been touched by a man for ages, either, which means you are also young and frustrated. It's a very hot day. I think that you should all take your clothes off and welcome your new friends in all your naked beauty. Vanessa, bring out the drink that we liberated from Miss Spenser's study. I think the para boys will soon see things our way.'

NEW BOOKS

Coming up from Nexus and Black Lace

There are three Nexus titles published in March

Sisters of Severcy by Jean Aveline
March 1998   Price £4.99   IBSN: 0 352 33239 5
The villa at Severcy is a place of extremes. Here, innocence and love
vie with experience and cruelty in the scorched wilderness of southern
France. As young Isabelle is introduced to the perverse pleasures of
Severcy by her cruel lover Robert, so her sister aids in the sensual
education of Charlotte, Robert's young bride in England. As
Charlotte and Isabelle are enslaved, so they enslave all who use them.

The Black Room by Lisette Ashton
March 1998   Price £4.99   ISBN: 0 352 33238 7
The submissive trainees at the Pentagon Agency can tolerate most
things. Their lives are dedicated to sexual servitude and they enjoy
pain and humiliation on a daily basis. There is only one punishment
that they try to avoid: the black room. When the gorgeous and kinky
PI Jo Valentine is assigned to investigate the agency, she is prepared
to do anything to get results. She is not prepared, however, for the
bizarre and sexual journey the Pentagon Agency has in store for her.

One Week in the Private House by Esme Ombreux
March 1998   Price £4.99   ISBN: 0 352 32788 X
Jem is a petite, flame-haired, blue-eyed businesswoman. Lucy, tall,
blonde and athletic, is a detective inspector. Julia is the slim, dark,
bored wife of a financial speculator. Each arrives separately in the
strange, ritualistic, disciplined domain known as the Private House.
Once they meet, nothing in the House will be the same again –
nothing, that is, except the strict regime of obedience and sexuality.
This is a reprint of one of the most popular Nexus titles.

The Mistress of Sternwood Grange by Arabella Knight
April 1998   Price £4.99   ISBN: 0 352 33241 7

Amanda Silk suspects that she is being cheated out of her late aunt's legacy. Determined to discover the true value of Sternwood Grange, she enters its private world disguised as a maid. The stern regime is oppressively strict and Amanda comes to appreciate the sharp pleasures and sweet torments of punishment. Menial tasks are soon replaced by more delicious duties -- drawing Amanda deep into the dark delights of dominance and discipline.

Annie and the Countess by Evelyn Culber
April 1998   Price £4.99   ISBN: 0 352 33242 5

Annie enjoys her dominant role at the Academy, nurturing nascent submissives among her charges and punishing genuine miscreants, until she meets the Countess, who teaches her how to submit herself. The Countess proves to have unparalleled skills in the subtle arts of sensual pain and takes Annie on as an acolyte. Will Annie succeed in her ambition to become this beautiful voluptuary's favourite companion?